MURDER
OFF THE
BOOKS

MURDER OFF THE BOOKS

TAMARA BERRY

Poisoned Pen
PRESS

Published by Poisoned Pen Press, an imprint of Sourcebooks
P.O. Box 4410, Naperville, Illinois 60567-4410
(630) 961-3900
sourcebooks.com

Printed and bound in the United States of America.
KP 10 9 8 7 6 5 4 3 2 1

Chapter One

GERTRUDE'S CORPSE LAY AT AN UNNATURAL ANGLE ON the floor of the Paper Trail bookstore. Her pale skin glowed eerily under the lights, her deathly pallor made starker by the winged liner that circled her eyelids like a burlesque raccoon. No one in the store could discern the cause of her death, but it was obvious to any trained eye that—

"Ouch. I think there's a rock under my hip. Wait a sec."

The corpse wriggled, shifted, and dislodged a pebble from beneath the waistband of her torn black jeans.

"Never mind," she said as she popped the rock into her mouth. "It's just a jelly bean."

"Gertie, don't eat that," Tess cried, but she was too late. Her teenage daughter had already swallowed it. "And stop fidgeting so much. You're supposed to be dead."

"If she keeps eating pieces of candy she finds on the floor of the bookstore, she *will* be dead," murmured Nicki, hoisting a box of books on her hip as easily as if lifting a baby. Tess couldn't help but be impressed. She knew from experience that a box of thirty hardback copies of her newest release, *Fury under the Floorboards*, was no light burden. At a little over four hundred pages, it was her longest book yet.

It was also her most successful book yet, even though

it wouldn't technically hit the shelves until tomorrow. According to her publisher, presales were through the roof—or rather, through the floorboards. Ever since an elusive serial killer had been captured and arrested after decades-old bones had tumbled through this very floor and onto Tess's head, the entire world had been holding its breath in anticipation of her fictionalized version of events.

"Maybe we should conk Gertie over the head before the launch party tomorrow night," Tess mused as she watched her daughter's continued attempts at finding a comfortable resting spot. "For authenticity's sake. If she's supposed to look like a corpse, she can't keep moving around."

Now that Tess was looking closer, she didn't think anyone had ever appeared less dead. Not even the veiny blue makeup along the side of Gertrude's temples could counteract her healthy, blooming glow. Ah, to be fifteen again. Before gravity had taken hold, back when skin cells regenerated themselves without the aid of hundred-dollar face cream, when she could pick up candy off the floor and suffer no more ill effects than—

"Gertie! Stop eating those." Tess nudged her daughter with her foot. "What's the matter with you?"

Gertrude sat up and popped another jelly bean into her mouth. "I'm *hungry*, that's what. You promised me dinner at the hotel restaurant. How much longer is it going to take to get everything set up?"

Tess looked to Nicki for the answer. She'd wanted to hire an event planner for this—the grand opening of her new bookstore and launch party for the latest installment of her Detective Gonzales series—but Nicki had insisted she could handle it. The tall, willowy librarian not only ran a local bookmobile program, rambling along in a blue truck that covered every nook and cranny of this rural Washington county, but she also happened to be an undercover FBI agent investigating a money-laundering scheme along the Canadian border. At this point, Tess was pretty sure the woman was superhuman.

"That depends..." Nicki consulted a clipboard on the top of the box. "Gertie, you have all the canapés prepped for the party tomorrow evening, right?"

Gertrude gave her a mock salute as she bounced up from the floor. "Aye aye, Captain. Most of it only has to be popped in the oven before it's ready to go. I still need to assemble the sushi, but we're having the tuna specially flown in tomorrow so it's fresh."

"And the fancy journalist you paid for is coming in on the same flight, right?"

Tess took instant umbrage at this. "I didn't *pay* for the journalist. He contacted me of his own volition. He wants to follow me for a week to get a good look at my writing process. It's for a feature."

Nicki leveled a look at Tess over the top of the box. "But he's staying with you?"

"He specifically requested it! He said it helps him get a personalized look at my life."

"The same week you're launching your latest book *and* opening a bookstore?"

"It was the only opening he had in his schedule!"

"When the town also happens to be teeming with fans, movie executives, readers, and every other living being who could feasibly be called a member of the Tess Harrow Fan Club?"

That was taking things too far. "It's not my fault I draw a crowd. I'm very popular these days. There's even a murder podcast about me."

"Ohmigod, Mom." Gertrude sighed as she finished scanning the bamboo floor for other signs of rogue candy. The floor was brand new, courtesy of the renovations that had transformed the old hardware store into a boutique bookshop, but Tess wouldn't have eaten anything off it. Especially since she couldn't remember buying jelly beans at any point in the past six months. "The podcast isn't *about* you. It's about solving murders that the police haven't been able to figure out."

"What are you talking about? They mention me all the time."

Nicki laughed. "Yeah, as the bestselling hack who hacks people up to get a story."

"One time. They called me that *one time* before my publisher shut them down." Tess grabbed her purse, her expert eye running over the bookstore one last time. After six months of hard work, a deadline to meet, and way more murder than any woman should have to encounter in her lifetime, it was finally done. She'd always said that giving birth to Gertrude had been the greatest accomplishment of her life, but getting the Paper Trail up and running was a close second. She had no idea how Nora Roberts made owning a bookstore look so easy. "Besides, that's what this party is all about, remember? We're making murder fun again."

Gertrude snorted. "Just don't hang that on a sign above the door, and I think we might get away with it."

Tess did her best to ignore the wave of anxiety this remark brought up. Throwing a murder-themed party as a way to entice customers into her store wasn't the most traditional way of going about things, but there was a lot more at stake than peddling a few books. Ever since she'd been pulled into not one but two recent criminal investigations, her writing career had taken off in ways she'd never anticipated.

The book sales and movie deals? *Fantastic.*

The staggering advances her publisher was dangling to keep her happy? *Keep 'em coming.*

The fact that she was starting to earn a reputation as someone who put her friends and family members in harm's way for the sake of a story? *Not exactly the look she was going for.*

One online journal had called her the Black Widow, despite the fact that her ex-husband was still very much alive and kicking. Murder Mary had been the term coined by another journal, this time in reference to Typhoid Mary, a person Tess didn't enjoy being compared to at all. She took public health seriously and was doing her best to *avoid* causing additional deaths. But worst of all was the one who'd labeled her a less-than-charming Jessica Fletcher.

"Imagine if America's beloved *Murder, She Wrote* heroine had been cast as a frumpy soccer mom who wouldn't know a good subplot if it bit her on the a—"

Tess had stopped reading after that. She could handle

being compared to serial killers, but her subplots were *amazing*, thank you very much. And Gertrude hadn't played team sports a day in her life.

In an effort to counteract the negative press—and, okay, to show that she wasn't nearly as frumpy as some of the Associated Press photos made her look—she'd decided to throw a party so *charming* that not even the hardest-hearted journalist could resist. Tomorrow morning, the bookstore would open its doors for the very first time. Tess would spend all day signing books, after which everyone was invited to attend a murder-themed party, with cupcakes that oozed fake blood and sushi made to look like grotesque body parts. Everyone would eat and drink and be merry, all under the watchful eye of the journalist Tess had—okay, *fine*—paid to be here. The plan was practically foolproof. As long as everyone avoided eating floor jelly beans, she was sure the event would be a success.

It would be a new stage in her life—hers and Gertrude's both. With the bookstore opening in town, they were putting down real, lasting roots. The kind that would outlive a few bestselling novels, that would boost the local economy in ways everyone would benefit from.

Not even Typhoid Mary could boast of having such an impact.

"Relax, Mom," Gertrude said, as if sensing the sudden trend of Tess's thoughts. She bumped her mother lightly with her hip. "We've been planning this thing for months. As long as you feed me before I pass out from malnutrition, we have nothing to worry about."

Tess could take a hint when it was pouting up at her. Carefully locking the bookstore behind them, Tess ushered her daughter and her best friend down the quaint, old-fashioned main street that led to the hotel.

The town of Winthrop was nothing if not dedicated to its Wild West theme. Every other storefront boasted a false front and rustic wooden slats, and she'd designed the Paper Trail to match. Some people might think it strange to live and work in a tourist trap with fewer than five hundred residents, but Tess wasn't one of them. There was fresh air, a decent school district, and all her favorite people in the world.

In fact, as long as bodies stopped mysteriously cropping up everywhere she turned, she might even call it perfect.

Chapter Two

"DAHLING, THERE YOU ARE!"

As soon as Tess walked into the restaurant attached to the hotel, every instinct she had warned her to flee. That voice was a herald of doom, the death knell to all her hopes and dreams, the one thing—outside of a fresh corpse—that had the power to break her.

And if there'd been any mistaking who it belonged to, Gertrude's sudden shout of "Grandma!" would have been sure to tip her off.

Tess felt as though she were watching the scene unfold from underwater—or, at the very least, through a thick plate of plexiglass that held the water at bay. Either way, the imminent threat of drowning was present.

"How many times have I told you not to call me that? Call me Bee like everyone else. *Grandma* makes me feel so old." Despite the stricture, Bernadette Springer opened her arms to engulf her favorite—and only—grandchild in an enthusiastic hug. She met Tess's eyes over the top of Gertrude's head, her expression bland. "Well, dear? Aren't you going to tell me you're happy to see me? And introduce me to your friend?"

Tess could only find it in her to comply with the second

request. No one—least of all her mother—would buy the first.

"Mom, this is my good friend Nicki," Tess said, gesturing at the woman next to her. "Nicki, in case you can't tell, this is my mother. Call her Bee like everyone else. *Grandma* makes her feel old."

"Very funny, Tess," her mother said as she accepted Nicki's handshake. After one glance at the librarian, who looked more like Iman stepping off a catwalk than a small-town bookmobile driver, she nodded her approval. "I don't know why any of you insist on living in this godforsaken town. When Dad died, I'd hoped I'd seen the last of it. It doesn't improve much with age, does it?"

"Neither do you," Tess muttered under her breath. Only Nicki heard her, so only Nicki choked on a laugh.

"I didn't know you were coming for a visit," Gertrude said as she tucked herself into the crook of her grandmother's arm, which was clad in a pink Chanel suit that Tess knew well. Her mother had been wearing that suit in some form or another since the sixties. Not the *literal* same suit, since even her mother's painstaking care couldn't make tweed last forever, but one of the replicas she kept on rotation. *As Jackie O. would've done.* "Mom never said anything about it."

"That's because your mom wanted it to be a surprise, my pet," Bee said as she nuzzled her granddaughter's head. This time, her eyes held a look of stern warning. Tess interpreted that warning as it was intended—namely, to pretend that she had prior knowledge of her mother's descent upon the town. Bee had never been a communicative parent, especially regarding her whereabouts, but Tess was happy to play along. She and her mother had never seen eye to eye on anything except Gertrude.

According to Bernadette Springer, thrice-divorced attorney-at-law and general pain in Tess's backside, Tess had lousy taste in men and questionable fashion sense. Her career was a fluke, her personal life in shambles. Nothing she'd ever done had been good enough for the Springer family line... with the exception of bringing into it a child as intelligent and full of life as Gertrude.

"When I heard your mother was throwing a big gala in celebration of her new book, wild horses couldn't keep me away," Bee said with another of those stern looks. "She knows how much I love a gala."

"*Gala* is an awfully strong word," Tess said, her heart sinking. Since her mother sat on the boards of no fewer than three national charitable organizations, *gala* was a loaded term. Emphasis on the *loaded*. "I'd call it more of a light party."

Bee arched one of her eyebrows. They were thin and villainous, the inevitable outcome of the over-plucking trend of the nineties, but the style had always suited her. If anyone looked like she planned to skin a pack of Dalmatians in the pursuit of high fashion, it was this woman. "You'll be wearing a dress?"

"Yes, but I draw the line at pantyhose, so don't even try."

Bee conveniently ignored this. "Food?"

"Of course. Gertie is doing most of the catering."

"Champagne?"

"Technically, it's more of a sparkling wine."

Not even this blow could quell her mother's fervor. "If it looks like a gala and tastes like a gala, then I'm calling it a gala. Now. Where are we having dinner tonight?"

Tess recognized this as the double-edged question it was. Most people would take one look at the scene around them, with wagon wheels arranged artfully on the walls and the mounted animal heads looking them over, and assume dinner would take the shape of a fifteen-ounce steak brought out on the end of a pitchfork. Which, incidentally, was what Tess had been looking forward to all day. Her mother's distastefully wrinkled nose broadcast what she thought of such a rustic offering.

Fortunately, Gertrude came to the rescue before any lines of battle could be drawn.

"We're eating here, of course," the girl said without a trace of irony. "They have the best burgers in town. You can get a regular burger, a buffalo burger, or—if you're really lucky—one of the chef's specials."

"This place has a *chef*?"

Gertrude giggled and began dragging her grandmother toward a booth near the back. It was located underneath the scraggly visage of an elk who'd long ago lost one of its glossy black eyes. "Well, he's more of an enthusiastic amateur, but it still counts. If you guess which animal was ground up to make the special burger, you get it for free. I was super close last time. I said ostrich, but it was really yak."

The look that Bee cast over her shoulder at Tess was one that she planned to store up and protect in her heart for years to come. *Save me*, that look said. *This child of yours is an abomination against nature.* Tess only waggled her fingers playfully at her. If her mother was going to start popping up in town unannounced and sporting a haircut that looked like a shellacked helmet from a sixties time capsule, then she could eat an ostrich. Or a yak.

"Sorry about this," Tess said with an apologetic grimace at Nicki. "If you'd rather cry off for dinner, I'd totally understand. I don't know if you can tell, but my mother is a bit... much."

"Are you kidding?" Nicki moved toward the table with a grin that boded ill for the meal to come. "The great Tess Harrow has a mother? Like *that*? I wouldn't miss this for anything."

"Don't say I didn't warn you." Tess loped after her, but her steps felt as heavy as her stomach. "The last time she visited us was when we lived in Seattle. We ended up having to entirely rebuild the west side of the house. That was her *Breakfast at Tiffany*'s phase. She always forgot to check if her cigarette holder was extinguished before bed."

"And what phase is this?"

Tess set her mouth in a grim line. "Ask me again in an hour. From the look of things, we're going full Jacqueline Kennedy Onassis."

━━━━━━━

Not for nothing was Tess Harrow a thriller writer who specialized in twisty murder mysteries. It didn't take her the full hour to uncover the clues and figure out her mother's newest obsession; it took twenty minutes.

"Oh, God. It's Elizabeth Taylor," she hissed in a low voice to Nicki, who'd been sitting with a grin splitting her features the entire time she'd been watching the three generations interact. "The size of her earrings, that helmet of hair, the way she keeps drawing out every syllable... I'll bet you a million dollars her luggage contains nothing but girdles and necklaces as big as your head."

"Since I know you actually have the bank account to back that bet up, there's no way I'm taking it," Nicki hissed back. "Besides, what's wrong with Elizabeth Taylor? I always thought she seemed like she'd be a lot of fun at parties."

Tess agreed, which was the exact problem. Having a silver screen goddess as a party guest was great; having one as a mother was an entirely different ordeal. Especially when the party in question was supposed to be providing Tess with an aura of respectability. Her mother putting on the airs of a famously impetuous, outspoken personality was about as far from respectable as you could get.

"I'm not sure this salad is agreeing with me," Bee said. She creaked back against the vinyl booth seat and lifted her napkin delicately to her lips. "There's something off about the dressing."

"Do you want to try some of my burger instead?" Gertrude offered as she held up an oozing piece of red meat that even Tess shuddered to look at. "I've got it narrowed down to moose or kangaroo, but I'm leaning toward the second one. How hard do you think it is to import meat from Australia?"

"If you love me, Gertie, please don't ask me that right now."

Since Bee really did look green around the gills, Tess slid along the booth to let her mom out. "The bathroom's around the corner and through the swinging saloon doors," she said. "If you hit the spittoon statue, you've gone too far."

Her mother's look of level scorn said everything she felt about spittoons, no matter how artfully they'd been arranged. "This had better not be an attempt at poisoning me to get me out of the way for your party," she said. "I'm not as easy to kill off as one of the characters in your books."

"That's not a bad idea, actually," Tess mused as she watched her mother's determined march toward the bathroom. "There are several poisons that would knock her out for a few days without actually killing her. Strychnine is a definite no go, and there's no way I'm playing around with cyanide—but something gentler. Ipecac, maybe. Or eye drops in her coffee. I've always wanted to try that one."

"Mom! We're not poisoning Grandma."

Tess waved her hands like a magician showing off her trick. "Maybe I already have. Maybe you should be careful not to eat any of that dressing."

Nicki swept a pinkie finger around the rim of the ramekin that sat on the edge of Bee's garden salad. After popping it into her mouth, she said, "There. Now if your mom dies, I'm going out with her." She paused and picked up the ramekin with a wince. "Actually, there's something seriously wrong with this ranch. I hope Cyrus didn't leave it out overnight again."

Discussing poisons and room temperature mayo-based

dressings went a long way in suppressing what remained of Tess's appetite, but Gertrude attacked her burger with renewed vigor.

"It's not sweet enough to be moose," she said, chewing thoughtfully. "And there's a bit of earthiness in the aftertaste. I'm officially going with kangaroo."

Since Gertrude had yet to successfully guess the mystery meat despite their weekly trip into town to make the attempt, Tess wasn't optimistic about her chances of a cheap meal. Not that it mattered, when Gertrude bolted upright in her seat, the burger falling to her plate with a wet *thwap*.

"I think one of us should go check on Grandma," she said, her voice so thin and tight that it sounded as though it had been strung on a wire. "You won't believe who just walked in the door."

"Richard Burton?" Tess guessed, naming the most famous of Elizabeth Taylor's seven husbands.

Nicki snorted. "John Warner?"

"Eddie Fisher?"

"This is serious." Gertrude flapped her hand in a gesture Tess recognized as a request to borrow her phone. "I'm pretty sure that's Levi Parker."

"Who?" Tess asked. She handed Gertrude the phone and twisted around to get a look at their mystery visitor, but her daughter kicked her under the table. With a howl of protest, Tess clutched her injured shin. "There's no need to be so drastic, Gertie. I was going to be discreet."

Nicki laughed. "Tess, you haven't done a discreet thing a day of your life."

There was no time for Tess to defend herself before Gertrude dropped the phone in her lap and pretended to be busy playing with a straw wrapper. "Wait—I can't google his photo yet. He's coming this way. Act natural."

"I *am* acting natural. You're the one who's suddenly all weird and fangirly over a random stranger. Is he one of those influencers you're obsessed with? Is that what this is about?"

"Mom! Levi Parker isn't on Instagram. He's—"

"A notorious murderer with a penchant for elderly widows," a smooth male voice said from behind them. "I'm flattered you recognized me so easily. What was it that gave me away? The glasses? The tie? The face?"

At that, Tess had no qualms about turning around and taking thorough stock of this Levi Parker character. His glasses were ordinary enough, if a little too round for his face, and his tie was one of those skinny black ones that always made men look like door-to-door salesmen; but the real draw was the face. Tess wasn't sure she'd ever seen such a symmetrical collection of features before. Gently wisping crow's-feet and a touch of gray at his temples put him at around her own age—midforties and inching on up—but that was where all signs of aging stopped. His tawny skin was flawless, his eyebrows like a pair of perfectly groomed pipe cleaners. A thin mustache last pulled off by Clark Gable quivered on his upper lip, and his eyes sparkled in a deep-golden color that seemed unnatural by the dim lights of the restaurant.

By this time, Gertrude managed to change her expression of surprise to one of belligerent challenge instead. Tess almost pitied the poor man who was about to be on the receiving end of it. That expression had once caused Tess to throw out her favorite pair of gladiator sandals—a strappy five-hundred-dollar masterpiece that had made her legs look incredible. *It's fine*, Gertie had said at the time. *Wear them. Just as long as you want everyone to know you peaked ten years ago.*

"It was your face," Gertrude said, staring sullenly up at the feature in question. "You're all over the murder-podcast fanboards. So people know who to look out for when their grandmothers go missing."

"Wait. You're *that* Levi Parker?" Nicki asked. "I thought you were still in—" She cut herself off with a start, but it was too late. The man fell into a rich peal of laughter.

"Rikers?" He grinned. "Nah. A prison like that has enough overcrowding without holding on to an innocent man. I got out months ago. Did I hear you say your grandmother is missing?"

"She's not missing," Gertrude said, setting her jaw. "She's indisposed at the moment. And if you go anywhere near her, I'll—"

"Levi, dahling! There you are." Bernadette came out of the bathroom, looking none the worse for wear. In fact, the sight of the newcomer seemed to revitalize her. She practically threw herself into his arms, her girlish squeal curling up to meet him.

"I've been so lonely without you," Tess's mother cooed. "You should've called me when your flight got in."

"And ruin the surprise?" Levi lifted Bee's hand to his lips and left a wet, lingering kiss on the surface. "You know me…the mystery is half the fun. I like to keep my victims on their toes."

Mention of the word *victims* caused Gertrude to shoot up out of her seat, but Bernadette only dissolved further into his arms. "Oh, you naughty boy. My granddaughter is present."

"Not only is she present, but she's calling the police. Grandma, did you know that this man is wanted for the murder of two women in New York and one Detroit? That doesn't even count the theory that he was in Sedona a few months ago when—"

"Oh, he was definitely in Sedona a few months ago," Bernadette said with a laugh. "We met on a healing retreat back in June. The crystals in those mountains have incredible powers. One night, we slept in an energy vortex so strong that—"

Levi squeezed Tess's mother hard enough to cause the older woman to squeak. "I wouldn't say we did much sleeping out there, Bee."

"No." Planting her feet, Gertrude crossed her arms and took what could only be called a literal *stand*. "Something's wrong. He belongs behind bars. They don't just let people walk out of prison like that."

"Actually, they do if they don't have reason enough to hold them," Nicki said with an apologetic shrug. "Sorry, Gertie."

To an outsider, Nicki was just a well-informed librarian sharing her knowledge of the world, but both Tess and Gertrude knew better. If Nicki said something fell within the bounds of the justice system, it did.

"Oh, that." Bee scoffed. "It was nothing more than a misunderstanding. Levi was in the wrong place at the wrong time. You know all about that sort of thing, Tess."

It was true. She *did* know all about that. She also knew that being in a relationship with a dangerous man was no walk in the park—it was more like a walk in the deep, dark woods.

"Those podcasts of yours love to play him up as the villain, but it's nonsense," Bee added. "It's all just storytelling. Isn't that right, Levi?"

Levi's eyes met Tess's in a quick challenge. "I think everyone here knows the power of a compelling story."

Tess wasn't sure what to make of this. On the one hand, she absolutely agreed. Stories had the power to change minds, to reveal terrors and truths that might otherwise be closed to the human heart.

On the other hand, she didn't particularly care for potential murderers who were dating her mother.

"Well, I'm not ready to call it a night yet," Bee said, as though they were discussing a quiet family evening rather than a walking, talking serial killer in their midst. "What do you say we head into the bar for a nightcap, cookie?"

It took Tess a moment to realize the *cookie* in question wasn't her.

"That sounds perfect," Levi murmured. He lifted one eyebrow in a debonair move that Tess had only ever assumed existed in novels. "Would you ladies care to join us?"

"My mom doesn't socialize with killers, thanks," Gertrude answered for them. "And I'm a *kid*. I can't drink at a bar."

Instead of taking offense, Levi chuckled and tilted his head in a question for Nicki. "Fair enough. What about you? The invitation's an open one."

It said a lot about Tess's friendship with Nicki that the other woman immediately agreed. She'd no more abandon Tess's mother to her fate than she would her own. "That sounds nice, actually," Nicki said. "I hope you don't mind, but I'm a big fan of your podcast. Or, er, the podcast about you. Gertie and I listen to it every week."

"Excellent," Levi said with a flash of his teeth. They were perfectly white and straight except for his eyeteeth, which were angled just enough to give him the look of a vampire. He crooked both his elbows—one for Bee and one for Nicki. Bee's expression flickered in annoyance at having a third wheel, but Tess didn't care. What kind of a woman brought her much younger murderous lover on a visit to her family?

"Don't let him out of your sight, Nicki," Gertrude warned as she watched the trio prepare to depart. "And see if you can get him to leave you his glass when he's done. So you can get his saliva and fingerprints."

Levi chuckled again, this time with an infectious charm that even Tess felt herself warming up to. "Bless you, child. Those things have been on record since I was younger than you." He winked. "If it makes you feel any better, I promise to send your grandmother home before midnight. I wouldn't want my Cinderella turning into a pumpkin."

"That's not how the story works," Gertrude muttered, but Tess doubted anyone else heard her—or that it mattered. As

Levi led his prey away, the girl turned to Tess with a determined scowl. "Mom, pay the bill and follow me. We're going to the sheriff's office. *Now.*"

Chapter Three

"There's an infamous murderer staying in town, and we have to do something to stop him."

Gertrude waltzed through the doors of the sheriff's office like she owned the place, her step assured and her head held high. Tess felt equal ownership over the office—after all, she'd solved *several* murder cases under this roof, and without once demanding payment—but her step wasn't quite as sure. Mostly because Gertrude had run all the way over. Tess hunched against the growing stitch in her side and did her best not to look like a winded middle-aged writer who spent most of her time sitting behind a typewriter—her preferred tool of the trade.

"Nope. I'm not helping your mother plot her next book." Ivy Bell, the sheriff's right-hand deputy and a woman who more resembled a bulldog than a human being, didn't glance up from her computer. Her hair was pulled back into its customary knot at the back of her head, her no-nonsense expression perfect for protecting—and occasionally terrifying—the innocent. "Tell her to take a writing course if she can't come up with a plausible story line on her own."

"I'm serious." Gertrude threw herself into the chair on the other side of Ivy's desk. She began playing with a pair of handcuffs with the expertise of a teenager who regularly helped her mother research the ways and means of breaking out of them. "This isn't about a pretend murderer in one of her books. There's a *real* murderer here. He's staying at the hotel. Tell her, Mom. Make her post a man at the door before someone gets hurt."

Ivy finally looked up. "I'm not falling for it, so you can stop playing this game. This has something to do with your big party for tomorrow night, doesn't it? I already heard about you making Gertie play a corpse as a marketing ploy."

This proved too much for Tess, even in her winded state. "How dare you, Ivy. It's not a *ploy*—it's a theme. I need to be entertaining. People are coming hundreds of miles to see me."

"To see if they can find bloodstains on your hands, you mean."

"They're doing no such thing," Tess protested, refusing to let the deputy get to her. Ivy was one of her closest friends in town, but she'd never respected Tess's career the way it deserved. Mostly because a six-figure book deal had recently fallen into her own lap like a gift from the gods. Ivy had no idea how hard most of them had to work to get anywhere in this business. "And if they are, they're going to be disappointed. Everyone knows hydrogen peroxide wipes away all trace DNA from skin. The murderers in my books use it all the time."

Gertrude let out a grunt of irritation. "I can't believe you guys are joking around at a time like this. Levi Parker is *literally* roaming our streets right now. I'm going to find Sheriff Boyd."

"Wait." All Ivy's irreverence fled at once. "Did you just say Levi Parker? *The* Levi Parker? From that murder podcast?"

The look Gertrude shot Tess overflowed with triumph. "The very one. He's here to kill my grandma."

"If she's anything like your mother, I doubt she'll go down easily," a low, dry voice said from behind them. Tess didn't turn around—she didn't have to, since the familiar sound of Sheriff Boyd's drawl was more than enough to tip her off as to the new arrival—but Gertrude squeaked and launched herself at him.

"Sheriff Boyd, you have to *do* something," she pleaded. "He's at the bar with her right now. We left Nicki to guard them, but who knows how long that'll work? I think my grandma likes him. Like, *likes* him likes him."

Sheriff Boyd had spent enough time in Gertrude's company to catch her meaning despite the rapid succession of *likes*. "Levi Parker, huh?"

"Wait." Tess blinked. "You know who that is?"

"Of course I do. He's all Gertie's been talking about for the past two months." He smiled down at the girl in question. He might treat Tess the same way he would a live round of ammunition, but he'd always had an open tenderness for Gertrude. "Well, that and the newest *Nightwave* comic, but I learned to tune that part out. You're sure it's him?"

"Yes. He admitted to being in jail and everything."

"Interesting." Sheriff Boyd scrubbed a hand over his jaw. Tess knew that jaw well, and not only because it was most often set in a scowl for her. It was the same chiseled, slightly shadowed chin of her fictional detective, Gabriel Gonzales.

Even though she hadn't yet met Sheriff Boyd when she'd started penning the series that made her a star, the resemblance was uncanny. They had the same raven's-wing black hair, the same gruff growl in their voices, and even a similar cleft palate scar.

The worst part was, that wasn't even the worst part. Whereas she was in a fair way to giving Detective Gabriel Gonzales a romantic happy ever after—or as close as you were allowed to get in a thriller series with no end in sight— she and Sheriff Boyd had only shared one real kiss. It had been an *amazing* kiss, and Tess wasn't averse to trying it out again, but there were…complications.

As far as she was concerned, the complications weren't insuperable. Yes, she'd recently gone through a particularly nasty divorce. And okay, Sheriff Boyd wasn't the only man she'd kissed since that particularly nasty divorce had been finalized.

But all it would take was a word, a look, a flutter of his eyelashes, and she'd set every bit of that aside.

Unfortunately, Sheriff Boyd didn't speak. Or look. Or flutter. Ever since the last murder had rocked this town, he'd retreated behind a wall of professional disinterest. For all that Tess couldn't get a foothold, she may as well have been dangling off the side of a cliff.

"Interesting?" Gertrude echoed. Tess might have been having a hard time reaching the sheriff lately, but her daughter had the man wrapped around her little finger. "My school's new band teacher is interesting. The mole on my mom's neck that keeps getting bigger is interesting. Levi Parker is—"

"I do *not* have a neck mole," Tess felt compelled to protest. "It's a freckle, and it's the same size it's always been."

Ivy snorted. "I'd be happy to take a look at it, if you want."

Tess tugged at the top of her embroidered top, lest the wayward freckle show itself. "Can we please focus on what's important here? Victor, if you know who this podcast man is, then you're saying he really is a murderer?"

"If I remember rightly, he was never formally charged. Just held on suspicion."

"At *Rikers*?" Tess demanded.

"The deaths of three women would necessitate a careful watch. I didn't realize the charges had been cleared." He eyed Tess's face with a narrowness that made her feel even more uncomfortable about that freckle. "Or that you'd invited your mother here for the big celebration."

Of the two, Tess had the feeling the second crime was the one that loomed larger in his mind—though why it should bother him, she didn't know. Sheriff Boyd had grown up in this town, so there was a chance he'd met her mother a few times over the decades, but he'd never once mentioned knowing her. Or wanting to know her.

"You don't *invite* Bernadette Springer anywhere," she said. "She just shows up."

"Sounds like someone else I know," Ivy muttered under her breath.

Tess tactfully chose to ignore her. "Look, I'm not sure what this guy is doing here, but if he's really as dangerous as Gertie claims—"

"He *is*," Gertrude said with a jut of her lower lip.

"—and if there's a chance he's going to kill my mom in her sleep tonight..." Tess allowed her voice to trail off. She paused to give someone a chance to contradict her, but no one did. "That's it, then. I'd like to lodge a formal complaint."

"About what?" the sheriff asked. "That a man came to a town where you're throwing a huge book-release party? One that's been publicized widely and without regard for the strain it's put on my resources?"

They were both good questions. Even though Tess had discussed the logistics with the sheriff ahead of time, she may have *slightly* undersold the amount of push her publisher planned to put behind it.

"Victor, I cannot and will not have that man murdering my mother right now," she said. "There's too much riding on this. Make him come back and try later. That'll give me time to open the bookstore and equip my mother with some common sense—or at the very least, pepper spray and a gun."

"This is about that journalist you have coming tomorrow, isn't it?" Ivy asked.

Tess closed her eyes and counted to ten, but it was no use. Despite the fact she'd only been living in this town for a little over a year, these people knew her too well. Back in Seattle, she'd gone for months at a time without talking to her neighbors, her whole life a careful balance of curated appointments and spaced-out drinks with friends. Here in Winthrop, she couldn't go five feet without running into someone she knew, owed a favor to, and/or had accused of murder at one time or another.

"Please?" she begged; there was no other way around it. "If not for me, then for Gertie? She's gone through enough trauma without watching her grandmother fall prey to a schmoozing serial killer thirty years her junior."

Tess knew it was an underhanded trick, throwing her almost-sixteen-year-old under the bus and forcing the sheriff to swerve to avoid her, but it was the only way. Canceling tomorrow's event wasn't an option, and batting her eyelashes would only get her a grunt and a suggestion that she fix her contact lenses.

Sheriff Boyd sighed long and hard. "You really think this man is stupid enough to be seen in public with your mother a few short months after being released from prison, only to bump her off in the middle of the biggest brouhaha this town has ever seen?"

No, she didn't, which was why she was here, asking for help rather than handcuffing her mother to her own wrist and refusing to let her out of her sight. This was for her daughter and her daughter only.

And Sheriff Boyd, for all his severity, knew it.

When Tess didn't back down, the sheriff threw up his hands. "Fine. I'll go to the hotel and see what I can find out. But I don't have any deputies to spare, so taking care of your mother will have to fall to you. Get her to stay at your place, and ask Nicki or Ivy to sleep over. That's the best I can do."

"Not me," Ivy said with a firm shake of her head. "You forget that I've spent the night on Tess's futon before. There's no way I can do crowd control tomorrow if I'm hunched over in pain."

"I'll call Nicki right now," Tess promised. "She's done with most of her party-planning duties. The only thing she has to do tomorrow is help me drink all that sparkling wine."

Ivy sniffed at this unfair distribution of labor. "That settles it. The next time you throw a big book party, I'm coming as a fellow author and nothing else."

The sheriff one-upped her with a grunt as he headed for the door. "The next time Tess throws a big book party, I'm shutting the whole thing down before it begins."

Chapter Four

THE NIGHT PASSED UNEVENTFULLY.

True, Tess *had* spent most of it pacing the kitchen floor while Nicki kept watch at the door, but that was beside the point. In the full light of day, she could admit that it was highly unlikely for Levi Parker to burst in with a machine gun or creep in through the window with a knife between his teeth, but nighttime fears were a powerful thing. Some of Tess's best thriller ideas came late at night, when every anxiety became a pulsing, powerful magnification that quashed common sense flat.

"If you love me, Gertie, you'll bring me three aspirin, a strong cup of coffee, and a mirror," Bee said from her position against Tess's headboard. A gel mask pressed elegantly across her forehead, but it was doing little to improve the dark circles under her eyes. Apparently, she hadn't slept well either, despite having claimed Tess's bedroom for herself. "How long do we have before we need to be in town? That ranch dressing last night did a number on me. I'll need at least two hours to spackle my face on."

Gertrude giggled as she set about assembling the required items. "Nicki left as soon as the sun came up, but Mom and I are heading out once I finish packing the cupcakes. They're my greatest creation yet. When you bite into one, the strawberry blood squirts out everywhere."

Bee moaned as soon as she caught sight of herself in the small hand mirror. "You'll have to come back for me," she said. "I look like a haggard old crone. There's no way I'm letting Levi see me like this."

"You shouldn't let him see you at all," Tess pointed out, but she didn't know why she bothered.

"And you shouldn't jump to conclusions about a man you've only just met. It's not as if you have a good track record when it comes to relationships. If you'll recall, I warned you about Quentin. There was always a shifty-eyed look about him I didn't trust. Now we know why."

Tess tilted her head back with a groan. She was willing to take a lot from the woman who'd given her life, but that particular wound hadn't healed yet. "Stop right there. You have no right to lecture me about the way my marriage ended. Not when you're dating a known criminal."

"Levi is an *implied* criminal. It's different."

"Fine. Not when you're dating an *implied* criminal—or when you brought him to this town with you." Tess waited until she could hear Gertrude whistling to herself in the kitchen before she lowered her voice to a dangerous hiss. "Your *granddaughter* lives here, for crying out loud. Even if there's only a 2 percent chance he's actually dangerous, isn't that enough? You know what that girl has been through lately. You know how much she's suffered."

To her mother's credit, a look of genuine regret crept

across her face. She tugged the gel mask down until it hung around her neck, looking as limp as she did.

"I didn't invite him, if it helps," Bee said. "He just followed me. He keeps doing that even though I've sworn a hundred times I'm not half the fool he thinks I am."

"Have you tried maybe not telling him where you're going?"

Her mother's gaze didn't quite meet her own. "It's true that we *may* have had a brief flirtation in Sedona, but you know what they say: What happens in the crystal vortex stays in the crystal vortex."

"That's not—" Tess began, but she gave up. Getting her mother to see reason was a thing she'd stopped trying to do a long time ago. Her mom was as sharp as a box of tacks, hilariously irreverent, and—despite appearances—a genuinely caring person. She was also as immovable as a brick wall. "Fine. You win. I'm sure he's a lovely, misjudged person who will end up bringing nothing but joy to this town and our home."

At the mention of *home*, Tess's mother glanced around her surroundings, her gaze taking in the familiar log walls and not-so-familiar upgrades to the electric and water systems. Although Tess had done her best to keep the basic structure the same, the transformation to the log cabin that had been built by her grandfather's own two hands was nothing short of miraculous. It had taken several months, a lot of money, and more splinters than Tess cared to remember, but the experience had brought her and Gertrude together in ways she'd never imagined.

"You've done wonders with the cabin, by the way," Bee said with something approaching approval. "I couldn't even stand to set foot inside this place when Dad lived here. The *spiders*, Tess. You have no idea."

"Actually, you sent me here to live with him one summer, remember? The spiders and I got very close during those three months."

"Did I? Odd. I don't remember that."

Tess wasn't surprised by this confession. Her mother often forgot large chunks of her memory—not because of the twinkling twilight of old age, but because convenience and comfort rendered it necessary. The summer Tess had been abandoned here had been the summer her mom had met the man who would become her second husband. At the precocious age of eleven, Tess had mostly been in the way.

"What are you really doing here, Mom?" Tess asked, suddenly unwilling to play the older woman's games. "You hate this town. You hate that Grandpa hid himself away here, and you hate that I'm doing the same thing with Gertie. Why the sudden change of mind?"

Once again, Bee failed to make eye contact with Tess. This time, however, she hid that fact by springing up and wrapping herself in a satin robe.

"You always were a suspicious little thing," she said as she extracted what looked like a full tackle box of cosmetics from her luggage. "Seeing mystery and intrigue everywhere you turned. Did it ever occur to you that I'm long overdue for a visit with my two favorite people in the whole world?"

"Seeing mystery and intrigue everywhere I turn is how I

make a living," Tess countered. "And no, that didn't occur to me. Not when you first got here and not now that I've met the man you dragged with you."

"I've never had to *drag* a man anywhere a day in my life," Bee said tartly. "Unlike you, they actually enjoy it when I walk in the door."

Tess understood that as her cue to be elsewhere and left her mother to her toilette.

———

In the end, Tess and Gertrude waited for Bernadette to finish getting ready before they headed into town. The result was that they were almost an hour later than planned as Tess pulled her bright orange Jeep up the familiar road—a thing not only evident in the chiming of the clock at the end of Main Street but also in the way the sidewalks were already teeming with visitors.

"Oh, my." Bee peered through the windows at the overflow on the street. In addition to the familiar faces of the townsfolk, Tess spotted a number of uniformed deputies and even a few news vans. "I know people enjoy your little books, but I had no idea you were *this* famous."

Gertrude popped a bubble of gum. "She's not."

"I beg your pardon. The *New York Times Book Review* called my last book 'a masterpiece of villainy.' Those aren't terms they throw around lightly."

Gertrude snorted and pointed toward the largest gathering of people. It wasn't, as might be expected, in front of the

Paper Trail. Instead, everyone was pushing and pulling to get into the hotel. "'A masterpiece of villainy' might get you a few people driving up from Seattle for the day, but isn't that the lady from—*ohmigod*."

Tess stepped heavily on the brakes, sending all three of them lurching. "What? What happened? Did I run over a squirrel again?"

"Mom, do you have any idea who that is?"

Tess squinted and tried to figure out who Gertrude was pointing at. It looked like Ivy was heading out of the hotel, and Tess could make out the bright red hair of a local reporter who covered most of Okanogan County, but neither of them would cause her daughter to squeal like that. Those noises were reserved for the author of the *Nightwave* comics and—

"It's her. It's Neptune Jones. I can't *believe* you got her to come to your stupid bookstore opening—and that you didn't tell me." Gertrude was already halfway out of her seat belt. Tess had to shoot out an arm to stop her.

"Wait, Gertie. *Wait.* Who's Neptune Jones?"

Gertrude stopped and stared. "Are you kidding me right now? Neptune Jones is the lady who runs *Murder, at Last.* She's my idol. She's my everything. She's my—"

"Oh. It's the woman from the murder podcast? The one you guys keep yammering on about?" Tess got the car moving again before she realized what she'd just said. She touched the brakes once more. "Wait. I didn't invite her. Why would she be here for my book release?"

Tess wasn't sure how long it would have taken her to put the pieces together if her mother hadn't moaned out loud. At first, she feared the ranch dressing was making a return attack on her mom's digestive system, but her mom's moan quickly turned to a sob. That was when Tess caught sight of Sheriff Boyd staring at them from across the street, his expression one of soul-deep weariness. She'd seen that particular look more times than she cared to count.

"Mom?" Gertrude asked. "What is it? What's wrong with Grandma? What does it have to do with the podcast?"

"No. I don't believe it. Levi *couldn't* have killed someone. No murderer is that stupid."

After quickly putting the car into Park, Tess yanked open the door and made a beeline for the sheriff, heedless of the people she had to push through to get there. When she spoke again, it was for his ears only.

"You said it yourself, Victor. Levi wouldn't make an attempt on someone's life. Not when his identity has already been advertised. Not after you paid him a visit and warned him away."

"He didn't kill anyone," the sheriff said, his mouth a flat line. "And he'll never again get the chance to try."

Tess felt the ground start to slip and slide beneath her.

"I'm sorry, Tess, but the hotel staff found him early this morning. He's dead."

Chapter Five

THE TUNA WAS DELIVERED RIGHT ON TIME.

Gertrude had convinced Tess to order it from a Seattle company that would catch the fish and pack it on dry ice directly from the deck of the boat. According to the man she'd spoken to on the phone, the fish was so fresh that it was still alive when it was slipped into the cooler. The whole operation was as streamlined as the black market organ trade—and equally as expensive, according to the hefty bill Tess had received.

She'd assuaged her conscience by the belief that it would be worth it—for the fresh taste of albacore two hundred miles from the coast, for the chance to impress her guests with something special on her big day. The fact that it required Tess to charter the flight that could also carry Mumford Umberto to her doorstep had been a mere bonus.

Oh, that the plane had crashed somewhere in the Cascades. Oh, that Mumford Umberto had been forced to eat the tuna to survive until help arrived.

"You want me to reschedule this interview until a later date?" Mumford asked as he stood next to the giant cooler holding the fish, his expression lit up like a Christmas tree in the middle of Rockefeller Center. "Are you kidding? This is the stuff Pulitzers are made of. I got here right in time."

Tess cast a pleading look around her, but there was no one here to help. From the moment that Levi Parker's death had been announced, the whole town had descended into chaos. Every available deputy was buzzing around the hotel in search of clues, and every available townsperson was buzzing around, watching them do it.

Even Gertrude and Bernadette were currently out of reach. Tess had been forced to leave her mother stretched out on the floor of the bookstore, which was the only place she could think to take her as the first spasms of shock began. Gertrude had promised to keep watch over her grandmother, but only if Tess gathered as many details as she could in the meantime. Tess would have preferred to pack them both up and send them to the cabin to wait out this first wave of grief, but Sheriff Boyd had asked them to stick around for questioning.

And by *asked them to stick around*, Tess meant he'd ordered them to stay away from his crime scene until he was ready to take their statements. Do not pass Go, do not collect two hundred dollars, and definitely do not insert your nose where it doesn't belong.

"What are the chances you can get me a sit-down with the sheriff heading up the investigation?" Mumford asked, his voice nasally in a way that Tess found particularly grating. She'd seen pictures of him online and had extensively researched his credentials ahead of time, but nothing could have prepared her for this tiny slip of a man with glasses the size of a praying mantis's eyes and a head of hair that she was almost certain had been glued on. A less distinguished-looking journalist had never existed in the annals of history. "You're good friends with him, right? Could I get an exclusive? Would he be willing to take a picture with the body?"

Tess bit back a sigh and did her best to appear like the upright, composed professional she decidedly wasn't. "Sheriff Boyd is busy gathering evidence right now. When he's ready to talk, I'm sure he'll call a press conference, the same as any other member of law enforcement."

Mumford didn't appear abashed by this. "What about Ivy Bell? She's his chief deputy, right? From what I understand, you two share a literary agent. You must be close enough to ask a favor."

Tess tried to remind herself that she'd chosen this man because of his impeccable research skills and that reading up on her background was literally part of his job, but it was slow going.

"A man is dead, Mr. Umberto," she said, calling on her mother's most dignified Jackie Kennedy impression. "Perhaps we should focus on giving the family some space before we swoop in like vultures to pick over his remains."

"Oh, didn't you know?" A low, sultry female voice assailed them from behind. "Levi Parker doesn't have any family."

Even though Tess had only listened to one full podcast from Neptune Jones—the one that had shamefully slandered her—she'd have recognized the woman's voice anywhere. There was a reason she had thirty-five million downloads every month. Listening to her speak was like being dipped in a vat of chocolate before getting toweled off with crushed velvet.

"It's quite sad, actually," the woman continued. "He grew up horribly neglected by his foster family, ran away from home at the age of fourteen, and spent the majority of his twenties eking out a living in a commune in upstate New York—though, if you ask me, calling it anything but a cult is doing a disservice to communes. With an upbringing like that, it's no wonder he turned to a life of crime. All those elderly women he targeted were clearly stand-ins for his foster mother, who died before he could take his vengeance on her. Oedipus and Freud would have had a field day with him."

All of this was uttered in the dulcet, cultured tones of a woman who was accustomed to having—and holding—an audience. Both Tess and Mumford were too dazed to respond right away, so she laughed and held out her hand.

"Sorry to unload all that on you, but I couldn't help over-hearing. I'm Neptune Jones. You may have heard of me. I'm—"

"I know who you are," Tess said irritably. Honestly, from the way the woman was speaking, you'd have thought only one of them made a living fabricating stories out of thin air. True, only one of them *did* currently have her face splashed across Times Square, but Tess could have pushed for a pro-motional screen if she'd wanted one.

Of course, she wouldn't have looked nearly as good blown up to twenty-nine feet. She knew for a fact that Neptune Jones was close to her own age, but the woman's light brown skin, gorgeously flowing black hair, and elegant—and defi-nitely braless—pantsuit put Tess and her frizzy-haired bohemia to shame. This woman could have been painted on the side of the Hoover Dam and made it look good.

Since the last thing Tess wanted was to sound petulant in front of Mumford, she slapped on a smile. "My daughter is a big fan of yours, Ms. Jones. I'm sure she'll accost you as soon as she gets the chance."

"Your daughter's named Gertrude, right?" Neptune asked.

"Gertrude Alex Harrow, soon to be sixteen and starting her sophomore year at the local high school," Mumford announced. He was obviously feeling the need to show off, images of his Pulitzer already starting to melt away. "She was born and grew up in Seattle, but she and her mother now reside here in Winthrop. She was an integral part in both of Tess's murders being solved. Apparently, she's quite precocious."

"They weren't *my* murders," Tess protested. "The only thing I've killed lately is a fifteen-ounce steak at the hotel restaurant."

Instead of laughing, Neptune turned toward her with sharp, narrow-eyed appraisal. "That's right. Someone mentioned you were at the hotel last night around the time Mr. Parker arrived. I got in about an hour too late."

"An hour too late?" Tess echoed, suspicious. "For what?"

Neptune brushed off Tess's questions with an airy wave of her hand. "He'd already gone upstairs by the time I tried to check in. My producer and I are usually hot enough on his trail to request the room next to his, but for some strange reason, the hotel is already as full as it can hold."

"For the bookstore opening," Mumford supplied, nodding along. "If I wasn't staying with Ms. Harrow, I'd probably be forced to put up a tent on the edge of Main Street. This town is a lot smaller than I was expecting." He turned to Tess with a smile that showcased a gap between his two front teeth. "Speaking of, are we heading back to your cabin before the bookstore launch party? I'd like to get settled in and survey some of your property before it gets dark. I'm especially interested in the pond where you found the first dead body."

Tess bit back a groan. In all the upheaval of Levi's death and Mumford's arrival, she'd somehow forgotten that she was expected to play hostess to this man for a full week. It would have been bad enough with a dead man on her hands; with a dead man *and* her mother on her hands, it was catastrophic. She didn't have nearly enough beds.

"I don't know when we'll be able to get home," Tess demurred, "or even if it's a good idea for you to stick around."

Her hint failed just as spectacularly the second time around.

"You couldn't pry me away with a crowbar," he said with a wink so deliberate that it took a full two seconds to complete. "This is the best story that's landed in my lap in a long time."

"Same here," Neptune agreed. "Since the moment I started tracking Levi, I knew something like this would happen—though, to be honest, I thought it was the old broad he's been sniffing around who'd end up dead, not him. I wonder where she is. The police are going to want to question her first."

Tess coughed so heavily that Mumford felt compelled to whack her heftily on the back. For such a small man, he packed a powerful punch.

"Wait," Tess said as soon as her lungs recovered from the blow. "Are you saying that you've been following a murderer all over the country? *On purpose?*"

Neptune eyed her askance. "I thought you said you knew who I was."

"I do. I mean, I did. I mean—" Tess forced a deep breath. She wasn't going to get anywhere if she let this woman fluster her. "I thought your podcast was about solving murders, not stalking a man."

Neptune Jones already had a good five inches on Tess in the height department, but these words caused the woman to straighten in a way that seemed to double the distance. "I don't *stalk* him. He's the number one suspect in a total of three murders, all of which remain open and unsolved. Someone has to keep an eye on his movements to ensure he doesn't kill again. That someone, unfortunately, is me. Since he was released from prison, I've been the only person standing between him and another hapless victim."

Tess had endured just about enough of this woman uttering every sentence like a sponsor for home-delivered meal kits was waiting right around the corner. "Didn't you say you were traveling with your producer?" she asked.

Mumford held back a laugh.

"That," Neptune said, her nostrils tightening to tiny pinpricks, "is beside the point. Sven knows what kind of danger we're in every time we pack up our things and head out the door."

Tess would have been happy to leave the conversation—and the woman—there, but Mumford had regained his composure by this time. "Did I hear you say that there's a suspect already? A woman Levi had been tracking as his next victim?"

Neptune lowered her voice to what Tess imagined was supposed to be a confidential whisper, but it sounded more like an emcee talking over a radio-announcer convention.

"Yes, the poor thing. She fits the exact description of his victims. An elderly woman, living alone and without anyone to care about where she is or what she's up to. Wealthy, from the look of things, and desperate for affection. You know the type. When a woman's been on her own for that long, she starts to cling to any man willing to pay her a compliment."

Tess felt her whole body grow hot. Her mother might not have been the best judge of character—and the fact that she'd willingly jumped into a murderer's bed was, okay, an objectively terrible decision—but she wasn't *desperate*. And she had people who cared about her.

Gertrude cared. Tess cared.

"Who is she?" Mumford whipped out a notepad and pulled a pen from his pocket, where an array of five similar pens sat waiting for use. "And what are her current whereabouts?"

Tess could have easily enlightened him on both fronts, but she hesitated before answering. From the way Neptune grew equally reserved, it was obvious the other woman also wasn't about to hand out clues like they were candy.

The whole situation would have been hilarious if it

hadn't involved Tess's mother so closely. Take one journalist expecting a puff piece and stumbling onto a murder. Add a murder podcaster who obviously had zero scruples when it came to chasing down a good story—literally. Mix in an author who adapted her real-life experiences with murder into award-winning novels, and this was what you got.

Mistrust and greed in all directions. They all wanted to get their hands on that story, but only one of them was going to—and Tess knew *exactly* who that was going to be. She just had to find a way not to alienate these two people while she was at it. They might not know it yet, but they had the power to destroy her bookstore before she even opened its doors.

"If the woman is arrested on murder charges, as I expect, then I'm sure that information will shortly become public," Neptune said tightly.

"She won't be arrested," Tess said. "Bernadette Springer has an airtight alibi for last night."

Tess shouldn't have felt so pleased at catching the other two off guard, but she was only human.

"How do you know about Bernadette Springer?" Neptune asked.

Mumford wasn't far behind. "Wait. What am I missing?"

Tess turned to him with a kind smile. "Bernadette Springer is the name of the woman Levi Parker had earmarked as his latest victim. She's not—as Ms. Jones here wants you to think—a lonely old woman. She has money, yes, and he may have thought he could get away with murdering her and covering his crime, but she came to the one place she knew that man could never hurt her."

Mumford darted his tongue out and touched the tip of his lips. "You mean to Winthrop? She came here to get away from Levi Parker? Because…it's so remote?"

Tess shook her head. "No, not because of its location."

Neptune caught on long before Mumford did. "Because of you," she breathed. "You're her daughter, aren't you? I don't know why I didn't see the resemblance before."

"Before you start airing stories about her involvement in Levi's death, I should probably inform you that she stayed with me last night. We met up at the hotel restaurant for dinner, at which point Levi joined us. She was never alone with him after that. Both Sheriff Boyd and I can vouch for it."

Instead of backing off and admitting defeat, as Tess had hoped, Neptune only narrowed her eyes and leaned closer. From this distance, Tess could count the crow's-feet—which were, to be fair, very few. Before she ran this woman out of town, she seriously needed to discover the brand of her face cream.

"So you weren't just inside the restaurant at the same time as Levi," Neptune said with a low whistle. "You were literally sitting *at* the same table. Did you notice anything off about his appearance?"

Tess blinked. "I'm sorry, what?"

"What did he eat? Drink? Did he share a plate with anyone else?"

Tess found that being on the receiving end of Neptune's barrage of questions felt uncomfortably like sitting opposite Sheriff Boyd at his most autocratic. "What does that have to do with anything? Of course I didn't notice anything off about him. It was the first time we'd ever met. He was perfectly smarmy—and alive—when I left him. He and my mother had a few drinks at the bar, but a friend of mine stayed with them to—" She cut herself off as soon as she realized what was going on. "Wait. You want to know what he ate? Are you saying he was *poisoned*? At the hotel?"

A smug lift of Neptune's lips was all the confirmation Tess needed.

"That explains everything," Tess said as a feeling of deep, abiding relief washed over her. This wasn't murder; it wasn't even foul play. She could have this whole terrible mishap cleared up in a matter of minutes—and then it would be back to her bookstore, back to her feature article, and back to normal.

"I know what killed him," she announced, her voice ringing loud and clear. "This is nothing more than a case of food poisoning gone terribly wrong."

———

Tess pushed her way past Mumford and Neptune, abandoning the cooler of tuna to its fate. She'd never been so delighted by a case of bad ranch dressing in her life. All these people milling around and asking questions, the drama surrounding a death on the *very* day she was supposed to be reclaiming her reputation—it wasn't the taint of murder following her around. It was rancid mayonnaise. She could have laughed out loud at the irony of it all.

She made her way toward the hotel, ducking underneath

the yellow police tape and making a beeline straight for Ivy. The deputy looked grim and overworked—two things that didn't abate when she caught sight of Tess.

"Not now," Ivy said before Tess even managed to open her mouth. "I don't know if you've noticed, but we're kind of dealing with a homicide here."

"No, you're not. You're dealing with an accidental death." Tess registered the sound of footsteps behind her, annoyed to find that both Mumford and Neptune had followed her. "Negligence, maybe. Food-sanitation problems, definitely. But Levi wasn't killed on purpose."

"Tess..."

"I'm serious," she said. "Call up Nicki and ask her, if you don't believe me. Both she and my mom tasted bad food from the hotel restaurant last night."

"Nicki Nickerson, local bookmobile librarian and Tess Harrow's best friend," Mumford said as if narrating a nature documentary.

"Interesting," Neptune murmured. "I didn't know a book-mobile librarian was a real thing."

"It's actually quite common in rural areas like this," Mumford said. "When a population is this spread out, resources are often best spent bringing the library to the people rather than the other way around."

Tess could appreciate library advocacy as much as the next author, but this was neither the time nor the place to plug literacy services. She quickly tuned the two of them out and focused on Ivy instead.

"I know the sheriff is busy, but could you please tell him

I have important and timely information about the case?" Tess asked. "I promise he's going to want to hear this. It'll save him a mountain of paperwork. You know how he feels about paperwork."

Ivy hesitated in the exact way Tess knew she would. If there was one consistency about Sheriff Boyd—aside from his gruff exterior, inability to ask for help, and his not-so-secret love for the Detective Gonzales books—it was that he hated the hundreds of different forms associated with working as a rural officer of the law.

"Is there a reason you're traveling with an entourage?" Ivy asked, gesturing with her thumb at the two people standing behind Tess. "Because I'm not sure the sheriff is going to want a whole troop of people moving in and out of his crime scene."

Tess had to work hard to subdue her sudden expression of delight. *She* might not be able to prevent these two from following close at her heels, but Ivy was more than capable of it.

"Sorry, guys," Tess said as soon as she was able to slap on a semblance of regret. "You'll have to sit this one out. Sheriff Boyd is really uptight about his process. He—"

"—does things by the book," Neptune filled in for her. "Don't worry. I know the type."

Tess doubted she had any idea just how *by the book* Sheriff Boyd could get, but she was too relieved to find them lingering behind the caution tape to care. She was also too smart to give Ivy a chance to second-guess her decision. With a quick nod of thanks, she dashed past the officers moving about their work and headed up the stairs.

Levi Parker's hotel room was the largest of the corner suites, which told Tess a few things: one, that he enjoyed traveling in style; and two, that he'd planned this trip in advance. Those rooms were always the first to go, so he must have called several weeks ago to make his reservation.

Which, in turn, meant that her *mother* had planned this trip in advance—and without a word of warning. As soon as Bee recovered from the shock of Levi's death, they were going to have a serious talk about boundaries. Tess was always happy to see her mother, but she did have a life and responsibilities.

And, you know, a strong desire not to bring more dead bodies down upon her head.

"Sheriff Boyd, I have good news," Tess announced as she approached the room. "Well, *good* is probably the wrong word to use when a man is dead, but—"

She halted on the threshold, her body growing rigid at the sight of what greeted her on the other side. Levi's body had already been escorted away, so it wasn't the presence of death that shocked her. It was the *manner* of it that gave her pause. Everywhere Tess's gaze landed was a scene of utter destruction. Furniture had been tipped and turned over; paintings hung askew from the walls. The bedding was a knot of tumbled blankets and sheets, and Levi's luggage had been tossed about like it had gone through a wind tunnel.

"Good God." She put her hand over her mouth. If this was what food poisoning looked like, she was going to hire a professional taster before she ever left the house again. "What happened in here?"

"Tess!" Sheriff Boyd popped his head around the corner, flinging up his arms to keep her at bay—not that it was necessary. She wouldn't set foot inside that room for anything. "What are you doing up here? I told Ivy not to let anyone up until I finished securing the scene."

Tess ignored him. In this instance, *anyone* didn't include her. She had pertinent information about the case. She had facts. She had—

"Victor, why does it look like Levi Parker fought off a wild animal in here? What *happened* to him?"

Tess's use of the sheriff's first name always had a way of turning him—and her—into human beings rather than friendly adversaries. His arm was around her shoulders before she realized it, heavy and comforting in a way he rarely allowed himself to be. Even though he was clearly escorting her away from the scene, she was happy to let him.

"I came up here to tell you that both my mom and Nicki felt sick after eating at the hotel last night. Someone said… That is, I was told…" She forced herself to swallow and focus. "Victor, Levi was poisoned, wasn't he? That didn't look like poison. It looked like cold-blooded murder."

"It was cold-blooded murder," he said, his mouth grim. "But it was also poison."

"Really? But how…"

"It's too early to call it, but I'm guessing either strychnine or botulinum, and in a high-enough concentration to leave no room for doubt. He obviously ingested something that affects the muscles—spasms, seizures, that sort of thing. He didn't go down easily." They stopped at the end of the hallway, but Victor didn't lift his arm from her shoulder right away. Instead, he gave it a light squeeze, his fingers like comforting pincers. "Whoever did this to him wanted him to suffer."

Tess appreciated this new foray into open, honest communication between professionals, but she was also no fool. "Why are you telling me this?"

Despite the situation and the grave, ashen expression on his face, Sheriff Boyd chuckled. "Because I want you on your guard for once in your godforsaken life, that's why. Look— there's no mistaking that this Levi Parker character had a lot of enemies, and I doubt that whoever killed him is likely to start bumping people off just for the fun of it. But anyone with access to these kinds of poisons—and who isn't afraid to use them—is dangerous. I'd prefer it if you didn't start playing amateur sleuth this time around."

"I wasn't playing—" Tess began, but the sheriff wasn't done yet.

"In fact, if you *really* need a new plotline for your next book that badly, I'll give you an inside look at one of my older cases as soon as all this is finished."

Tess's whole being stilled in an instant. "How old are we talking?"

He didn't mistake her meaning. "From back when I worked in Seattle." He held up a warning finger. "I won't go into detail out of respect for the families, but if you want a good hook and some insider information about how a *real* detective would go about solving a case, I can get you what you need. Homicide, arson, a little light espionage..."

If Tess had been Gertrude's age, she would have squealed with excitement. As a grown woman who had complete control over herself and her reactions, she only gasped. What Sheriff Boyd was offering her was no small gesture; she could count the number of things he'd willingly shared about his past as a big-city detective on two fingers. He *never* talked about his history if he could possibly avoid it. Tess suspected that the recent reappearance of his sister, Kendra, had something to do with this new, more open side of him, but she liked to think that there were personal motivations in there, as well.

Personal, *private* motivations.

Maybe, just maybe, Tess was finding her foothold. Maybe, just maybe, he was finally willing to let her in.

"Should I take the fact that your whole body is vibrating with excitement as a yes?" the sheriff drawled, but not in an unkind way.

"Yes, sir. Absolutely, sir. I'll keep out of your way and leave the poison business all to you." She was mid-salute when a thought occurred to her. "Only…aren't you going to need to talk to my mom?"

"Yes, but there's no need for you to be present at the time."

That sounded like something he couldn't legally enforce, but Tess didn't feel like pushing it. "And what if, say, the journalist staying with me for the next week does a little nosing around on his own?"

Sheriff Boyd groaned. "Tess, this wasn't meant to be a negotiation."

"I know, but he's already showing an interest in what's

going on." She held up her hands and started backing toward the stairwell. Several additional arguments occurred to her, but she wasn't about to risk the offer to sit down and really *talk* about some of the things Victor had seen and done in his lifetime. Maybe they could even do it over a bottle of wine. "I'll do my best to keep him quiet, but I should warn you that there's also a famous murder podcaster in town, and she's very keen on getting to the bottom of things. Apparently, she's been tracking Levi for some time."

That got his attention. "Not Neptune Jones?"

Too late, Tess remembered that Sheriff Boyd and Gertrude had been discussing Levi Parker and the podcast that had made him famous for several months now. The sheriff probably knew more about Neptune Jones than Tess did.

"The one and only," Tess admitted, since he'd find out the truth for himself soon enough. "I ran into her downstairs. She's the one who told me about the poisoning. I know you hate it when people dig around in your cases, but—"

"By all means, send her up."

Tess stopped, certain she must have heard him wrong. "I'm sorry, you want me to do *what* to her?"

"You said she's downstairs, right?" he asked.

"Yeah. She's hovering around like a buzzard waiting for the wolf to finish his meal."

"Am I supposed to be the wolf in that scenario?" he asked with a quizzical tilt to his head. Sighing, he didn't wait for her to answer. "Never mind. It's better if I don't know. Have Ivy let her through, but only if she boots up first."

Tess paused, waiting for the catch. There wasn't one.

"I'd like to get her thoughts on some files I found in his luggage," the sheriff added—as if Tess didn't have eyes in her head and a brain in her skull, or a mind for ferreting out evil as well as any silly podcaster. "If anyone will have valuable insight into what he planned to do with them, it's her."

Chapter Six

TESS WASN'T THE ONLY PERSON TO FEEL SLIGHTED BY the sheriff's inclusion of Neptune Jones in what was likely to prove the most thrilling murder this town had seen since, well, the last murder.

"What do you mean, he asked Neptune to go up?" Mumford pouted as soon as Tess broke the news.

"What do you mean, he asked Neptune to go up?" Gertrude echoed after Tess finished dragging Mumford with her to the bookstore. They carried the cooler of tuna between them, the weight of it bumping along the sidewalk with every other step. She had no idea how a single fish could weigh so much, but it was like hefting a box of rocks.

"I don't know how many times I can keep saying the same thing," Tess said, feeling peevish. "He found some files in Levi's luggage that he thought Ms. Jones might be able to shine a light on. Since she's been investigating him for so long, she has more insight into his activities than anyone else."

Gertrude sighed and threw herself into one of the over-stuffed chairs that sat toward the back of the bookstore, where the barista stand and café promised free Wi-Fi with the purchase of every baked good. "I bet I could be just as helpful. I've listened to her podcasts all the way through *three* times. Did you know that Levi has six toes on his left foot? They say the extra toe is a sign of the devil."

"If we're on the subject of who knows Levi best, I think I have an insight or two," said Bernadette from the opposite chair. She sat upright, a tiny espresso cup in one hand. "And it wasn't technically a toe. It was more of a vestigial growth."

"Ew, Grandma."

"The human body is a natural and beautiful thing," Bee said pertly. She dissolved into a frown as she examined the veins standing out on the back of her hand. "And least, it *used* to be. Where on earth am I going to find another man who doesn't mind a few extra wrinkles to hold on to? Are they *absolutely* certain he's gone, Tess? He wasn't just sleeping off a few extra drinks? He was hitting the whiskey pretty hard last night."

As much as Tess appreciated that her mother didn't seem to be overwhelmed with grief, she wished she'd act a little bit more like a woman who'd been recently touched by death. Mumford Umberto was paying a lot closer attention than she knew.

"He's dead," Tess said firmly. "Are you sure you don't want to go lie down in the break room? This is a lot to take in. I think you might be in shock."

Her mother failed to take the hint. "I'll say I am. Levi owes me five thousand dollars. I told him not to bet against that Triple Crown winner from last year, but he says he always roots for the underdog. Or in this case, the under*horse*."

Tess could see the wheels turning inside Mumford's head,

so she was more grateful than words could express when Gertrude took one look at the clock hanging above the cash register and cleared her throat.

"Uh, Mom? Did you notice the time?"

Tess followed the line of her daughter's gaze to find that it was well past eleven o'clock. Even though the launch party wasn't supposed to start until six, Tess had planned to open the store at a more traditional hour. Unfortunately, instead of the eager hordes she'd expected lining up to get inside and start browsing, there was nothing outside her window but the flapping page of a newspaper as it whizzed by on the breeze.

"I'm sure everyone is distracted by all the cop cars and reporters down by the hotel," Tess mused, more for Mumford's benefit than her own. "They'll be here later. Maybe we should put the sandwich board out so they know it's okay to come in."

Gertrude eagerly jumped to attention, dragging the handwritten sign she'd made to the sidewalk and posting it outside the door. Tess assumed her daughter was just being helpful until the girl failed to head back inside. Instead of starting the party preparations like she was supposed to, Gertrude peered down the street in an attempt to see what was happening on the other end.

"It's a nice-looking store," Mumford said by way of peace offering. "Mind if I poke around a bit?"

"Poke away," Tess said. "I'll just get ready for the influx of customers. I'm sure they'll be here any minute."

Even as Tess spoke, she knew her words for the lie they

were. So did her mom, who only laughed and picked up the brand-new romance novel she hadn't paid for—and whose spine she'd already broken.

Five minutes in, and her bookstore was already running a deficit.

———

The afternoon wasn't as much of a bust as Tess had first feared. In addition to three different people who came in asking if they could hang out while the hotel remained off-limits, she sold four scones, six cups of coffee, and—much to her relief—a signed copy of *Fury under the Floorboards*.

Tess could have wished that Mumford Umberto was present to witness this latter transaction, but he'd given up on the bookstore watch around the same time her mother had yawned, proclaimed herself bored to tears, and headed into the back room to take a nap. Even Gertrude had hidden herself in the little kitchen behind the café counter, determined that the food for the party, at least, would be flawless.

"So this is the famous serial-killer book, huh?" a young man asked, picking up a copy from the stack by the door and flipping it over to examine the back. Tess didn't recognize him, but the fact that he knew about the serial-killer aspect meant he had some familiarity with the true version of the case.

"Would you like me to sign it for you?" Tess asked eagerly. He was younger than most of her readers—closer to Gertrude's age than her own—which was a good sign.

Her publisher was harping more and more on the need to draw in young readers by going viral through a thing called #BookTok. When Tess had asked Gertrude to do it for her, her daughter had literally laughed her out of the room.

"Yes, please. Sign it to Darcy." The young man grinned at her from under a swoop of locs that completely obscured one of his eyes. His hair was the same rich, dark tone as his skin, his eye only a fraction lighter. "I'm buying it for my mom. She's a big fan."

Tess tried not to look as depressed as this made her feel. There went all chances of viral fame. "Your mom has good taste. Did she come with you to Winthrop?"

"No way. She never travels. She doesn't trust computers. Or airplanes. Or any kind of technology, really."

Tess found it difficult to answer this, so she finished the swirling signature across the title page and rang up the book. "That'll be $28.50."

His eyes fairly goggled from his head. "Thirty bucks for a *book*?"

"It's a signed hardback," Tess pointed out. "A first edition too. It could be worth a lot of money someday."

"I got into the wrong business," he muttered, but he pulled out the cash and handed it to her. As if just now realizing there were no customers in the bookstore, he added, "Wasn't there supposed to be some kind of big deal about today?"

Tess sighed and tossed in a coupon for 10 percent off his next purchase. "You *are* the big deal," she said as she handed him his bag. "Turnout is a little lighter than expected."

She didn't add that he could turn left and stumble onto the *real* cause of her problems. In a town as small as this one, it was only a matter of time before he understood the scope of the investigation down the street.

As soon as he ducked out of the shop, Tess was afraid she'd have to do something drastic like start dusting the shelves, but a distraction arrived in the cheerful clang of the door chimes—followed almost immediately by the equally as cheerful boom of a male voice.

"I'm here to meet the world-famous author," it called. "Quick, someone grab a camera. I'm going to want to put this up on my Instagram."

Tess didn't bother to hide her smile when the man belonging to the voice popped into view. As much as she'd have liked to wallow in self-pity, Jared Wilson's presence had a way of neutralizing the emotion.

True, she often felt annoyed by him. And exasperated. But when a man stood well over six feet tall, was built of muscles heaped on top of one another, and always—*always*—wore a smile meant just for you, it was impossible not to return it.

Until he noticed how empty the store was and his face fell.

"Oh, no. They got you too?" He gave an exaggerated groan and clutched the honey-gold curls that made him look almost as much like a golden retriever as a living, breathing god. "Don't tell me—no one wants to read about murder when they can go stand outside the hotel and see it up close and personal, do they?"

"The party doesn't technically start until tonight," Tess

pointed out, but it was no use. There was no way to hide the fact that her bookstore opening was a flop. "I don't suppose you want five or six copies of my newest book, do you? Or at least a full gift set of the Game of Thrones series?"

"I tried getting into that one, but there were too many names to keep track of," he admitted with a lopsided grin. "A logger and handyman like me isn't built for heavy reading. Speaking of... How's the café counter holding up? I was a little worried about that slight lean toward the right."

"See for yourself," Tess offered as she gestured toward the back.

Since Jared had done a large percentage of the renovations inside the store, he was as familiar with the bookstore layout as she was. Since he was also Nicki's undercover FBI partner—and currently masquerading as a logger for the company they were investigating—he recognized this for the ruse it was. As soon as they were out of sight of the front counter, Tess pounced.

"Jared, please tell me you've got some more information about what's going on down there. Is Neptune still up in the suite with Sheriff Boyd? What kind of files did he want her to look at? Has the coroner come back with a preliminary toxicology report yet?"

He held up his hands in a gesture of surrender, a light laugh on his lips. "Whoa, there. I only just got into town. Yours was the first stop I made." His smile deepened into a pair of twin dimples on either cheek. "I wanted to make sure I was here for your big day."

Most of the time, Tess didn't let those dimples influence

her feelings about Jared. He was just a friend, and she was determined to keep him that way, but *no one* had taken the time to congratulate her yet. She felt herself faltering.

"That's really sweet of you, Jared," she said with real sincerity. "Thank you."

A tinge of red touched his ears. "I was hoping you'd say that. In fact, I brought you a little something to—"

He was interrupted in the middle of reaching for his pocket. Half of Tess was annoyed that her mother and Gertrude joined them before she could find out what that little something was, but the other half was relieved. She *liked* Jared, and the work he'd done to help her restore this bookstore was nothing short of miraculous, but nothing could change the fact that he was fifteen years her junior and had a serious crush on her.

Believe her, she'd tried. She'd coaxed and reasoned, made age-appropriate references, and once, in a fit of desperation, showed him her driver's license photo. Nothing seemed to convince him that a flirtation between an undercover FBI agent and a divorced middle-aged author with a teenager was a terrible idea.

"Hey, Jared," Gertrude said as soon as she caught sight of him. Like Tess, she immediately demanded the good stuff. "Did you just come from the crime scene? Is Neptune still there? I can't *believe* Mom got to meet her before I did. Did you know she's won three Podcast Awards already?"

Jared didn't have time to answer any of these questions before disaster struck. And by *disaster*, Tess meant her mother.

"I don't know who you are, young man, or why you and Tess are skulking around the back of this store, but you couldn't have come at a better time. There's a *spider* in the break room. I demand that you kill it for me at once."

Tess intervened before Jared could say a word. "Mom, Jared isn't here to be your personal pest control. Trap it and let it out in the alley if you can't stand its company." She turned to Gertrude. "And I already apologized for not bringing you with me to meet Neptune, but I'm sure you'll get the chance. From the look of things, she plans to stick around for a while."

Jared latched on to both of these with an enthusiasm that made Tess's head spin.

"Humane spider catch-and-release happens to be my favorite thing," he said as he reached for one of the coffee mugs that hung on the wall. "And I think that podcast lady is setting up her recording equipment inside the honky-tonk bar. I saw a guy unloading microphones and a bunch of other equipment from a van as I walked by. I peeked inside. I don't know why a single podcast would need so much, but some of the tech they have is next-level intel stuff."

Gertrude's only response to this was a squeak.

"Fine," Tess said, forestalling the inevitable. "You can go and watch. But *don't* get in Neptune's way, and *don't* offer her any information about our family. If Mumford is over there with her, there's a good chance she already knows most of it already. The two of them are like a walking, talking gossip sheet."

As Gertrude scuttled off to make a nuisance of herself

inside someone else's place of business, Bernadette stood back to watch her new minion at work. She was so pleased with Jared's handling of the spider that she didn't even bother to lower her voice when she turned to Tess.

"*Who* is that delicious heap of a young man, and why haven't I met him yet?" she asked.

"Mom!"

"What? I'm sure he knows exactly how he looks in those tight-fitting jeans. Don't you, love?"

Jared smiled ruefully at them both, the spider cup still in one hand. "I'm not sure how I'm supposed to answer that."

"Truthfully. If there's one thing I adore above all else, it's a man who isn't afraid to call it like he sees it."

"Don't fall for it," Tess warned. "She's only trying to butter you up so you'll take over doing her errands. The last man she had trailing after her wound up dead in the hotel down the street."

Jared blinked, startled by this piece of information, but Bee only laughed. "Too soon, Tess. Much too soon."

Tess took one look at her mother, who was the picture of good cheer and perfect health, and lifted her brow. For a woman who was near hysterics this morning, she'd bounced back awfully fast.

"Is it? Because you don't look particularly heartbroken to me. I hope you can be a little more remorseful when you go in for questioning. A merry widow laughing over the corpse of her discarded lover isn't a good look." She paused, struck by sudden inspiration. "It *is* a good plotline, though."

"I absolutely forbid it," Bernadette said, throwing up her

hands as if staving off a demon. "Tess Harrow, you cannot and will not mine your own mother's life story for your next book."

Tess refused to be intimidated by this. The lady might protest, but Tess knew for a fact that her mother loved nothing as much as being in the spotlight.

"Wait." Jared looked back and forth between them, his brow lowered in perplexity. "Are you serious? You knew the guy who died? Personally?"

Tess grimaced. "He was my mother's lover. Her *much* younger lover."

Jared's eyes flew open at this, but her mother casually ignored his surprise. Instead, she wound her arm through his and patted his hand in a way that *could* be interpreted as maternal but that Tess suspected was anything but.

"I've always fancied men with enough stamina to do the job properly," Bee said.

Jared choked and tried to take his arm back.

"Relax," Tess said, chuckling dryly. "She only means the job of escorting her around and keeping up with her late-night-martini habit. Whenever she gets to be too much for me, I find it helps to slip the bartender a fifty and have him replace her vodka with water."

"Why don't you run along and see what Gertie's up to?" Bee suggested, taking all of this in good part. Tess wasn't sure how much of it had to do with her mother actually wanting to have Jared to herself and how much of it was a desire to avoid talking about her relationship with Levi Parker, but she wasn't about to peer too closely either way. "Jared and

I can tend to the store while we get to know one another better. You know you're dying to see what that murder podcaster is up to—and it's not like you're getting any customers anytime soon."

Tess felt compelled to protest. "There was a nice young man who wanted a signed book for his mom."

"I saw that 'nice young man' slip his copy back on the New Release shelf as soon as your back was turned. I suspect one of your friends paid him to come in here and buy it just so you wouldn't feel so bad."

"Wait. Really?" Tess whirled around and ran to the shelf in question. She pulled out a few copies and flipped through them until she found the one she was looking for:

To Darcy,

May all your murder hopes and dreams come true.

XOXO,
Tess Harrow

"That doesn't make any sense. Why wouldn't he keep the book?" Tess asked as soon as she heard her mother's low trill of laughter. "Or at least wait until he got outside before he got rid of it?"

"I'm sorry, Tess," Jared said with real sympathy. "That was a mean trick to play."

"And now I can't even resell it unless I happen to come

across another Darcy," she grumbled. She tossed the book behind the counter so she could deal with it later. Partly out of peevishness and partly because she really did want to see what Neptune was up to, she decided to take her mom up on her offer. "Are you sure you don't mind keeping an eye on things for a bit? I'll be back in plenty of time to set up for the party."

"Go," her mom said, without once looking up from where she was gazing shrewdly at Jared's profile. "We'll be fine here without you."

It was the height of cruelty to abandon the poor man to her mother's machinations—Jared was no match for Bernadette Springer at her *least* determined, let alone her most—but Tess didn't think she could sit inside the bookstore watching all her hopes and dreams walk down the street for much longer.

"I just want to find out what evidence Neptune was given access to," Tess promised. "Unless it's something really good, I'll be back within the hour."

With that, she flashed an apologetic smile at Jared and whisked herself out the door.

Chapter Seven

TESS REGRETTED HER DECISION THE MOMENT SHE SET foot inside the honky-tonk bar.

The bar in question wasn't one of the quaint touristy watering holes that had sprung up over the past year to cater to the mountain-biking and winter-sports crowds. This was a dive, plain and simple. The greasy stools had been home to the same locals for decades, the shapes of their bottoms worn into the wood so deeply that they were rendered uncomfortable to anyone foolish enough to sit on one. The best whiskey in the place was Canadian Hunter, and the jukebox only played Hank Williams originals and covers, with an occasional Dolly Parton thrown in for good measure.

In an attempt to maintain her cover, Nicki rented the apartment upstairs. Tess had no idea how she slept with the constant twang of "I'm So Lonesome I Could Cry" ringing in her ears, but there was something to be said about being so close to the real pulse and population of this town.

At least, that was what Tess had always thought. As soon as she swung open the door, she sensed a serious change in the atmosphere—not to mention in the lighting and clientele. Instead of the usual dingy overhead lights, every bulb was at full wattage, illuminating each sticky corner. With the exception of Gertrude, Mumford, and a scattering of locals, it was packed with people Tess had never seen before—all of whom were quietly watching the events unfold.

"Well, well. Speak of the devil. Or in this case, the devil's handmaiden," Neptune crooned into a microphone that had been set up at one of the tables in the back. "Who should have just walked into my studio but the infamous, notorious, ignominious Tess Harrow?"

Tess found several things objectionable about Neptune's speech, not the least of which was the fact that *infamous*, *notorious*, and *ignominious* all basically meant the same thing. The first rule of good writing was that each adjective needed to carry its own weight. Listing things like you were reading a thesaurus was just plain lazy.

"Those of you who remember my legal troubles from earlier this year will recall that Ms. Harrow's publisher threatened to sue me out of business if I continued to imply that she was in any way involved in the string of murders plaguing her sleepy little town. Yet here we are. My pursuit of Levi Parker led me to this very place—and to Ms. Harrow's very own mother."

Tess groaned inwardly. It seemed that Neptune wasn't wasting any time with this new and tantalizing bit of information.

To Tess's surprise, a tall, massively hairy man sidled up to her with his finger over his lips. A large pair of headphones over his ears and the fact that he had multiple wires hanging over his body made her suspect that he was Neptune's podcast producer.

The man lifted a pair of headphones from around his neck and put them on Tess's head. She could feel her too-unruly curls flattening under the weight of them, but he didn't give her a chance to protest. With a series of hand gestures she assumed were meant to communicate his intentions, he led her to where Neptune sat like a queen holding an audience before her court.

"Ah. Sven has just brought me a present. Let's see if I can get Tess to agree to a sit-down, shall we? I'm sure we'd all love to hear her thoughts on this newest scandalous death. Remember, she and her family were some of the last people to see Levi alive last night."

Every part of Tess's being balked at the thought of sliding behind the table and letting Neptune loose to do her worst—and not just because her agent would have a conniption if she found out she'd done anything like this without an ironclad contract first. The truth was, the other woman intimidated her. Neptune's poise and self-assurance, the fact that her smirk held a challenge as much as an offer—this whole thing was an elaborate setup to make Neptune look as good as possible.

And for Tess to...not.

But then Gertrude flashed Tess a huge thumbs-up while Mumford sat scribbling notes next to her, and she felt herself weakening. That was when Neptune pounced.

"Uh-oh, folks. She looks nervous—and no wonder. Victor said she's squeamish when it comes to doing anything that might make her look bad. I guess we'll have to handle our disappointment and move on."

Tess found herself in the chair before she even realized she'd started moving. It was the *Victor* that had done it—the casual use of Sheriff Boyd's name like Neptune had any right to it. It had taken Tess *forever* to get up the nerve to use his first name, and even then, it had slipped out in a situation of high-intensity stress.

"If you had any idea how much death I've encountered in my lifetime, you'd know I'm not squeamish about anything," Tess said into the microphone that sat in front of her. It squawked with sudden feedback, at which point the hairy man rushed forward, made a few adjustments, and waved for her to go again. "I'm not nervous about being on your podcast. I'm upset that a man has just died."

"Are you?" Neptune didn't miss a beat—and her microphone didn't make any of the weird noises that seemed to be emanating out of Tess's. "You don't seem upset to me. Folks, let it be noted that Tess Harrow looks well-rested, alert, and completely dry-eyed."

Tess felt her whole body starting to grow hot and tight. "In that case, let it be noted that *you* look all those things too," she retorted. She thought, but didn't add, that only one of them looked like she'd visited a hairdresser this morning to go along with it.

Neptune chuckled in an infectious way that invited the whole bar to join her. The whole bar did, sounding like an obedient laugh track.

"Touché. I'd be the first to admit that I don't find Levi's death a major loss to this world. That man was dangerous in more ways than one."

"Are you admitting to having motive?" Tess asked.

This time, the audience sucked in a sharp breath. Tess could even distinguish Gertrude's voice among the crowd.

Instead of taking offense, Neptune's lips curved in a smile, a glint of appreciation in her eyes. "Interesting. For those of you at home who aren't familiar, there *is* some overlap between Levi Parker's arrival in town and my own last night. I didn't see him before his death, but the case could be made that I had plenty of opportunity to slip into his room unnoticed—especially since he had a corner suite overlooking the street. Unless I'm mistaken, that's what Ms. Harrow is implying right now. Yes?"

"I'm not implying anything," Tess said. "I just think it's strange that you'd admit to wanting the victim dead, that's all. Especially when there doesn't seem to be an obvious murderer yet."

"I'm not the only one who wanted that man dead. In fact, some might say that *your* motivation was the strongest."

"Mine?" Tess echoed, her brow furrowed. "I only met him for the first time last night."

"So you keep saying…" Neptune grinned across the table at her before flashing an enthusiastic thumbs-up. "Does that mean you'd have been okay with him continuing to date your mother?"

"They weren't *dating*," Tess protested. She mistrusted that thumb more than she could say. "They were…associating."

"Are you aware of the sizable sum she recently donated to his fake charity?"

"Wait. What?"

"Or the fact that his luggage contained, among other things, a complete workup of your mother's family history, including pictures of your underage daughter?"

"Over his dead body." Tess shot to her feet before she was aware of what she'd said—or the fact that she'd yanked the headphones from the head jack and unplugged them. "Is that true? You really found all those things?"

Neptune smirked up at her. "I'm afraid Ms. Harrow is looking uneasy. My words appear to have upset her. Speaking as one who's seen the worst that humanity has to offer—and the best—I'd say she's telling the truth when she says she didn't know about the file folders the local sheriff was kind enough to let me get a peek at. Why don't you sit back down and tell me how you're feeling, Ms. Harrow?"

Tess didn't want to do it. Her feelings on this particular subject should have been obvious to anyone packed inside the bar—or who would be listening to a highly edited version of the podcast at a later date. That Sheriff Boyd had invited Neptune onto his crime scene was bad enough. That he was letting her share these findings on her extremely popular podcast was worse.

Naturally, Tess was outraged. She was annoyed. She was—

"Scared," Tess said as she plopped back down in her seat and plugged the headset back in. Sheriff Boyd would have to wait. "How would *you* feel if a murderer had targeted your family as the next in a long line of victims?"

Neptune didn't even blink. "Angry, mostly—a thing you'd know if you'd ever listened to my podcast. Levi Parker has been making threats against me since the moment I first aired his name. Unfortunately for him, I'm not a woman to take threats lying down. I'm like a wild animal. I fight back."

There it was again—that implication of motive, the confession that Neptune's life would be substantially more comfortable now that there was no danger of Levi deciding to end it early. Before Tess responded, she narrowed her eyes and tried to figure out the woman's angle.

Option one: Neptune had, in fact, murdered Levi and wanted to get caught. She wouldn't be the first killer Tess had encountered who needed the validation that came with the chase. It was a little cliché, but then again, any good writer could spin the most basic of clichés into a tale worth telling.

Option two: Neptune was totally innocent of the crime and knew she couldn't be blamed for it. That meant an alibi of some kind, probably in the form of her producer—which was easy enough to check and probably the first thing Sheriff Boyd had done.

Option three: Neptune wanted people to think she'd done it. Tess knew from experience that there was no better way to drum up promotional interest than to fall feetfirst into a murder investigation that was as titillating as it was difficult to solve.

Tess stopped coming up with options after that. There was no need. If she knew anything about driven, career-oriented women who'd stop at nothing to succeed in a man's world—and she did—then she already had her answer. Neptune Jones was going to ride this particular wave, and she was going to ride it hard, no matter who got caught in the floodwaters along the way.

"Tell me, Neptune: Do you have children?"

The other woman looked surprised at this sudden shift of conversational tone, but she was nothing if not good on her feet.

"No, Ms. Harrow. I don't."

Tess leaned eagerly across the table. "Then you don't know that a mother isn't the sort to take threats lying down either. Mention my fifteen-year-old child on your podcast without my consent again, and I guarantee that you—and your entire legal team—won't like the outcome."

Tess could have almost laughed out loud at how quickly the recording was shut down after that. The bartender cut the power to the table with the flip of a switch. Neptune scowled as she started unplugging the recording equipment to her right. And Sven whisked the headset away from Tess before barking orders in a low, gravelly voice that matched his rough exterior. He drew forward and practically threw a clipboard at her.

"Here's your stupid consent form," he growled.

Tess didn't even glance over the contract before unclipping it and shoving it in her purse. "I'll have my agent review the terms and get in contact with you," she said primly. "But I wasn't kidding about my daughter. If I hear one peep of—"

"Mom!" Gertrude came storming up, her expression clouded. "Are you *trying* to make me die of shame?"

Tess immediately went on the defensive. "Gertie-pie, I know it seems cruel, but—"

"Do you have any idea what my friends would give to be in this room right now? How much *I'd* be willing to give to hear it keep going? You're ruining this for me."

Tess winced inwardly, careful to hide how much the lash of her daughter's words hurt. This was the one thing she disliked most about being a single parent. Any and all blame for harsh parental strictures landed solely on her own shoulders. She was the judge, jury, and executioner—and Gertrude was a master at making her feel each one.

"I'm sorry, but this isn't negotiable. I know you don't see it now, but this is for your own safety—"

"This is so embarrassing. *You're* so embarrassing."

A low cough interrupted them before their argument could devolve further. Tess and Gertrude both turned to find Sheriff Boyd leaning against a wall near the bar's entrance, his leg propped behind him as if he'd been standing there for some time. From the way his eyes met Tess's briefly before flicking just as quickly away, she understood that he had— long enough to hear Tess threaten Neptune with a lawsuit, maybe long enough to hear Neptune throw her murder motive around like it was confetti, definitely long enough to absorb the full scope of Gertrude's wrath.

"Sheriff Boyd!" Gertrude turned to him, her hands clasped in front of her. "Will you please tell my mom that she's overreacting? I swear, every time something goes a little bit wrong around here, she treats me like I'm a...a..."

"Child?" he suggested gently. "Sorry to break it to you, Gertie, but you are one. And I think she was right to shut this down before it went any further."

At this unexpected championing of her cause, a warm rush of sensation flooded through Tess. The heat of it was so intoxicating that she felt it touch her cheeks—a thing that rarely happened to her and made her feel more self-conscious than she cared to admit.

"Thank you," she said, the words a little stiff on her tongue. "I appreciate you saying that."

The sheriff eyed Tess carefully. "I thought I told you to stay out of this."

The heat in her cheeks flushed even hotter. "I *am* staying out of it," she protested. "Which is more than I can say for Neptune Jones. Victor, do you have any idea how dangerous it is to let a woman like that loose on your crime scene? And then release her to tell the whole world about what she found?"

Instead of answering her, the sheriff turned so abruptly away from Tess that her head swam.

"Ah, Neptune," he said to the woman approaching them. "I came to thank you for your help earlier. Your insight on the crime scene was...invaluable."

"Like I said before, Victor, when it comes to getting to the bottom of this, my resources are your resources." Neptune smirked in a way that Tess felt *sure* was meant to make her feel even smaller than she already did. She also reached over and pressed a meaningful hand on the sheriff's arm. If that *Victor* had been proprietary, then that hand was downright possessive. "Any of my old case files, any information either I or my producer might have—night or day, we're at your disposal. Collaboration is the only way we're getting to the bottom of this."

A smile touched the edges of the sheriff's mouth, so soft you had to be watching closely to see it.

But Tess was watching. Closely.

"I may need to take you up on that," he murmured. "I'm about to go question Bernadette Springer, but maybe we could meet up for drinks later? Say, around six? The hotel restaurant will have to stay shut down for the foreseeable future, but I always keep a bottle of Wild Turkey in my desk drawer."

Tess felt her blood run cold. Six o'clock was when her launch party was slated to begin—a time she'd practically imprinted on the sheriff's skin. For him to deliberately miss her party was a cut of the highest degree. For him to do it with an offer of cheap desk bourbon, which he'd never once offered *her*, was even worse.

"That sounds perfect, thanks." Neptune pressed her lips together in a belated attempt to hide her grin. "It's a date."

Tess was still in the process of finding her tongue when the sheriff turned to her with a curt nod. "I assume you plan on sitting in while I take your mother's official statement?"

Tess couldn't be sure, but she felt she detected a weariness in the way he asked the question, as if he was suddenly speaking to a recalcitrant teenager. It was fitting, therefore, that the *actual* recalcitrant teenager was the one who responded. With a snort and something bordering on a laugh, Gertrude said, "Of course she does. She'll want to make sure Grandma doesn't say anything that might get in the way of her big celebration."

The bookstore didn't appear to have burst with activity in the hour or so that Tess was away. If anything, it was more subdued than before. The only sounds she heard when she pushed her way inside were the low-voiced murmurs and giggles of her mother behaving at her very worst with Jared.

"You naughty thing. How could you?" Bernadette said from the back. "A woman of my age. You ought to be ashamed of yourself."

Gertrude ignored this with a combination of sanguine disinterest and the lingering resentment she was harboring toward her mother. Tess ignored it with a fervent hope that Sheriff Boyd hadn't overheard.

Sheriff Boyd didn't ignore it at all.

"Ms. Springer?" he called out in an authoritative tone that brooked no argument. "It's Sheriff Boyd. If you don't mind, I'd like to ask you a few questions."

"If you promise to ask nicely, I don't mind *what* you do to me." Bee sauntered out, looking delighted to find herself the center of even more attention than before. From the way her mom's vowels trilled, Tess had the sinking sensation that she planned to flirt with Sheriff Boyd as shamelessly as she had with Jared.

Fortunately for all of them, Sheriff Boyd was entirely un-flirtable. At least where the women in Tess's family were concerned.

"I don't have a lot of time, so let's make this brief," he said. "I'd like to know the exact nature of your relationship with Levi Parker."

Bernadette cast a quick glance over at Gertrude. "I'm not

sure we should be holding this conversation where there are minors present, if you know what I mean."

From the flicker of amusement that Sheriff Boyd was quick to hide, Tess was pretty sure he knew what she meant.

"C'mon, Gertie," Jared said as he, too, popped out of the back, a grin and a pleased look that matched Bernadette's on his face. Honestly, if Tess didn't know any better, she might think they actually *had* been canoodling back there. "I can tell when we're not wanted. I'll buy you an ice cream and bring you back when they're done with the interrogation."

Gertrude scowled. "I don't want ice cream. I want someone around here to treat me like a living, breathing human being capable of making her own decisions."

Jared didn't miss a beat. "Last I checked, choosing between vanilla and chocolate *is* a decision."

"No thanks." Gertrude shook her head. "It's nice of you to ask, but I'll be in the back finishing up the sushi for tonight. It's not like I want to hear about my grandma's sex life. Mom already pays a fortune in my therapy bills as it is."

Although this was true, Tess wisely kept her own counsel. She also refrained from meeting Sheriff Boyd's eye. She knew exactly what he was thinking—*You sent Jared Wilson to babysit your mother? That's the best you could come up with?*—and also that she didn't have a good answer. The sheriff didn't exactly approve of Jared hanging around Tess as much as he did.

Not, he'd have been quick to assert, out of a sense of jealousy but of propriety. Considering how Bernadette Springer appeared to the outside world right now—a daring, decadent divorcée embroiled in a murder investigation that painted her out to be a fool of the highest degree—Tess was starting to see the sheriff's point. Women in relationships with much younger men weren't ever going to be accepted by society. It took a lot of self-confidence and Elizabeth Taylor sangfroid to pull that kind of thing off.

"Should we sit down and make ourselves comfortable?" Tess suggested as soon as Jared and Gertrude took themselves off in separate directions. As if just now realizing the store was empty, the sheriff took a slow, careful look around him.

"Where are the customers?"

"Where do you think?" Tess knew she sounded bitter, but there was no help for it. She *felt* bitter. "In all the upheaval of Levi's death and Neptune recording her podcast like it's a live H. G. Wells performance, everyone is too busy to care about a bookstore opening."

"I'm sure that's not true," he said.

Tess's mother must have felt that the attention had been off her long enough, because she drew a dramatic breath and began speaking.

"We met on a cloudless day in Arizona," she announced. "I was minding my own business, soaking in the sun and the energies from our shared sacred space. The veil was particularly thin that day."

"The veil?" Sheriff Boyd echoed with a pair of upraised brows for Tess. She only sighed and shrugged. He'd understand for himself soon enough.

"The mystical veil?" Bernadette prompted. "The

boundary between our world and the forces of the great beyond? Have you never been to Sedona before?"

"Ah." The sheriff's expression grew flat in a way that Tess felt certain was meant to suppress laughter. "*That* veil."

"Exactly." Bernadette trailed over to one of the café chairs and elegantly draped herself across it. "I think that was what first drew him to me. He could sense how attuned I was with nature, how completely a part of it I was. Men enjoy that, you know. Coming home to their earth mothers."

Tess ran a hand over her eyes. She couldn't believe her mother was saying these things out loud, not only to a man who was the county sheriff but also a member of the local Colville tribe.

"This is very true," he said, his lips twitching. "I'm still searching for my own earth mother."

Bernadette reached over and squeezed his hand. "And you'll find her, love. Just keep looking. She's out there somewhere."

Since there was a good chance this interview would continue for hours unless Tess did something to intervene, she kicked her mother's chair. "Stop weaving us this ridiculous tale and answer the sheriff's questions."

"I *am* answering the sheriff's questions. He wanted to know about my relationship with Levi. I'm painting the picture for him. We're all winners here."

Tess felt pretty sure she wasn't in the running to win *anything* right now, but there was no chance for her to point that out.

"So he sought you out?" Sheriff Boyd said as he pulled

out a pad of paper and began taking notes. "He approached you, not the other way around?"

"Of course. Despite what Tess may have told you, I'm not in the habit of picking up men who are young enough to be my son. He was very...persuasive."

"And you knew about his past? That he'd been recently released from prison?"

"I googled him as soon as I got back to my yurt, yes. I may be old, but I'm not a fool."

"Your yurt had cell service?" Tess asked, suspicious. "Is that something *the veil* allows?"

Her mother quelled her with a hard glance. "It's not as if it mattered either way. Levi told me the truth over dinner that night. He wanted to 'be his most authentic self,' as he called it. He said he couldn't, in good conscience, continue seeing me unless I knew his whole story."

"That he'd been held on suspicion of murder?" the sheriff asked.

"That he'd been falsely accused and found innocent, yes. He said he'd always been attracted to more mature women and that society was so repulsed by it that they found ways to villainize him." She gestured at the door where Jared had recently exited. "Ask Tess. I'm sure she could tell you all about it."

Tess coughed so hard she felt an artery might have burst inside her chest. "Mo-om. I told you already. It's not like that. Jared's my *friend*."

Her mom scoffed, heedless of how stiff Sheriff Boyd had grown. "Sure he is, pet. And I'm the Dalai Lama." She turned to the sheriff with a bright smile. "Anywhoodles. That's about it, really. I appreciated his candor. He appreciated my...for-giveness. We hit it off, and the rest—as they say—is history."

The sheriff had regained control of himself by this point. "And he never made you feel unsafe or threatened?"

"No. He was a total gentleman." She winked. "Until, of course, he *wasn't*."

"Ugh." Tess had to fight the urge to go run and hide in the back with Gertrude. Sometimes, being a teenager had its benefits. "Do you really need to go that much into detail?"

Sheriff Boyd coughed gently. "I'd like your mother to feel comfortable telling me anything she feels is pertinent."

"Well, I doubt his stamina is relevant to your case, but he had it in spades, if you're wondering." Bernadette heaved a wistful sigh. "I know he wasn't perfect. Anyone that good-looking and smooth obviously wants something in return."

Sheriff Boyd coughed again, even more gently this time. "Money?"

"Of course. And why shouldn't he be compensated for his efforts? Attractive young women have been doing the same thing for centuries. No one thinks it's odd if a man my age takes up with a younger lover and buys her extravagant things. I'm a grown woman. I have the means to indulge in my hobbies. At the end of the day, what harm is there?"

"You mean, other than his murder and the fact that you've brought an entire three-ring circus into town?" Tess asked, unable to help herself. She knew that everything her mother was saying was true—and under any other circumstances, she'd have been the first to stand up and applaud this upending of the patriarchy—but there was a difference between robbing a cradle and robbing a juvenile detention center. "Mom, you knew he was potentially dangerous. He was literally being followed around the country by a murder podcaster watching his every move."

"It added spice."

"Is it spicy for him to be carrying around a folder full of facts about our family?" Tess added, feeling her anger starting to mount. "Because he had one of those too. In his luggage. Neptune told me."

"I thought she might," Sheriff Boyd murmured.

Tess let this pass, but she put a bookmark in it so she could come back to it later. "And you said yourself that you didn't invite him to join you here—that he just followed you. Doesn't that seem predatory to you?"

"If you'd ever been chased by a man, Tess, then you'd know that the predation is half the fun."

Tess had been chased by men before—or, at the very least, lightly pursued. She opened her mouth to defend herself, but there was no opportunity. Gertrude ran into the room holding what looked like an enormous block of moldy cheese wrapped in plastic.

"Mom?" she called out, her voice wavering.

"If that's blue cheese, I absolutely forbid you from putting it on the charcuterie board for tonight's party," Tess said, not altogether upset at the interruption. If her mother planned to continue holding a one-woman show on the virtues of dating criminals, then she'd more than heard enough. And so, she hoped, had Sheriff Boyd. "Once you get a Stilton on the plate, everything starts to taste like decay."

Gertrude's lower lip wobbled. "It's not cheese."

The sheriff was the first to react to Gertrude's signs of distress, making his way across the floor and kneeling in front of the teenager before Tess could blink. He lifted the bundle from Gertrude's hands with a reverence that felt unsettling. "Gertie, where did this come from?"

"It was in the cooler with the fish," she said. Her hands started to shake the moment they were free. "Underneath the dry ice. Sheriff Boyd, is that—"

He nodded once. "Cash. And a lot of it. Take me to that cooler at once, Gertie. And don't touch anything else in it."

Chapter Eight

TESS WASN'T SURE WHETHER TO BE RELIEVED OR DISAP-pointed that the discovery of an enormous bundle of money inside her fish cooler resulted in the cancellation of her book-release party.

On the one hand, all her hard work and planning was going completely to waste—or more specifically, to her *waist*. She was currently sitting in her living room, eating her third murder cupcake. Now that there were no party guests to help them, they had five dozen of the things to get through.

On the other hand, Tess's complete and utter failure as a bookseller was now much more likely to go unnoticed by Mumford. Not only was he sitting in a murder-cupcake daze of his own, but he was so taken up with the mysterious cash that she doubted he even remembered she'd had a book release today.

"I don't understand," he said for what was probably the fifteenth time. A splotch of the strawberry filling from his cupcake had splattered across his white shirt front, but no one bothered to point it out. They were too busy wishing him elsewhere. "Was the money meant for me? Are you sure there wasn't a note? I feel like there should have been a note."

"If there was a note, it's been booked as evidence by this time," Tess said with painstaking friendliness. She was determined that no matter how many people died or how much random money appeared inside coolers, she was going to get a positive article out of this man. "Maybe you could claim journalistic privilege and go talk to the sheriff first thing in the morning. I'll drive you into town as soon as the sun's up."

"Drive him there now and save us all the trouble," Bernadette muttered. Since Gertrude's sudden laugh covered the remark, Mumford looked quizzical rather than affronted.

"You say the seal was unbroken when you opened the cooler up?" he said to Gertrude, his tongue running eagerly over the gap in his front teeth. "It hadn't been tampered with while it was sitting in the street?"

Gertrude shrugged. "It looked sealed to me. The dry ice was still intact, so I doubt anyone cracked the lid before I did. That stuff melts fast in this weather."

"And you're *sure* there wasn't a note?"

Tess threw up her hands. "Why would anyone include a note with a giant bundle of cash sent on a plane from Seattle? Unless it was a kidnapping ransom, there's no need."

Something about the shifty way Mumford noticed the stain on his shirt, dabbed at it, and then continued dabbing at it long after the sticky residue had been smeared away put Tess on her guard.

"Mumford," she said slowly. "Was that a kidnapping ransom?"

His laughter felt a little too bright and forced. "How

should I know? I just think it's an awfully big coincidence that it traveled on my plane. If it was meant for me, I want to make sure my rights are being upheld. That had to be fifty thousand dollars, at least."

"It was a hundred thousand," Gertrude said.

Mumford looked taken aback. "How do you know that?"

"Because Mom once made me cut out a thousand hundred-dollar-bill-shaped pieces of paper and bundle them up so she'd know how heavy it was. She said it was research for a book."

"It *was* research for a book," Tess protested. Honestly, from the way Gertrude spoke, you'd think she'd been planning a heist instead of trying to figure out how many duffel bags of cash Detective Gonzales would need to empty out a drug warehouse. The answer had been disappointing. The fake money had fit easily into a single bag. "And it was a lot smaller than we expected it to be."

"It always is," Bernadette said with a sigh. She hoisted herself to her feet, flinging up a hand before anyone could even pretend to get up to help her. "No, stay where you are. I'm just going to wind down with some light reading before bed."

"Take a bottle of sparkling wine with you," Tess said with a gesture toward the box near the front door. "I ordered a full case for the party. Everyone needs to do their part to empty it."

"*Everyone?*" Gertrude asked eagerly.

"Nice try. I meant everyone of legal drinking age."

Bernadette tucked one under her arm. "Don't mind if I

do. I'll need it if I'm going to survive another night on that lump you call a mattress."

Tess bit back her retort, which was to be glad that she had a mattress at all. Since Mumford refused to take the hint about finding accommodations elsewhere, he was staying in Gertrude's room. That left the futon for both Tess and Gertrude; and since the girl was already snuggling in deep with her headphones over her ears, Tess suspected she'd end up in her Jeep before the night was through.

Tess had hoped Mumford would take a few sparkling wine bottles of his own and settle himself in for the night, but he seemed predisposed to chat about the day's events. Partly because the strawberry stain on his shirt was starting to seriously bother her and partly because she wanted to follow up on that bit about the kidnapping, she jumped right in.

"Money troubles?" she asked.

He gave a start of surprise. "I beg your pardon?"

Tess put on her blandest smile. "It's just that you seem really interested in what becomes of the secret stash of money. I guess being a reporter—even one as big and important as you—doesn't pay as well as it should, huh?"

Instead of answering her, he parried her question with one of his own. "Your friend Sheriff Boyd didn't trust you with the cash for very long, did he? I've never seen a member of law enforcement move that fast. What makes him think it's tied up with his murder case?"

That was a good question. Tess felt herself softening toward Mumford almost against her will.

"The strangeness of it, probably," she said, throwing out the first thing that occurred to her. "What are the chances that a man dies of mysterious causes and a hundred grand shows up the next day *without* there being a link?"

He shrugged. "Coincidences happen all the time. Just because two incidents seem related doesn't mean they are."

This was something Tess said so often—and to unheeding ears—that she relaxed even more. Maybe Mumford wasn't such a bad reporter after all.

"Okay, so let's say they aren't related," she mused aloud. She might as well get some use out of the dratted man. "Why else might that much money show up without warning?"

"In my experience?" Mumford held up a hand and ticked off his fingers. "If we ignore the kidnapping-ransom idea, there are only three likely possibilities: drugs, smuggling, or money laundering."

Tess felt a quaver of something that wasn't quite fear shoot through her. "Say that last one again?"

"What?" he asked. "Money laundering? It sounds far-fetched, but some of those guys have to move large amounts of cash on airplanes without tipping off the authorities. It's harder to do than you might think—between the money-sniffing dogs and customs agents in the airports, they have to get creative. Shoving money under a freshly caught fish seems plenty creative to me. The French used to run brandy up the British coast that way."

Tess sat back against her chair and did her best *not* to look like a woman who'd just been floored—and potentially solved part of this case. Mumford had obviously only said all that to show off his knowledge of criminal misdeeds, but his words carried a lot more truth than he realized. Money laundering was the reason Nicki and Jared were in this town. They'd been trying to nail down Mason Peabody, local logging magnate, on just such a charge for years. They knew he used eco-friendly shell companies to move his money around and that the logging shipments he carried over the borders were highly suspect, but they'd never gotten their hands on concrete evidence.

If Mason was getting—as Mumford put it—*creative*, then this money could very well belong to him. And if that was the case, she was guessing he'd want it back before too long.

"I wonder if I should put in another order for fresh tuna and see what happens," Tess mused, only half joking.

Mumford only half joked in reply. "Nah, it'd be too obvious to do the same thing a second time. You'd need to mix it up. Order a rare plant from a specialty shop in Seattle or fly in some cheesecakes from New York. That's how you'd *really* be able to tell if someone was using you to run money. Or even better—buy something from Canada. International smuggling is a lot more common than the domestic kind."

These were all fantastic notions, but Tess planned to put a little more thought into the idea before she pulled the metaphorical trigger. She also planned to clue in Nicki and Jared to what she was doing, but that part went without saying. Nicki would kill her if she interfered in her investigation without at least giving her a heads-up first.

"You've been weirdly helpful tonight, Mumford," she said with all honesty. "Thanks."

"It's the least I can do," he replied. "Don't forget that fish aren't the only thing you flew in on that plane. By the time I'm done turning over every stone and clue in this town, I'll have enough story material to carry out the rest of my life."

Chapter Nine

THE NEXT MORNING, TESS STEPPED INTO NICKI'S FAMIL-iar blue bookmobile to find her best friend busy with the handwritten cataloging system. By itself, this was a per-fectly ordinary occurrence. Less ordinary was Jared stand-ing in the back and searching through a bookshelf that held the Zane Grey Westerns popular in this area. For years, Nicki had been trying to get readers to shift toward V. S. McGrath or Isabel Allende for a little diversity in their Western-themed reading, but her efforts weren't showing much progress.

"I like the look of this one, where the lady is almost falling off the horse," Jared said as soon as he heard the sound of footsteps. When he turned and noticed who the footsteps belonged to, he relaxed. "Oh, good. It's only you, Tess. The last person who came in talked to me about something called *Riders of the Purple Sage* for twenty whole minutes."

"I'd never do that to you," Tess promised with a laugh. Jared was good for a lot of things, but literary discussions weren't one of them. "I'm glad to find you both here. Start this baby up and take us for a spin. I have something import-ant to ask you."

Nicki rolled her eyes and continued flipping through her

papers. "We appreciate you coming all this way, but if it's about the fish, we're already on it."

"What? How is that possible?"

"Sorry, Tess," Jared said with a good-natured grin. "I wanted to call you as soon as we heard about the money, but Nicki thinks it's suspicious enough to have me browsing for books all morning. She says the whole town knows that if I wanted something to read, I'd hang pathetically around the Paper Trail instead of the bookmobile."

"Am I wrong?" Nicki shook her head before either of them could speak. "Never mind. Don't answer that. I don't want to hear anything about what Jared does around you— pathetic or otherwise."

Tess tactfully ignored this remark. No matter how many times she'd tried to explain the nature of her friendship with Jared, Nicki refused to accept Tess's highly factual version of events.

"Does that mean you don't want to hear about my plan to order a bunch of specialty Canadian candy bars and have them flown in from Vancouver?" Tess asked.

"Candy bars?" Jared echoed, his brow lowering in confusion.

Nicki was much quicker to understand. "No, Tess. Absolutely not. I'm not getting you more tangled up in this than you already are."

Tess threw herself onto one of the small stools that sat near the kids' section of the bookmobile. Her adult-sized bottom barely fit, but she was determined to make these two hear her out. She'd spent all night squashed in the driver's seat of her Jeep, coming up with a plan. Sleep had been impossible with a steering wheel rammed under her rib cage and visions of a podcaster's microphone dancing before her eyes.

Neptune Jones wasn't the only one who could doggedly pursue a nefarious criminal to the ends of the earth. *Tess* knew that, even if people like Victor refused to admit it.

"Was Sheriff Boyd the one who told you?" Tess asked.

Nicki peeked behind Tess and, seeing that no one was headed their way, slid the doors of the bookmobile closed. "Yeah. He called and updated me last night. Can you recall mentioning the name of the shipping company you used within Mason's hearing? Or in the hearing of one of his brothers?"

"I can do you one better." Tess grabbed her phone and pulled up her email account before handing it to Nicki. "Mason's the one who recommended that place. He told me they use it whenever they need high-end catering. This is the name of the guy he referred me to."

Nicki almost dropped the phone in her sudden excitement. "Tess, this is *fantastic*."

"That's a heck of a slipup for people as careful as the Peabodys." Jared gave a low whistle and crowded over to peek at the phone. He pressed a hand on Tess's shoulder to steady himself and kept it there, his palm warm and heavy. "I've been working on that logging crew for four months, and they still don't even let me punch a clock without supervision."

"Yeah, well. Why do you think I came up with the plan about the candy? It's the perfect way to set a trap for Mason.

That much money appearing in a random shipment once could be a fluke. If it happens a *second* time…"

Nicki and Jared shared a look that Tess read as easily as a book. She doubted either of the federal agents would appreciate knowing how much they gave away—but then again, Tess was something of an expert on this particular subject.

"I'll wait until Mason or one of his brothers is around before I mention it," she said as though it was the simplest thing in the world. "They won't think it's weird for me to buy candy in bulk. I have a teenager."

Nicki snorted.

"Okay, and maybe I have a thing for Coffee Crisps. Have you ever had one? It's like a Kit Kat and a mocha had a love child."

Jared rubbed the side of his nose. "I don't know, Tess. It might be dangerous…"

Tess almost laughed. Of all the dangerous things she'd done in her lifetime, luring a money launderer with candy barely counted as a blip. "I won't do anything obvious. I'll just put it out there and see what the universe sends back."

Oddly enough, Nicki was the first to give in. She turned to Jared with a shrug. "Worst-case scenario, all she's doing is wasting a couple hundred dollars on snack foods."

"With everything else going on around here, Mason might even let his guard down."

"And we have to show *something* to Agent Li soon, or they're going to make good on that threat to send us back to Seattle."

As far as Tess was concerned, that settled it. She had no

idea who Agent Li was or why he should have the power to take her friends away from her, but she'd order thousands of candy bars if it meant keeping Nicki around for a few more months. She'd even *eat* them, millions of calories and all.

"Then it's a done deal." She stood up, pleased to find at least one of her plans finally working out. "I'll start the arrangements as soon as I can. You guys have been a big help."

Nicki glanced out the window with a groan. "What we've been is indiscreet. Quick, Edna St. Clair is heading this way. She's going to wonder what we're all doing in here." She grimaced. "Worse, she's going to tell everyone else what she saw. I've never known anyone so in love with the sound of her own voice, and I'm including Mason Peabody on that list."

"Don't worry," Jared said with a grin so deep it brought out the full force of his dimples. "I know just the thing."

Nicki quirked a brow. "The Capulet play?"

"You know it. It always works on nosy old ladies."

Tess was just about to ask what the Capulet play was when the question was lifted from her lips—literally. No sooner had she opened her mouth to speak than Jared had his own mouth pressed to hers.

That wasn't the only part of him doing the pressing. With a strength and a suavity that Tess found *far* more attractive than she cared to admit, he had her up against one wall of the bookmobile, his arms pinning her against the cold metal.

"Sorry," he said against her mouth. He didn't sound the least bit apologetic. "It's the only way to save the operation."

Tess was pretty sure that was a bald-faced lie, but she found it difficult to care as his lips found hers again. Instead of contenting himself with the *appearance* of scandal, he leaned into it. He also leaned into Tess, his whole body heaving as he wrapped her in an embrace that left little to the imagination.

With a sudden slamming open of the door, Nicki released an annoyed shout. "I've had just about enough of you two making use of my stacks for your indecency," she cried, clearly enjoying herself. "It's bad enough when I get horny teenagers in here trying to use my bookmobile as a way to fool their parents. You're grown adults, for crying out loud. Get a room."

Jared pulled back with an even deeper grin than before, his eyes glittering. Tess was sure she looked equally flushed, but she could hardly help that. She *felt* flushed. Despite her best intentions to keep this man at arm's length, he always seemed to find a way to slip past her guard.

"Sorry, Nicki, but I couldn't help myself. Tess was—"

Edna's familiar cackle filled the bookmobile. "No need to explain to *us* what Tess was doing, young man. I have eyes in my head. She was seducing you."

"Now, wait just a second," Tess protested, unable to help herself. "He was kissing me, Edna, not the other way around."

The crotchety old busybody had the audacity to cackle even harder. "And you were enjoying it, so don't try to bamboozle me. Does your other boyfriend know what you get up to in your spare time?"

This time, Tess's flush had nothing to do with the expertise of Jared's kiss. She tried to cough and change the subject, but Edna could be just as dogged as Tess herself.

"Poor Sheriff Boyd," Edna said with a sad cluck of her tongue. "And I just ran into him down at the grocery store with his sister. They were stocking up on supplies. Apparently, that podcast lady and her whole crew are staying with him until the hotel opens back up again. He'll be heartbroken once he discovers what a loose fish you are."

"Wait. *What?*"

"A loose fish," Edna explained carefully, "is someone who flops from boat to boat, unable to decide which—"

"No, not that." Tess waved her off with an annoyed tsk. Somewhere in the back of her mind, she knew that she was only making a bad situation worse, but this was too important for tact. "Neptune Jones is staying at the sheriff's house? He *invited* her?"

"You'd better be careful," Edna said by way of reply. "She's a good-looking woman. If the sheriff hears what you've been up to in here…"

Every single person listening to Edna knew that there was no *if* about it. She'd have this sordid tale spread all over town in a matter of minutes.

"For the last time, Edna, Sheriff Boyd and I are just friends," Tess said. Her gaze darted over toward Jared and back again. "So are Jared and I. You've got the wrong idea."

The attempt was a futile one. Edna harrumphed and started browsing through the gardening bookshelf. "If that's how you treat your friends, then you must have been the most popular girl in your high school. Back in my day, we had a name for that too."

"Tess, wait."

Tess had only made it a few feet from the bookmobile before Jared stopped her. He touched her arm but withdrew his hand just as quickly. She'd have much rather gone the rest of the day—and, in all honesty, her life—without addressing that kiss inside the bookmobile, but that wasn't Jared's way. Not once, in all his pursuit of her, had he shown the least remorse or shame. That kind of unabashed earnestness would have been endearing if it wasn't so embarrassing.

"Sorry if I put you on the spot back there," he said, rubbing a rueful hand along the back of his neck. Tess felt pretty sure he regularly practiced that move in the mirror, so perfectly did it capture both his boyish charm and the size of his biceps straining underneath his tight T-shirt. "But you heard Nicki. We had to do *something* to throw Edna off the scent."

"It's fine," Tess was quick to say.

Disappointment touched the edges of his lips. "Just 'fine'? I thought it was pretty amazing. You're a really good kisser."

Any chance Tess might have had at making it out of this situation with her dignity intact disappeared like a puff of smoke. She gave a shaky laugh. "You're the one who did most of the work. I just didn't fight back."

"Yeah." A tinge of red crept up toward his ears. "I noticed that."

Tess cast an anxious glance over her shoulder. It was still early enough in the day that *some* people hadn't yet ventured out onto Main Street to witness what mysteries and murders the day held, but there were plenty of watchful eyes.

"Don't worry," he said. "I won't do it again unless you ask me to. But, um, for the record, I'd really like it if you asked me to."

Tess froze, unsure how to react to this—or even how she *wanted* to react. Her heart told her that nothing Jared said or did would matter even a fraction as much as a single look from Victor Boyd, but Victor had made it more than clear that her interest wasn't reciprocated. Especially if he was going to be letting Neptune Jones stay at his house for the duration of this investigation.

"Jared—" she began, but he cut her off with a lopsided grin.

"Don't worry. I'm not going to push my luck again today. I only came to give you this." He slipped a note into her palm. "Nicki wanted me to make sure you got it before you left. I think it has something to do with that Neptune lady you hate."

"I don't *hate* her," Tess said irritably. "I just don't see why everyone else thinks she's so amazing, that's all."

"If it's any consolation, I don't think she's amazing at all," he said and whisked himself away before she could say more. He also took care to walk in an easy, long-legged stride that did amazing things for the fit of his jeans. The man was no deep thinker, it was true, but he wasn't *always* lacking in wisdom.

After tucking the note in her pocket for later, Tess continued toward the grocery store, determined to waylay Sheriff Boyd and his sister before they left town. She arrived just in time to see the pair stepping out with enough food to feed a dozen Neptune Joneses and her crew.

The sheriff took one look at her and groaned. "Please don't, Tess. I have neither the time nor the patience for it this morning."

Instead of taking offense at his words—a thing she was totally justified in doing—she lifted a grocery bag from his hands. "I know you don't. That's why I'm going to offer to take Kendra back to your house to unload these things. You wouldn't want to neglect your investigation." She turned to the sheriff's sister with a smile. "Hey, Kendra. Good to see you. How are things at the impound lot these days?"

The sheriff's sister was almost as tall as he was, equally languid, and just as inscrutable. Naturally, Tess adored her.

"They're fine, thanks," Kendra said, her expression flat. She'd been in town for a few months now, but Tess was finding her a tough nut to crack. No matter how many friendly overtures she made, Kendra seemed content to stay to herself. She lived and worked with Herb Granger, a miserly old man who ran the local impound lot and de facto garage, and rarely ventured out into the public eye. The fact that she was helping her brother with grocery shopping and setting up a makeshift Airbnb for Neptune and her producer was as good a sign as any that there was more to that situation than met the eye.

"What's the catch?" Sheriff Boyd asked, watching Tess carefully. "If you're after the toxicology report, it hasn't come back yet. I'm not letting *anyone* into the hotel room right now, so it's not worth batting your eyes at me like that. And like I told that nosy reporter friend of yours earlier—I don't have any leads I'm willing to share at this point. You can wait for the press conference like everyone else."

Tess bit back all the things she wanted to say in her defense—Mumford *wasn't* her friend, she *wasn't* batting her eyes, and he'd been more than happy to escort Neptune Jones through his precious crime scene—and smiled cheerfully instead.

"No catch," she said. "I just know you've got a lot on your plate right now, that's all. And since the adoring hordes I was expecting at the bookstore still haven't showed, I might as well make myself useful."

The sheriff obviously didn't believe a word out of her mouth, but Tess knew how to press even the smallest advantage.

"Relax," she said. "I'm not going to do or say anything to your precious podcaster. I'll make her a nice breakfast and even clean up after myself when I'm done. How's that for helpful?"

He snorted, but with a slight relaxing of his shoulders that Tess knew well. "You won't get rid of my houseguests by feeding them rubbery eggs and burnt toast."

"Then it's a good thing I don't want to get rid of them, isn't it?" Tess said brightly. "I'll text later to let you know how it goes. I'm sure Neptune and I will find plenty to talk about."

She turned and started moving toward her car before the sheriff or his sister could argue further. Success was guaranteed when Kendra joined her a few seconds later.

"Neptune's not there, you know," Kendra said. "That's the only reason Victor agreed to let you go."

"Really?" Tess lowered the grocery bag, which must have weighed close to twenty pounds, down to her hip. "I thought both she and Sven were staying at his house."

"They are. But they got an early start this morning—Ms. Jones said something about research that could only be done in Seattle. They won't be back until tonight."

Tess couldn't decide whether to be pleased or annoyed by this, though she was leaning toward the latter. Sheriff Boyd had played her on purpose.

The conflict must have appeared on her face because Kendra chuckled again. "You don't have to come with me to drop these things off. I can take one of the impound cars from the lot. I'm sure you have plenty of stuff to do today."

That resolved her. "No, I want to help," she said. Opportunities to spend time with Kendra alone were rare, and for once, the woman seemed willing to open up. "Besides, this'll give me a chance to snoop through the sheriff's house *and* Neptune's personal belongings in one fell swoop."

Chapter Ten

CONTRARY TO HER CLAIMS, TESS DIDN'T SNOOP THOUGH anyone's belongings—and it wasn't just because Kendra was with her and she wanted to make a good impression on the woman. Tess knew enough about Victor Boyd by now to know that he valued his privacy above all else. He'd have never agreed to let her go to his house if it contained anything worth finding.

"Wow. Neptune and Sven seem to have really made themselves at home," Tess said as she cast a glance over the open-concept kitchen, which overlooked a living room decked out in floral decor. She'd always found the floor-to-ceiling flowers delightfully incongruous with the sheriff's personality. "This place is kind of a mess."

"I know." Kendra wrinkled her nose as she stepped over a black duffel bag that seemed to be spilling electronic parts. "I had no idea producing a podcast took so much *stuff*. I thought the whole point was that you could take a microphone and do it anywhere. This makes it look like they're planning a heist or something."

"Did they really go to Seattle this morning?"

Kendra's hand hovered over the door to the fridge. "I didn't put a GPS tracker on their van, if that's what you're asking. I think you're better off asking your friend Nicki for that kind of help."

To this day, Tess had no idea how much of the truth about Nicki and her law enforcement activities Kendra knew. Being the sheriff's sister and a big part of the last murder investigation meant that she had an inside track on the activities that took place around here. Her level of reserve, however, and the fact that she'd basically sealed herself up inside Herb's repair shop made it impossible to get an accurate read on her.

"Victor asked me to help him pick up some groceries, that's all," Kendra added, lest Tess decide to press for more information. "He doesn't ask for help very often, so I didn't question it."

Tess wanted to point out that *neither* of them asked for help and that they both made it virtually impossible to offer it, but she didn't. She started putting produce away instead.

"It's weird, right?" Tess asked. "For your brother to open up his home like this? To a virtual stranger?"

Kendra eyed her speculatively. "Yes."

"We've been friends for over a year now, and the most I've gotten out of him is a request to stop making such a nuisance of myself. Except for my birthday, when he bought me a belt to wear my bear spray when I go hiking."

"That tracks."

"He invited Neptune onto his crime scene yesterday like it was nothing. I'm usually removed by force the second I cross the yellow tape."

"Victor's very protective of the things he cares about."

With each of Kendra's terse replies, Tess felt her shoulders slump lower and lower. This wasn't the chatty insight into Victor's heart she'd been hoping for.

"I haven't stopped by the sheriff's office *once* this month," Tess complained. "Not even when I thought someone slashed my tires while I was getting a haircut. I figured he wanted some space."

"That was nice of you."

Tess gave up on the oversized bunch of carrots she was trying to wrangle into the produce drawer. "Kendra, can't you tell I'm in crisis over here?" The carrots fell to the floor with a plop. "What does Neptune Jones have that I don't? Your brother has *never* invited me into this house—not a single time, not even after everything we went through on the Simone Peaky case. He doesn't ask for my help with anything, and when I'm stupid enough to offer, he acts like I just invited him to watch a beheading. What is it about me that's so off-putting he won't even be my *friend*?"

It took Kendra so long to reply that Tess was afraid she'd done it again—said the unimaginable something, put up the Boyd barrier she couldn't see or understand. But the other woman blew out a long breath and began moving through the kitchen again. Not to put the groceries away but to put a kettle on to boil for tea.

And, blessedly, to talk.

"When Victor was a kid—oh, probably ten or eleven years old—he got this paint-by-number kit for Christmas," Kendra said as casually as if discussing the weather. "It was some cheap little thing, probably bought last minute at the dollar store, but he absolutely lit up when he opened it."

"Your brother *paints*? Since when?"

Kendra stared at her. "Are you going to let me tell this story or not?"

"Sorry." Tess immediately made the motion of a zipper over her mouth and settled onto one of the kitchen stools. Kendra made no move to hurry her story as she set about making the tea. "Please keep going. No one ever has fun Sheriff Boyd boyhood stories to tell. Or if they do, they certainly don't tell them to *me*."

"The kit came with two canvases." Kendra placed some kind of light floral tea in front of Tess. More for comfort than because she was cold, Tess wrapped her hands around the mug and inhaled the steam. "One was of a litter of puppies—all wearing bows and crawling out of a basket, that sort of nonsense. The other was a landscape. Mountains against the night sky, aurora borealis in the distance. It was beautiful—or rather, it *could* have been beautiful, provided the person doing the painting knew what he was doing."

It was killing Tess not to interject or at least ask questions. "And Victor didn't know what he was doing?"

Kendra glared but didn't comment on the interruption. "Of course he didn't know what he was doing. He was eleven and he'd never picked up a paintbrush before. Our dad made him an easel out of firewood and set him up in the living room—right over in that corner by the bay window—so he could try his hand at being an artist. He started with the puppies, and it took him *months* to finish. Like, literal months. He'd come home from school every day and dab at the canvas, his little tongue sticking out of his mouth in concentration. It was adorable."

Tess believed it. The image was too good to pass up, especially since it sounded just like him. Determined and diligent, refusing to be rushed even on something that had cost a literal dollar.

"By the time he finished, the painting wasn't half bad. My dad had to go back to the store several times to replenish the paint, though, so Victor ended up with this small stack of canvases to work on—more puppies, a beach or two, a super-offensive one with a Native woman in full headdress. He threw that last one away, but he eventually made it through all the rest."

"Are these paintings still in existence somewhere?" Tess asked, glancing around the house. "Because I'd pay good money to see them."

Kendra rolled her shoulder in a half shrug that reminded Tess so much of Victor that she felt something tight grab hold of her chest. "Probably. You can ask him if you want, but I wouldn't recommend it. He won't like that I told you this story."

"I mean, it *is* a nice story, but..." Tess trailed off, hoping Kendra would take the hint.

Thankfully, she did.

"The one canvas he never touched, no matter how good he got at those paint-by-numbers, was the aurora borealis one. I teased him about it—sister stuff, you know, about how it was going to rot underneath his bed without ever seeing a dab of paint, about how he'd never be good enough to do it justice—but no matter what I said, he never rose to the bait. He'd just smile that soft, inward smile of his and go about his business." Kendra paused and gave what Tess would very much consider a soft, inward smile of her own. "He never did paint it. I'd catch him looking at it sometimes, as if he was thinking about all the things it *could* be if only he was brave enough to start, but he never did. I think my mom ended up throwing it out a few years later when she was going on a spring-cleaning tear. He was so mad about it that he didn't talk to her for weeks afterward. That's the last time either of us ever mentioned it."

Kendra shrugged her half shrug again before turning around and putting the rest of the groceries away.

"Wait." Tess took a sip of her tea. It tasted like soap, but she was too distracted by the story to care. "That's it? He just never painted it? That's the whole story?"

"He never painted *anything* after that. Not to my knowledge, anyway. Victor's always been strange like that. There are some things in his life—some parts of him—that he refuses to touch or let be touched, even if it means letting years go by in the process."

Tess sat for a moment, dazed and not altogether pleased. She was as much a storyteller as Kendra, so there was no use pretending she didn't understand the metaphor. In this particular story, Tess was the unpainted painting, a blank canvas that Victor had shoved under his bed, an untouchable thing that he couldn't bring himself to start.

Only that was a load of rubbish. Tess wasn't an inanimate object. She was a human being—one with hopes and aspirations and a desire to paint of her own.

"That's the stupidest thing I've ever heard," Tess muttered, pushing her mug away.

Kendra turned back toward her, her carefully arched brow her only sign of surprise.

"And he's the stupidest man I've ever met," Tess added. "I'm glad your mom threw that canvas away. If he was just going to let it sit there, going to waste while he hemmed and hawed and wasted his time on puppies, then he didn't deserve it. I hope the worms got it. I hope a dumpster diver found it and turned it into a hat."

"That's...one way of looking at it."

"It's the *only* way of looking at it," Tess said. She cast a glance around the living room again, taking in the suitcase and electronics with a reinforced sense of outrage. "And it still doesn't explain why he's relaxing his standards enough to let two virtual strangers crash at his house. I don't trust that woman, Kendra. Not one bit. In fact—"

Kendra stood unblinking as Tess cut herself off. "In fact, what?" she inquired politely.

Tess dug in her pocket for the forgotten slip of paper that Jared had handed her outside the bookmobile. "In fact, I'm not the only one," she said. "Nicki gave me this. I think it's some kind of warning about her."

The note turned out to be exactly that. As Tess scanned the first line, she felt a rising sense of triumph that bubbled over like that freshly brewed pot of tea. By the time she got to the end, however, her feelings took a much more sinister turn.

"What's wrong?" Kendra asked.

Tess didn't answer, but it didn't matter. Kendra lifted the note from her hand and read it aloud.

"'I got some inside info on that murder-podcast woman for you. Neptune isn't her real name.'" Kendra chuckled as she considered the slip of paper. "Sorry, Tess, but that one was pretty obvious. Neptune is the fakest stage name I've ever heard."

"Keep going," Tess murmured, her voice faint. Like Mumford, she believed in the existence of coincidences—she really did. But this one, coming so soon on top of all the rest, was too much, even for her.

"'Her real name is Darcy.'"

Chapter Eleven

WHEN TESS ARRIVED AT THE BOOKSTORE LATER THAT day, she found her mother decked out from head to toe in widow's weeds.

She had no idea if her mother traveled with a full wardrobe—complete with a black suit, black heels, and a black hat so big that it was practically a kite—or if she'd somehow managed to procure those items since the news of Levi's death, but it was alarming either way.

"Mom, what's the matter with you?" Tess demanded as soon as she stepped through the door. "Are you *trying* to draw attention to your involvement with that man?"

Her mom barely looked up from where she was striking a pose by the front window, her attitude one of thoughtful ennui. "I'm in mourning, love. Don't make my pain worse by yelling at me."

"Could you at least move away from the window?" Tess asked. Even though Gertrude was standing diligently behind the counter and the Open sign was blazing full neon, the bookstore looked untouched. "You're scaring all my potential customers away."

Her mom dropped the attitude. The hat, however, stayed on, courtesy of an enormous hat pin that was giving Tess a plot bunny of epic proportions. A stab from a pin that long could probably reach an internal organ—one of the juicy, important ones. An eccentric widow could do some serious damage before Detective Gonzales was any the wiser.

"You've had exactly three customers since we opened," Bernadette said. "One wanted to use the restroom. The other wanted to know where he could find Neptune Jones. And the third—"

Tess groaned. "Don't say it. I'm having a bad enough day as it is." She moved toward the counter, pausing just long enough to bestow a quick kiss on her daughter's forehead. "Thanks for opening, Gertie. I can take things from here."

Gertrude heaved a sigh and continued flipping through the pages of the *Nightwave* comic in front of her. "Why bother? Neptune's in Seattle today, hunting down a hot lead in the Levi Parker case, so there's nothing else to do. I might as well *not* sell books for you."

It had been Tess's intention to reach for the book stashed behind the counter—the one signed to Darcy—but her daughter's words gave her pause. "How do you know that's what she's doing?"

Gertrude only looked up long enough to roll her eyes. "Because the whole town is talking about it, that's how. Apparently, she and Sheriff Boyd have something they want to check into, but he's still busy interviewing witnesses. She went to look into it for him."

"That is *not* true, and you know it," Tess said hotly. "Sheriff Boyd would never send a random civilian to do his dirty work for him." Then, because it seemed equally important, she added, "What's the lead?"

Gertrude shrugged. "No one tells me these things."

"Yet you seem to overhear plenty..."

"Not this time. Sheriff Boyd is up to something. He keeps looking at me all weird and sideways when he thinks I'm not paying attention." Gertrude paused, considering. "He's been looking at you that way too."

Tess's heart gave a small leap, but Bernadette spoke before she could come up with an appropriately disinterested way to follow up.

"It probably has something to do with your hundred-thousand-dollar fish," her mother said. "That came from Seattle, didn't it?"

Yes, it did, but Tess resented the implication that a) it was *her* hundred-thousand-dollar fish, and b) that Sheriff Boyd would have told Neptune anything about it. If there was even a remote chance it was related to the federal case, he wouldn't put Nicki and Jared in the position of bringing a total stranger into his confidence.

At least, she didn't *think* he would. The old Sheriff Boyd, who did things by the book and refused to break rules for anyone, was a man Tess trusted with her life. This new Sheriff Boyd, who drank Wild Turkey and opened up his home to strangers, was someone she didn't quite recognize.

"I'm sure Neptune will put on a show for the whole town as soon as she gets back," Tess said, doing her best to push the woman out of her mind. "I, for one, don't plan on giving her the attention she craves. I have more important things to do."

"Like what?" Gertrude asked as she continued flipping the pages. "I hope you plan to work on your next book, because I don't think the sales from this place are putting me through college."

"Very funny." Tess ducked her head over the edge of the counter and reached for the book. Instead of the four-hundred-page hardback she expected, there was nothing back there but a half-eaten poke bowl.

"Hey. That's mine." Gertrude snatched the bowl of tuna and avocado away from Tess. "You wouldn't want it anyway. I put scallions in this one. I'll make you one without if you're hungry. There's no way we're going to be able to eat that whole fish by ourselves unless we start making a serious effort."

"I'm not hungry," Tess said, despite the rumbling in her stomach that indicated otherwise. "What happened to the book I put back here? You didn't return it to the shelf, did you?"

"That's what I was trying to tell you," her mother said. "The third customer came in and specially requested a signed copy made out to Darcy. Isn't that nice? What are the chances that *two* different people would want a book signed to the same name?"

The rumbling in Tess's stomach suddenly turned to a hard lump. "What did you just say?"

"He was quite nice, actually. We had a long chat about his name—apparently, it's a tradition in his family. You don't meet many male Darcys these days. Leslies, either. I always liked the name Leslie for a man."

"Mom." Tess grabbed her mother by the shoulders and pressed so hard that the older woman grunted. "Are you being serious right now?"

"Don't worry. Gertie's been telling me all about how there aren't any such rules nowadays. Man, woman, Darcy, Leslie—the only thing that matters is that you feel comfortable in your own skin."

Gertrude held up her fist in show of solidarity. "Yeah, Grandma! Trans rights are human rights."

As much as Tess appreciated her daughter's worldview, she needed answers—and she needed them fast. "You mean to tell me that someone came in and specially requested that book? Not a different signed copy? Not one of the ones we have in the back with the note from my editor? He specifically wanted the one that the young man had me sign yesterday?"

"Yes." Her mom gently pried Tess's hands from her shoulders. Brushing at the invisible wrinkles left behind, she added, "Was that one not for sale? You never said you wanted to keep it."

Tess sank onto the footstool sitting behind the counter, forcing her thoughts into a semblance of order. "Yes. No. I don't know." She glanced up at her daughter. "Gertie, did you know that Neptune Jones isn't that woman's real name?"

Gertrude shrugged and continued eating her lunch. "So? You're the only person in the world who doesn't use a pen name. What difference does it make?"

"The difference," Tess explained with painstaking calm, "is that her real name is *Darcy*."

Tess couldn't have been more pleased by her family's reaction than if she were Neptune Jones herself, recording a podcast in the middle of a small-town honky-tonk bar. Gertrude dropped her poke bowl, sending fish and scallions flying, while Bernadette blanched and looked every inch the widow she was pretending to be.

"No way," Gertrude breathed.

"That's too much of a coincidence, even for me," her mom said faintly.

Tess stood up and helped lower her mom to the footstool in her place. "I think that young man left the book on purpose yesterday—for Neptune to find, maybe, or for this new guy who showed up. Did he look on the shelf first? To see if it had been put there for him?"

"I don't know," Bernadette said. "I wasn't paying attention until he asked for help."

"Don't look at me." Gertrude held her hands up as if in surrender. "I was cutting up fish in the back. Do you think the book had a message in it? Like a secret note or an envelope holding the poison that killed Levi Parker?"

"It's possible." Tess turned to her mother. "Mom, what did today's guy look like?"

"Like an ordinary man, I suppose." Her mom didn't seem to be getting her color back. "White. Tallish. Thin but not in a way that stood out. A bit of growth on his chin, but I wouldn't call it a full beard. It was that scraggly thing young men seem to think counts as facial hair nowadays."

White, tallish, unremarkably thin, and growing out a beard were the least-useful descriptors Tess could think of in a place like this. In a town renowned for its hiking and mountain-biking opportunities, that described about nine-tenths of the people who came through.

"Did you at least get a peek at his driver's license?" Tess persisted. "To confirm that his name was Darcy?"

"Of course not. I was selling the man a book, not questioning him for murder." Her mother glanced up at her. She seemed to be regaining some of her color, which was good, but she was also starting to regain some of her attitude with it. "And before you ask, he paid in cash. Ordinary, crumpled cash."

Tess tried to tamp down her disappointment. "It's too bad I never got around to installing a video camera system. I don't know why I let Sheriff Boyd talk me out of it."

"Even if you did have him on camera—or know what his legal name is—what difference would it make?" Bernadette asked. "What exactly are we accusing him of? Coincidental name usage?"

The question wasn't a bad one. Other than the tingling sensation that always came over Tess when murder was in the air and her family tied up in it, she had little to go on. All she knew was that something wasn't right—and Neptune Jones likely held the key.

"I don't think anyone should work in the bookstore alone," she said by way of answer. "We work in pairs or not at all. The same goes for walking the streets—and yes, Mother, I'm including you in that. I don't know how or why the Paper Trail fits into all this, but I don't like the way things are leaning."

"Mom, you don't think Neptune killed Levi, do you?" Gertrude asked, her nose wrinkled as all the implications sank in. "Like…for podcast content?"

"Of course not," Tess reassured her, though there was no *of course* about it. If she was writing this story line into her book, Neptune Jones would definitely be suspect number one. By Neptune's own admission, she'd arrived in town well before Levi's death. She knew his habits and weaknesses better than anyone, was sure of his guilt, and made no attempt to hide how little she cared for him. It was almost too easy.

Then again, a woman who killed off her cash cow couldn't get a whole lot of cash after he was dead and butchered.

Tess decided to use this last thought to assuage her daughter's fears. "I doubt she's that shortsighted," she reassured her. "Now that Levi is dead, Neptune will have to rustle up another serial killer on the run to start podcasting about. They don't grow on trees, you know. She wouldn't waste this one unless she had a very good reason."

Bernadette's snort showed what she thought of this logic, but Gertrude paused to think about it, which was what really mattered.

"That's true," Gertrude said slowly. "She made almost twenty million dollars last year between her podcast, her book deals, and her live appearances. She wouldn't want to do anything to endanger that."

Tess swiveled her head to stare at her daughter. "I'm sorry, she made *what*?"

"I mean, she has a staff and production costs to pay and everything, so it's not like she's *that* rich."

Tess could only blink at her daughter. She earned a generous income with her writing career, it was true, but nowhere near that kind of money. That was the kind of wealth that turned generational.

That was the kind of money that people killed for.

Before she could say anything, the door to the bookstore swung open. Tess perked up at the thought of a customer, but it was only Ivy. She took one look at the fully stocked shelves and lack of people to buy them and laughed.

"If you're looking for your customers, they're currently gathering outside the hotel," Ivy said.

Tess ignored the slight on her bookstore to focus on the more important task at hand. "Why? What's happened now? Is Neptune back?"

"Neptune? Why would I care about her?"

Tess could have kissed Ivy for that look of scorn, but she didn't have a chance. Ivy's next words were calculated to get them *all* moving.

"If you don't hurry, you're going to miss it," she said with a jerk of her head toward the street. "The sheriff is getting ready to hold a press conference—and I think it's going to be a good one."

———————

If everyone in attendance at the press conference bought a single copy of Tess's book, she'd have been sure to reach the very top of the *New York Times* bestseller list. In all her time living and working in this town, she'd never realized how many people it could hold—or how ravenous their appetite for scandal and intrigue.

"Couldn't you have saved us a seat or something?" Tess asked Ivy as they pushed their way into the crowd. She could just make out Sheriff Boyd standing on the front porch of the hotel, looking grave and annoyed at the duty that lay before him. "I feel like there should be a VIP section."

"There is," Ivy said and pointed toward the front. "But seeing as how you're neither a crime reporter nor a member of the force, you weren't on the list."

Tess would have protested against this, but she caught sight of the scruff of Mumford's pasted-on hair and glanced over at her mother instead. Bee was quick to wave her off.

"Go on," Bernadette said, interpreting Tess's plea without having to hear a word. "I'll keep an eye on Gertie. I know you're agog to hear what he has to say."

She *was* agog to hear what Sheriff Boyd had to say, but even more important, she wanted to watch him while he said it. Every part of her longed to take Victor aside and tell him what Nicki had discovered about Neptune—and about how it tied in to the young man who'd visited her bookstore yesterday—but only if he was in the mood to listen. This was too important to be brushed aside as an annoyance.

"Thanks, Mom," she said as she moved toward the front. She had sharp elbows—all the women in her family did—so she managed to make her way up before the sheriff got started. "Hey, Mumford. You must have gotten here early to score such a good seat."

"I'll say I did. I've been waiting forever for this blasted

thing to start." He pressed a damp handkerchief to his fore-head, which did little to stop the beads of sweat that were trickling down his face. Between the sun overhead and the bodies crammed in all around him, it was no wonder he was feeling the heat. "That sheriff of yours sure knows how to amp up the drama. He's had us on tenterhooks for over an hour."

"Is that what he's doing?" Tess asked, her own brow wrinkled. "That's not like him at all. He's normally—"

"Thank you all for your patience." The moment Sheriff Boyd started speaking, he lifted his hands like a preacher silencing his congregation. Such was his aura of command that it worked right away. "Given the highly public identity of our victim and his alleged crimes, I know many of you have questions about the cause of his death and the efforts being made to find his killer. I'm here to answer as many of them as I can. But first—"

"Is it true he came to this town in pursuit of a new victim?" one man shouted before the sheriff could launch into his speech. "An eccentric older woman?"

"I heard she had dinner with him the night he died," another man said.

"I heard she ransacked his room," a woman added.

"I heard she's related to that author who murders people and then writes books about it," said yet another.

Tess would have defended herself, but there was no need. Without once raising his voice or straying from the drawl that always became more pronounced when he was trying to make a point, Sheriff Boyd continued as though there had been no interruption.

"But first," he repeated, "I'd like to state that the hotel will be opening back up for business at the conclusion of this press conference. The victim's suite will remain closed to the public, but we've found no cause for alarm or danger for the rest of the guests."

"That means it's murder for sure," Mumford said to Tess in a low voice, "and that your friend up there has a pretty good idea who did it."

Tess glanced sharply at the reporter. "How do you know?"

"He basically just invited this pack of rabid wolves to descend onto the hotel en masse," Mumford said. "He wouldn't do that unless he knew himself to be standing on solid ground. I wonder if he's already made an arrest."

Tess felt pretty sure that he hadn't, but her heart still gave a leap as she stood watching him. Sheriff Boyd was always a powerful presence, but she'd never seen him like this before—aloof and stern, no sign of the lurking smile in his eyes.

"Levi Parker died of hemlock poisoning around two a.m. on the night of the fourteenth," he said. A gasp broke out in the crowd, but the sheriff kept going as if nothing had happened. "All signs point to the poison having been ingested sometime in the hour preceding his death. At this time, we have several leads we're looking into, but no arrests have been made."

Tess glanced over at Mumford to see what he made of the last statement, but the reporter wasn't paying her any attention. His gaze was fixed on the sheriff's face.

"Due to the nature of Mr. Parker's death, we're asking

that everyone use an abundance of caution moving forward. While we believe there is no danger to the community at large, several known species of natural hemlock do grow in this area. They can prove hazardous to anyone unfamiliar with these woods and the dangers they afford."

There was no stopping the outburst of questions after that. Every reporter in attendance—and several people that Tess suspected were merely present for the spectacle—had something to add. Mumford was the first to shoot up his hand, but Tess didn't stick around to hear what he asked.

For one thing, she doubted Mumford or any of these reporters would get anything more out of Sheriff Boyd. Never what one would consider a communicative man, when it came to his work, he was downright tight-lipped. For another, she had a much more important destination in mind.

"Ivy, will you keep an eye on my mom and Gertie, please?" she asked as she passed by the deputy, who was listening to the press release with an air of satisfaction. At the sound of Tess's voice, she tore herself away long enough to narrow her eyes.

"Why?" Ivy asked suspiciously. "Where are you going?"

"To talk to our resident hemlock specialist, obviously," Tess said. She didn't know much about that particular poison, but she knew someone who did—and she was determined to get to her before anyone else did.

"We have a hemlock specialist?" Ivy called out after her, but Tess was already halfway across the street and pretended not to hear.

If Tess was right—and she almost always was—they didn't just have a hemlock specialist. They had a hemlock gardener, and she was sure to be home from the bookmobile by now.

Chapter Twelve

EDNA'S HOUSE WAS LOCATED A LITERAL HOP, STEP, AND jump away from the hotel. In Tess's experience, this was true of busybodies all over the world. The closer they were to the action, the better the chances that they'd be on hand when something exciting was underway. In fact, as Tess marched up to Edna's front door, she could still hear the sounds of the press conference going on behind her.

"Edna, open up!" Tess rapped her knuckles on the faded wood grain front door. Tendrils of ivy crept over the front of it, which Tess assumed was Mother Nature's attempt to lock the ornery old woman inside. "I see your curtains moving, so I know you're in there. You might as well give up and let me in."

When her threat did nothing more than cause the curtains to twitch back down into place, Tess gave up on trying to enter the dignified way. After slinking around the side, she carefully pushed her way through a garden that had long been the envy of the whole town.

The first time Tess had ever visited this woman's house, she'd been struck by how delightfully old world Edna's garden was. Instead of neat rows of flowers and orderly vegetables, it was an overgrown cascade of greenery. At first glance, it had an air of disarray, but after spending a few minutes among those leafy fronds, a pattern started to emerge. Creepers had been guided by patient and expert hands to create a vertical feast for the senses. Bright blooms poked their heads out of ferns that had been planted to shelter them from inclement weather. Prickly rosebushes were encouraged to keep predatory deer from making a feast of the bounty, and—as Tess had long suspected—to protect a small patch near the back where Edna's herbs grew.

"Aha!" Tess was no expert when it came to hemlock—or any natural poison—but she had a phone. She had Google Images. That white lacy burst looked an awful lot like the picture she currently held in the palm of her hand. "Edna, you have some serious explaining to do. Does Sheriff Boyd know you're growing hemlock in your garden?"

A cackle sounded from behind her. Tess whirled around, surprised to find Edna standing only a few feet back. For such an elderly woman, she moved a lot like a cat.

"That's wild carrot, you fool—and if you know how to get rid of such an invasive species, feel free to share your horticultural knowledge. I'm sure the local Lawns and Garden Society would love to hear from an expert such as yourself."

"We have a local Lawns and Gardens Society?" Tess asked, refusing to let Edna off the hook so easily. "Why is this the first I'm hearing of it?"

"Because we've seen what you've done with that dirt pit you call a yard, that's why. Some of nature's richest soil outside your door, and even the dandelions look like they want to give up." She snickered as Tess continued examining the garden for signs of poison. "You won't find it here. I keep the really potent stuff in the basement."

"How potent are we talking?" Tess asked with real interest. "Strychnine? Ricin? Nightshade?"

"Cannabaceae," Edna said. As soon as she saw the expression on Tess's face, she cackled anew. "And I have a permit, so there's no need to go calling up your boyfriend and tattling on me. It's *medicinal*."

Tess resented the implication that she'd turn tattletale so easily. "Edna, how could you think I'd do such a thing? I thought we were friends."

"You were looking for poison in my garden so you could pin a murder on me," Edna countered. "I wasn't born yesterday. Come on in."

Edna often cropped up as one of the suspects Tess *wished* she could pin a murder on, but the old woman had a way of always helping with the investigation instead. The offer to go inside may have been issued in a tone as curt as it was surly, but Tess wasn't about to look a gift invitation in the mouth.

"I just came from the press conference," Tess said as she ducked her head to make it under a wisteria vine and in through the back door. "Did you know it was hemlock that did Levi Parker in?"

"Of course I did. Sheriff Boyd was here yesterday, sniffing around my garden." She gave a triumphant smack of her lips. "*He* didn't find anything poisonous either."

Tess wasn't surprised to hear that Sheriff Boyd had already traveled down this particular rabbit hole—or that Edna had made things as difficult for him as she did everyone else.

Tess would have to use a lot more tact if she wanted to discover anything new.

"How interesting," she said in as polite a tone as she could muster. "Have you ever thought about growing poisons? Just for fun, I mean?"

"Of course not," Edna replied, affronted. Tess was afraid she'd actually offended her, but Edna curled her lip and added, "I wouldn't want the trail to lead back to me. There are plenty of ways to get your hands on poison in these parts *without* growing the evidence in your own backyard."

Tess was oddly pleased to hear this. "Oh? And if you were planning on murdering someone—say, a novelist who ratted you out for growing illegal marijuana—how would you go about it?"

"My marijuana *isn't* illegal, and I wouldn't poison you." Edna settled herself on the edge of her faded couch and folded her hands over her lap. "Poison is for cowards. I'd just shoot you instead."

Tess couldn't help laughing. "Thank you? At the very least, a gunshot would hurt less."

"Not if I shot you in the stomach. That can take days of suffering before you finally kick off." Edna winked. "But I'll tell you what I told the good sheriff...if you're sure you want to hear it."

Tess had never been so sure of anything in her whole life. She leaned forward to hear what the woman had to say— and made sure to cover her stomach with her hands while she was at it. After the past few days she'd had, she wasn't risking anything. "What do you know?"

"About life? More than you ever will. About hemlock? Enough." Edna leaned forward and met her halfway. "It's a funny little thing. Like the wild carrot, it's an aggressive plant—it'll sweep into a town and make itself at home without a care for anyone's comfort but its own."

"Edna, if this is going to end up being a really long-winded insult about me—"

Edna laughed. "It's not. Hemlock—the poisonous kind that grows here in Washington State—prefers areas that have been recently cleared. Vacant lots, empty meadows, that sort of thing. The damper, the better."

Tess wrinkled her brow. She couldn't be sure, but it sounded an awful lot like Edna was describing—

"It's particularly attracted to the edges of forested areas. Especially if the edge has been recently cut down."

Tess sat up so suddenly that her head started to spin. She might have accused Edna of poisoning her after all, but she recognized this feeling. It wasn't intoxication; it was *exhilaration*.

"Peabody Timber," Tess breathed. "Up where Mason and his crew have been clearcutting."

Edna sat back with a triumphant whoosh. "You might be a floozy and a nuisance, but I'll say this for you, Tess Harrow. You're no fool. You got it in one."

———————

Every instinct Tess had urged her to lose no time in making her way up the mountain to where Mason Peabody and his two brothers had spent the past few decades paving the way for hemlock to take root and flourish in the wilds of Washington. Only the knowledge that Sheriff Boyd was probably well-aware of this facet of the investigation—and how neatly it tied into the hundred-thousand-dollar fish— kept her in town.

Well, that and the fact that Neptune pulled up Main Street just as Tess was making her way down it. Sometime in the past two days, the unmarked white van the podcaster drove around in had become as recognizable a sight as Nicki's blue bookmobile—although much less welcome, as far as Tess was concerned.

"What a waste of a trip." Neptune stepped out of the passenger seat with a yawn and a catlike stretch. "If we'd known the records office was closed until fall quarter, we could've saved ourselves a lot trouble—oh. Tess. Hello."

Tess didn't miss the flicker of annoyance in Neptune's eyes as the woman caught sight of her—or how quickly she tamped it down to look like something else.

"How did the press conference go?" Neptune asked. "Did Victor shake things up with that bit about the hemlock?"

At this, Tess had to suppress her own flicker of annoyance. Just how deep in Sheriff Boyd's confidence was this woman?

"Something like that," she said, smiling blandly. "We all knew it was poison, of course, but I think we suspected something a little more modern."

"Of course," Neptune agreed, equally as bland. Before Tess could think of a way to question her about her day without *looking* like she was questioning her about her day, Sven stepped out of the van. He looked anything but pleased at the waste of his time, especially once his gaze swept over the dusty street and the well-worn buildings that lined it.

"I don't see why we couldn't have at least stayed the night in Seattle while we were there," he muttered. "My back can't take another night like the last one."

Neptune met Tess's gaze with a twinkle. "You'll have to forgive my producer. Sven is finding all the rusticity a bit... wearing."

"I just don't see why whoever killed Levi couldn't have done it somewhere near five-star accommodations, that's all," he said, grunting. Then, with something approaching actual humanity, he added, "At least we're saving a ton of money by staying with the sheriff. This place is a lot more expensive than it looks."

Tess couldn't resist. "Doesn't your podcast earn somewhere in the range of twenty million dollars a year?"

Neptune's low, throaty laugh sounded before he could answer. "Well, well. Someone's been doing her homework. But don't be fooled—the overhead on an operation like this one would boggle your mind. The amount we pay in bribes alone..."

"Don't, Neptune," Sven warned.

"I'm just saying. For the thousand bucks we slipped that security guard today, you think he could have at least let us *peek* at the records."

Tess was dying to ask which records they'd gone to see, but she refused to give Neptune the satisfaction of her curiosity.

Her resolve was helped by the sound of frantic footsteps, followed by her daughter's breathless, eager panting.

"Neptune," Gertrude said, sighing with delight. "*Finally*. I've been hunting you down since you got here. I'm your biggest fa—"

Sven stepped so quickly between Gertrude and Neptune that Tess didn't have time to react. That came later, when he threw up his meaty hand and caught the teenager on the bottom of her chin. With a sickening thwack, he sent Gertrude—who weighed all of a hundred and ten pounds—sprawling across the pavement.

"Gertie!" Tess cried as she fell to her knees. A trickle of blood ran out the side of her daughter's mouth.

As the single mother of a smart, likable teen who'd lived the bulk of her life under the protection of her upper-class white privilege, Tess hadn't been called on to show her teeth very often. A few altercations at the local park when Gertrude had been a toddler, one particularly nasty boy who'd shoved her from the top of a slide and caused her to break her collarbone, and the more recent murder investigations made up the bulk of Tess's inner Mama Bear appearances.

That bear emerged now with a vengeance.

"Have you lost your ever-loving mind?" she cried, fury whipping her into such a frenzy that she was literally seeing red start to form around the edges of her vision. "This is a fifteen-year-old child. *My* fifteen-year-old child."

"Oh, dear." Neptune was down on her knees and next to Tess almost immediately. "I'm so sorry about this. Sven's just overprotective, that's all. He's my security as well as my producer. You wouldn't believe some of the tricks people pull to try and get close to me."

Tess doubted she was *that* famous—Neptune Jones was no Kardashian—but she was too furious to come up with an appropriate reply.

From the weak way Neptune spoke again, she was guessing the other woman felt much the same. "So this is your daughter, huh?"

"Of course it's my daughter." Tess slipped her hand under her daughter's head, but Gertrude was already struggling herself into a seated position. "Not that it should matter one way or another. Do you always travel with grown men who punch defenseless children at the first sign of trouble?"

"I'm sorry," Sven muttered, his hand clutched to his chest as if *he* had something to complain about. "I didn't mean to. I just reacted."

"It's fine, Mom," Gertrude said, twisting her mouth as if testing it. She pulled her lower lip out to show a bright slash along the inside. "My braces cut my lip, that's all."

"That's all?" Tess repeated. *"That's all?"*

"There's no need to turn this into a Victorian melodrama. It was just a misunderstanding." Neptune didn't wait for Tess to finish sputtering before she turned to the teenager. "It's Gertrude, right?"

Gertrude showed a bloody smile. "You know who I am?"

"Of course. Your family is famous in this town."

The smile dimmed. "Oh. You mean my mom."

"Your mom *and* your grandmother. It's not all of us who are descended from so much fame and fortune." Neptune winked and started helping Gertrude to her feet. Tess wanted to protest against that too, but she caught the warning look in her daughter's eye and kept her mouth shut. This Mama Bear had a wise head on her shoulders. "I heard you're also kind of a big deal around here. Did you really help solve both of the murders with your mom?"

The blood and the blow were all but forgotten by this time—in Gertrude's eyes, at least. Tess was careful to angle her body between her daughter and Sven, but there was no need. He was already diving inside the well-stocked van.

"I'm helping her with this one too," Gertrude announced with another of those glares that dared Tess to defy her. "Is it true that your real name is *Darcy* Jones?"

Tess gasped. "Gertie!" she cried, but it was too late. Neptune had already blanched and stepped back, her tender concern for Gertrude's well-being gone in a flash.

"How do you know that?" Neptune asked with a wild look at where Sven had disappeared into the van. "Who told you?"

"So it's true." Gertrude narrowed her eyes and wiped at the blood on the side of her face again. That trickling swipe made her look like a vampire who'd just finished a satisfactory meal. It was all Tess could do not to cackle like Edna St. Clair. She needn't have worried about Gertrude letting Neptune and her crew off the hook too easily; her daughter had plenty of Mama Bear instincts of her own. "Do you use the name Neptune to make yourself sound more like a murder podcaster, or are you hiding something?"

"I don't—that is, I—" Neptune turned to Tess with a frown. "Is this *your* doing?"

"Do you mean, did I hunt down your true identity and tell my fifteen-year-old child in hopes of upsetting you to the point of confessing a crime? No. Do you mean, is this girl every bit as determined and diligent as her mother? Yes. It's best not to cross us." She noticed Gertrude tentatively fingering the inside of her mouth and added, "Or to hit us. I'll let it slide this time, but if you or any member of your team lay hands on this child again, I'll have the sheriff draw you up on assault charges—and don't think that staying in his house and flirting with him will keep you safe. He's not that kind of man. Believe me. I've tried."

Tess grabbed Gertrude by the arm and turned on her heel. She'd been half afraid that she'd have to drag the girl away, but Gertrude was every bit as eager to escape the scene as Tess was.

"I can't believe you just played our trump card," Tess said as soon as she felt sure they were out of earshot. "I was saving that bit about her real name for later. You never know when you're going to need a good scare tactic."

"And *I* can't believe you accused Neptune of flirting with Sheriff Boyd," Gertrude said with giggle. "When everyone knows he's—"

She stopped and cast Tess a sideways look that she didn't trust for a second. In an effort to turn the conversation, Tess planted her hands on her daughter's shoulders and pressed down on them. "Don't ever do that again, Gertie. I mean it."

"Don't do what?" Gertrude was still inclined to laugh, but she blinked expectantly up at her mother. "Reveal our secrets to a highly suspicious murder podcaster, or get in the way when an angry man is running at me?"

Tess felt that both those things warranted further discussion, but they weren't what she meant. "Don't risk your safety for answers. Solving this case isn't worth your well-being." She sighed and added, "Even if it means we get to take that woman down a peg or two while we're at it."

Chapter Thirteen

GETTING A STRAIGHT ANSWER OUT OF BERNADETTE Springer was like getting a declaration of affection out of Sheriff Boyd.

Tess and Gertrude cornered her after dinner that night, the two of them waiting until Mumford took himself off to "nose around the hotel" before attacking. And by *attacking*, Tess meant popping open another bottle of the sparkling wine and pouring with a heavy hand.

"Honestly, love. Do you have any idea how many calories are in a glass of this? Vodka sodas are the way to a woman's heart." Bernadette considered the very underage, very impressionable granddaughter next to her and amended her statement. "Or diet soda. Lots of diet soda."

Gertrude giggled. "Too late, Grandma."

"Don't be such a prude, Mom," Tess added. "Gertie's been mixing artisanal cocktails for me since she was eleven."

As expected, Bernadette took instant umbrage to this. "Who are you calling a prude? I'm not the one keeping a brawny young man like that Jared Wilson dangling on a string because I'm too chicken to do anything about it."

"Mom! I'm not dangling him from anything."

Bee opened her eyes wide at Tess. "In that case, you

should be. We had a nice chat about you at the bookshop the other day."

"Oh, jeez. What did he say?"

"The real question is, what *didn't* he say?" Sighing happily, Bernadette took a generous swallow of her wine. "There's something to be said for a man who puts it all out there like that. No games, no pretense, no—"

Since Gertrude was showing way too much interest in the direction this conversation was headed, Tess was quick to cut her mother off. "No secret, diabolical murders in his past?"

Her mother turned to Tess with such a clear, unwavering gaze that she felt herself flushing. "Levi didn't have any secret, diabolical murders, remember? The courts cleared him."

It was as good a segue as any. Now that Neptune was shaping up to be a suspect in truth rather than just hopefulness, it was time to set the record straight.

"Mom, exactly how long had you and Levi been traveling together before you came here?"

That same clear, unwavering gaze of her mother's moved to a point about three feet above Tess's head. "I told you already. We weren't traveling together. He just sort of followed me."

"Fine. Exactly how long was Levi following you?"

"Let's see… We met back in June, like I told your sheriff friend, so that gave us two and a half months." She sighed and held a hand to her bosom. "And *what* a two and a half months it was."

"*Mom.* Stop it." Tess scooted so close to her mother that

their knees bumped. "We get it. You're a woman in her prime with hordes of attractive young men after you. That's not the point."

"It's not?" Bernadette asked.

Since Gertrude was well-aware where Tess was trying—and failing—to steer this conversation, she spoke up. "Grandma, where did you and Levi go? After Sedona, that is. How many cities?"

Bee's brow wrinkled as she considered the question, the lines of her face folding up in an effort of concentration. "I had a meeting with an estate lawyer in Seattle after that—and don't look at me like that, Tess. I wasn't signing over my life and property to a man I'd known all of two weeks. I may be old, but I'm not a fool. Since Dad decided to leave all this Winthrop bounty to you instead of me, I've been moving a few things around, that's all. Like we talked about."

Tess had no argument to make with this. She and her mother had decided a long time ago that the person who should benefit most from her lifetime of hard work was Gertrude, who would be the recipient of a generous trust fund the day she turned eighteen. Tess didn't need or want her mother's money, though she would have fought tooth and nail to keep a scumbag like Levi Parker from getting his hands on it.

"After that, let's see..." Bernadette tapped her chin thoughtfully. "I spent a few weeks in San Diego—you know how much I love what the climate does for my skin—before heading to New York to visit some old friends. After that, I came here. Why?"

"New York?" Tess asked sharply, remembering two of the three women Levi was supposed to have killed.

"Yes. I wanted to see the Beckers before they packed everything up and moved to Florida. They bought the most delicious condo, Tess, right up on the beach and—"

Once again, Gertrude intervened before things could stray too far off course. "Grandma, did Levi go all those places with you?"

"Yes, love. He was very keen on me."

"And what about Neptune? Was she there too? Did you ever catch a glimpse of her?"

One of the nice things about having a sharp-edged former attorney for a mother was that it didn't take her long to pick up on what they wanted. "Ohh," she breathed. "You're still fixated on that whole Darcy thing, aren't you? You don't trust her."

"We're not *fixated* on anything," Tess protested. "In case you've forgotten, her producer hit your granddaughter in the face. And when Gertie mentioned her real name, it was obvious she wasn't expecting it—and that she didn't like our knowing the truth."

Much to Tess's annoyance, her mother looked to Gertrude for confirmation. The girl, bless her wise old soul, topped up her grandmother's glass before answering. "It's true, Grandma. I tried looking up information on Neptune's past, but there's nothing. Not under either of those names. Her bio makes it sound like she just popped up out of nowhere. 'A child of darkness and light, whose early obsession with Ted Bundy made her unpopular at parties but a killer at podcasting.' Ugh. I could write a better fake bio than that. I don't know how I bought into her schtick for so long."

"*Think*, Mom," Tess urged, not displeased to find that her daughter had gotten over her admiration for Neptune so easily. "She knew about you, so you must have caught a glimpse of her every now and then. She's not exactly inconspicuous."

"To be honest, love, Levi was the sort of man to draw a crowd wherever he went. He had natural charisma."

Tess wasn't buying it. "Mom, you're the most observant person I know. You always have been. You used to be able to smell the cigarette smoke on my fingers when I came home from parties. And there was that one time you—"

"You *smoked*?" Gertrude interrupted, and with so much feeling that Tess felt compelled to defend herself.

"Yes, but only—"

"Like, actual cigarettes?"

"Listen, Gertie. Just because I did something reckless and ill-informed doesn't mean—"

"You fell for Big Tobacco's lies and willingly ingested the arsenic and lead that those companies put into cigarettes without regard for public health and safety?"

Tess's guilty flush was replaced by a much more pleasant one. "Look at you, rattling off hazards like a diligent teeto-taler. I taught you well."

Gertrude rolled her eyes. "You didn't teach me at all. We did a whole anti-tobacco unit in our health and nutrition class." Fortunately for Tess's sense of self-preservation—and her ability to defend herself—Gertrude turned her sharp eyes and well-informed mind on her grandmother instead. "Out with it, Grandma. You totally saw her, didn't you?"

Tess wasn't sure why Gertrude's methods should succeed where hers failed, but Bernadette gave in with a sigh. She was probably hoping the girl wouldn't turn her Gen Z disdain for smoking on *her* instead.

"Fine. Yes. I may have occasionally spotted a woman who looked like Neptune sitting in the same bars and restaurants as us. And once, I saw her and that hairy producer creeping down the street while we were catching some midnight air. I thought maybe she was some random fan who had a crush on Levi."

"Mom."

"What?" Bernadette turned an innocent stare her way. "It's not unheard of. Some women are drawn to the aura and mystique of criminals. Levi said he used to get fan mail by the bucketful when he was in Rikers. Half of it was dirty pictures. The other half was proposals of marriage. It's quite sad, when you think about it."

"And how is what you were doing any different?" Tess demanded.

That caused her mother to pull up to her full height. "Now see here, Tess. I might have made a *teensy* error of judgment when it came to my relationship with Levi, but I'm still your mother." She sniffed and added, "Besides, it was fun, sneaking around to avoid her at all hours of the night. It was like trying to lose the paparazzi. Levi had all kinds of tricks for shaking her off. Why, once he even went up to her and threatened—"

She stopped as soon as she realized what she said—and as soon as both Gertrude and Tess practically jumped on her.

"He knew about Neptune following him?"

"What kind of threats did he make?"

"Enough to push her over the edge?"

"Enough to make her want to *kill* him?"

"Enough to make Sven kill him for her?"

Naturally, Bernadette couldn't answer this rapid-fire round of questioning, and just as naturally, Tess realized there was no need. There was only one man with enough calm, cool dignity and legal standing to get straight answers out of her mother.

That man, as they all knew, was Sheriff Victor Boyd.

―――――――――――

"My mother is here to make a confession."

Tess shouldn't have taken such perverse delight in the way her mother sucked in an outraged breath or how Sheriff Boyd actually stumbled mid-step on his way into his office building the next morning, but she did. She might not be getting much done in the way of writing—or selling books—lately, but there was enough thriller writer in her to enjoy the occasional plot twist.

The sheriff was the first to recover. His gaze held equal parts disbelief and shrewdness as he raked it over the two of them. "Do we need to make sure there's an attorney present first?"

"I *am* an attorney, young man," Bernadette replied

sharply. Honesty compelled her to add, "Or rather, I was before I retired. And it's not that kind of confession."

Tess could have almost sworn that an expression of regret flickered across the sheriff's face, but it was gone so fast that she may have imagined it.

"Is it absolutely necessary to have Tess present for it?" Sheriff Boyd asked next.

"Excuse me—" Tess began, but her mother lifted a hand.

"Actually, I'd prefer to do this one alone," Bee said. "If it's all the same to you, love."

It *wasn't* all the same to her, as her mother well knew, but Tess didn't bother arguing. She recognized that look in her mother's eye, and—more importantly—she recognized the one in the sheriff's.

"Fine. Knock yourselves out." She stared at Sheriff Boyd in a way she hoped would penetrate his thick skull and even thicker sense of self-righteousness. "But don't say I never gave you anything."

She turned and made her way back down the sidewalk before either of them could respond. Even though it would have been infinitely cooler to maintain her air of dignity and refrain from looking back, Tess did anyway. No one had ever accused her of having too much dignity before. Or, if she was being honest, any at all.

In the end, it didn't matter. By the time she glanced over, the two had already slipped inside the police office to conduct the interview. Tess was left to while away the next hour on her own.

She was toying between ducking into the bookshop,

where her part-time help had been put in charge of daily operations, or trying to nose out Neptune's whereabouts and following her around from a discreet distance, when the decision was taken out of her hands. Spotting the white van around the corner from the drugstore, Tess pressed herself flat against the brick wall and tiptoed closer. She was sure she looked ridiculous—in all honesty, she *felt* ridiculous— but she was eager to overhear anything that might help shed light on Neptune's misdeeds.

The low rumble of a male voice assailed her ears, followed shortly by another male voice. One of them was gruff and annoyed, so she risked a peek to confirm her suspicion. Sure enough, Sven stood near the hood of the van, chatting animatedly to someone she couldn't see from her vantage point. He was a hand-talker, Tess noted, but his knuckles were too hairy for her to detect any sign of bruising from his attack on Gertrude. She crept closer, only to stop herself in her own tracks.

The man Sven was talking to was a stranger to her—not unusual, given the current state of events around this place— and Tess found very little about him to be remarkable.

That, in and of itself, was remarkable. Tess had always been exceptional at seeing a person and immediately taking note of any distinguishing characteristics. Height, weight, clothing style, birthmarks—she was basically a sketch artist's dream come true.

This man, however, defied categorization. He was Caucasian—that part was certain—but his height could have been anywhere from five-ten to six-two. The exact number was difficult to determine because of the way he held himself, his shoulders hunched and his gait unsteady. His weight was the same—fairly average but hidden by clothes so cleverly cut as to avoid showing off any of his disparate parts. A hat on his head obscured most of his face, and the parts that Tess could see were hidden by a beard so sparsely patched and dingy that she'd have been hard-pressed to say what color it was.

In other words, he was white and tallish. Thin but not in a way that stood out. And with a bit of growth on his chin but not what Tess would call a full beard.

"It's Not-Darcy," Tess breathed. "Mom was right."

She stepped out of her hiding position almost without thinking, her hand outstretched toward the mystery man. If he'd come in to buy the signed book yesterday—the one bearing Neptune's secret name, the one left by the first mystery man—then she had questions for him. *Lots* of them.

Unfortunately, she tripped over a crack in the sidewalk just as the man glanced up, his eye color and any distinguishing facial features shaded by the brim of his hat. By the time she managed to gain her bearings, he'd already dashed away from the van and ducked into a crowd of tourists taking pictures of the hotel.

Tess would have attempted to follow him, but Sven rushed forward in a belated attempt to right her position. His hands pressed into her upper arms as he hauled her to a standing position.

"Ms. Harrow, are you okay?" he asked, peering closely into her eyes. "You look like you've just seen a ghost."

"I thought I made it clear that I didn't want you manhandling any members of my family," Tess said, shaking him off. Then, because Sven flushed guiltily, she decided to press her luck. "Who was that man you were just talking to?"

"What man?" he countered without missing a beat.

"The literal human being who was standing next to you a few seconds ago. You might be able to use this surly, antagonistic attitude to scare other people, but I'm not afraid of you. Millions of podcast listeners won't save you from *my* team of lawyers."

From the way a storm cloud settled onto Sven's brow, Tess felt pretty sure he wanted to test this theory out, but it was the broad light of day and there were dozens of witnesses milling in the street.

"He was just a guy. I don't know. He needed directions."

"You don't know, or he needed directions?"

"Both. Neither. What's the difference? I don't owe you anything."

It was on the tip of Tess's tongue to point out that his attack on her child tipped the cosmic scales decidedly in her favor, but there wasn't a chance. Neptune emerged from a nearby deli, two steaming cups of to-go coffee in her hands. Instead of offering one to Sven—or even to show surprise at finding him locked in battle with Tess—her expression underwent a drastic change.

And by drastic, Tess meant that Neptune smiled. At *her*.

"Ms. Harrow!" she called, holding out one of the cups. "Exactly the woman I was hoping to see. I got you four sugars and three tablespoons of cream. Just the way you like it, right?" She winked in such an obvious and heavy-handed attempt at friendliness that it was all Tess could do to swallow her grimace in time. She also mentally apologized for every time she'd prepared a coffee that way for Sheriff Boyd. Yes, it was how Detective Gonzales drank it. And yes, it was hilarious to rib Sheriff Boyd for his physical and emotional similarities to her closed-off fictional detective. But Tess resented the implication that she could be so easily bought off.

It would take more than a two-dollar cup of deli coffee and a nudge-nudge-wink-wink reference to her series for her to open her heart to this woman. Or to take a sip of something that potentially contained enough hemlock to fell a horse.

"Were you looking for me?" Tess asked with feigned innocence. "You could've stopped by the bookstore and left a message. I'm not difficult to get a hold of."

Neptune's smile didn't lose any of its vibrant wattage. "I just came from there. That young man you have working the counter is lovely."

"His name is Tommy Lincoln," Tess said, seeing no reason to lie. "He's the mayor's oldest son and a good friend of Gertrude's. He's saving up for college next year, so I figured the part-time work would help."

"How quaint. Small towns really are something else, aren't they? Neighbors helping neighbors. Everyone tied up in everyone else's business."

Tess couldn't say for sure, but she felt there was an insult lurking somewhere in those sentences.

"Anyway, I don't have a ton of time right now, but I wanted to invite you to dinner tonight. To apologize for Sven's overreaction."

Tess had never heard of anyone excusing blunt force trauma as an *overreaction* before, but she was too curious about the rest of Neptune's offer to question it. She had no idea what had happened to cause this dramatic turnaround in her personality, but she didn't trust it.

"Dinner?" she echoed. "Tonight?"

"It was Sven's idea. You wouldn't think it to look at him, but he's one heck of an amazing chef. He does things with a loin of pork that would bring a blush to your mother's face."

Since Tess's mother had zero sense of shame when it came to, well, *anything*, Tess seriously doubted this. She also doubted that she wanted to go anywhere near that man and a set of culinary knives.

As if sensing this, Sven softened his scowl into a mild sneer. "I have a Beard Award. You can look it up."

"I'm not sure I can make it," Tess demurred more politely than she felt either Neptune or Sven deserved. She didn't care if Sven had a dozen Beard Awards. "What with my mom staying in town and Mumford to see to—"

"Oh, was I not clear? The invitation is for everyone. There's plenty of room. Victor's letting us move the table around and hang some fairy lights over his back porch so it'll be like an Italian alfresco meal. It's lovely out there at night. Living in a big city, you always forget how many stars there are in the universe, you know?"

Tess *did* know—it was one of the main reasons she and

Gertrude had grown so enamored of this place—but she wasn't about to admit as much to this woman. *Victor* was letting Neptune rearrange his furniture? And cook in his kitchen? And—

"We'd love to," Tess said, the words popping out before she could help them. She also accidentally took a drink of the coffee, which was so cloying that it was all she could do to keep from spraying it across Neptune's signature low-cut black suit. "Assuming Mumford and my mom don't have other plans, that is."

Neptune released a trill of laughter. "In a town like this? From everything I can gather, the social life around here revolves around line dancing at the honky-tonk bar and going to high school football games."

It did, but that didn't give this woman a right to judge.

"You'd be surprised how much life you can pack into a place like this," Tess said. "When we're not burdened down with so much death, that is."

Chapter Fourteen

With her mom busy confessing her crimes to Sheriff Boyd and Gertrude hanging out with Tommy at the bookstore, Tess found herself free for the rest of the day. She could have used the time to work on her next book, but she had a better idea.

"Jared, I need you to take me to work with you this afternoon."

She found the federal agent enjoying lunch at the local deli, a copy of *Fury under the Floorboards* propped open in front of him. He was so startled to see Tess that he fumbled with his lobster roll. Buttery chunks plopped onto the page, highlighting one of Tess's favorite passages in bright-yellow grease. That was where Detective Gonzales had dug up an entire cemetery in hopes of finding a missing set of murdered bones. He'd sweated and sworn the whole time, and ended up no closer to solving the case than when he'd started.

One of the reviews Tess's agent had sent her yesterday called it the best use of a literary cemetery since Shakespeare's Yorick. That was the kind of praise an author could dine out on for years.

"Tess!" Jared fumbled a few more times before rising to his feet. He slammed the book shut, squelching the lobster in the process. "I was just having lunch. And, um, reading. This is really good."

"The sandwich or the book?" Tess teased. She slid into the booth opposite him. "Never mind. It's not important—though if you're in the mood for seafood, I wish you'd come eat the rest of the tuna at the bookstore. I'm afraid it's starting to turn."

"You want me to eat fish that's on the point of going bad for you?" he asked, blinking. He shrugged and added, "Sure. If it'll make you happy."

It was moments like these when Tess felt that she was in way over her head—or that Jared was. The problem was, she could never tell which. Jared was either playing a brilliantly long game of winning her over with guileless good humor or he was so innocent that he'd risk salmonella for no reason other than because Tess asked him to.

"Forget the fish," she said. "What I really need is to come up to the logging operation today so I can take a look around. But I need to not *look* like I'm looking around, if you know what I mean."

He blinked once more. "You want to investigate the fish money? Because I thought we agreed—"

"No, not the money." Tess dropped her voice to avoid anyone overhearing them. "I have reason to think the poison that killed Levi Parker came from Mason's land."

"No way." Jared didn't lower his voice in return. "How do you figure?"

"Because I have inside information and ironclad scientific research to back me up."

"Really?" He released a low whistle before answering the question for himself. "I don't know why I keep acting surprised when you come up with these out-of-the-ballpark solutions that no one else sees coming. You're the most intelligent woman I've ever known."

The compliment rolled so easily off his tongue that Tess couldn't help from picturing Sheriff Boyd in the exact same situation—reading her book in public, nothing but flattery on his lips. *Yeah, right.* Getting a compliment out of that man was like taking a crowbar to a bank vault.

"Who's your inside source?" Jared continued. He lowered his voice before adding, "Or am I not allowed to ask?"

Tess wasn't quite as excited about this next part. "I heard it from Edna St. Clair—but it's not what you're thinking, I swear. I looked up everything she told me. For once, I think the old bat hit the nail on the head. Apparently, hemlock loves growing in areas of cleared forest growth. That's why Sheriff Boyd warned everyone to be careful. It's as easy to stumble across as wild carrot."

"Wild carrot?" he echoed.

"You'll have to take my word for it. But I'm right about this—I just know it. All I need is a chance to verify the findings for myself."

If Jared doubted the integrity of Tess's investigative methods, he didn't let it show. With a nod, he threw himself wholeheartedly into the plan. "I can get you up the mountain without anybody saying too much about it, but you're not going to like my methods."

Since Tess was, in fact, the most intelligent woman Jared

knew, she didn't have to ask. She groaned instead. "You're going to make me pretend to be following up on that kiss in the bookmobile, aren't you?"

"I know it's not ideal, but if there's one excuse that Mason Peabody is *always* able to swallow, it's the pursuit of love." A fiery blush touched his cheeks. "Or at least, the other stuff that usually comes with it."

———————

As an organization, Peabody Timber was well-known to Tess. She'd had several dealings with Mason Peabody and his two triplet brothers over the years, usually in relation to a murder investigation and almost always with one of them playing the role of antagonist. They'd never turned out to be the actual culprits of anything—outside of the money laundering and questionable business practices that had set the FBI on their tail—and if Tess was being perfectly honest, she kind of liked them. Mason was a pompous blowhard, Zach a chickenhearted bully, and Adam a surly alcoholic, but they lived their lives according to their own rules.

Tess could respect that. She didn't always like it, but she respected it.

"Well, well. If it isn't my favorite *New York Times* bestselling author," Mason boomed as Tess and Jared stepped out of the work truck that had taken them up to the base of operations. Like most logging organizations, this one changed locations every few months, their mobile offices and tin can facilities moving as easily as forty tons of solid pine logs.

Mason rubbed his papery hands together with so much force that it was a wonder he didn't set the whole forest alight. "What brings you to my doors this time?" he asked. "Not trouble with that murder investigation, I hope?"

This latter part was said with so much sharp meaning that Tess was glad she'd thought to secure Jared's cover before making her way up here.

"If it's all right with you, she's going to hang out here while I finish clearing out the south patch," Jared said. His words sounded rehearsed, but there was no help for it. They *were* rehearsed. Tess could only hope that his flaming cheeks and wooden attitude could be chalked up to embarrassment.

"What's that? You want to leave her here with me?"

Tess recognized this as her cue to act. Placing her hand lightly on Mason's forearm, she gave him a meaningful squeeze. "I promise not to get in your way. It's just that with my mom staying in the cabin and the hotel booked as full as it can hold, Jared and I haven't been able to find... That is, we can't..." She trailed off with feigned confusion. "He's taking me to Omak for dinner tonight, and it'll be much faster if we leave from here instead of Winthrop."

As she'd hoped, Mason picked up on her meaning almost at once. He winked with such a deliberate show that Tess found herself blushing to match Jared. "Say no more. Your secret's safe with me. Omak's a lovely place. Very private. Perfect for a quiet night on the town." He chuckled. "Or a loud one. I don't judge."

Tess was careful not to meet Jared's eye as Mason continued chuckling to himself.

"I should be done in a few hours," Jared said, still in his too-wooden, too-obvious voice. "You can hang out in my truck, or—"

Once again, Mason spoke up at the exact moment Tess needed him to. "Don't you worry about us, young man. She can keep me company in the office. I might even have some light filing, if she gets bored."

Tess subdued her revolted expression. It was just like a man—and this man, in particular—to assume she'd enjoy an afternoon of unpaid secretarial work. She pretended to admire the view instead. "Actually, if I won't be in anyone's way, I wouldn't mind going for a short hike. It's so beautiful around here. I love the way the hills look when they're so desolate and scabbed over."

Mason, unaware of irony, nodded his agreement. "I always feel refreshed once we clear a hillside. There's nothing like an empty slate for filling the soul."

Jared cleared his throat just in time to stop Tess from responding. "I'll see you back here about four, yeah?"

"Yep. Four o'clock sounds good." That would give her enough time to hightail it down to one of the areas that had been cleared away a few months ago and make it back again before her dinner with Neptune. "I'll see you then."

A strange silence descended. Since Tess was still studiously avoiding Jared's gaze, she didn't pick up on its meaning right away. By the time she did, Jared was already pressing a quick kiss on her cheek.

"Be careful out there," he whispered, his breath wrapping over the curve of her neck. "I haven't been able to tell how many of these guys are on Mason's secret payroll yet."

Jared took himself off before Tess could respond, which was for the best since Mason took it upon himself to do it for her. "You two still going strong, huh?" he asked, a decided twinkle in his eye. "I thought for sure it'd wear off after those first few months. In my experience, it usually does."

Since Tess had been relying on the ol' young-enough-to-be-my-son boyfriend cover story with Mason ever since Jared had first rolled into town, this remark wasn't as unwarranted as it seemed. "Yes, but we're still keeping it a secret," she said. "Especially from you-know-who."

"These days, I don't talk to the sheriff unless I absolutely have to, so your secret's safe with me." Mason touched the side of his nose with a laugh. The laugh died almost immediately after he released it. "But be careful out there, Tess. I know it doesn't look like it, but even a recently cleared forest has its dangers."

———————

Tess tramped through the forest for hours and didn't come across a single, solitary poisonous plant. She'd checked out a field guide from Nicki's bookmobile and everything—*The Okanogan Book of Dangerous Flora and Fauna*—but unless you counted the nest of fire ants she'd kicked over when she sat down to catch her breath for a few minutes, there wasn't anything potentially hazardous.

Of course, the cleared forest covered hundreds of acres up along these mountains, and Tess, despite her sensible footwear and best intentions, had only covered a few dozen of them. The places for hemlock to grow out here numbered in the thousands. It would take a much more dedicated outdoorswoman than herself to explore them all.

Not to mention time—the one thing she was rapidly running out of. Not just on today's hike but also in terms of this entire investigation. Already, the numerous visitors to the town were starting to head home. Neptune was doing a decent job keeping people interested and entertained, but every day that passed without a suspect, the greater the chances that the person responsible for the murder would drift away just as easily as they'd drifted in.

Of the two problems, the former was the one concerning Tess the most right now. She had a good mile left to get back to the logging camp, and the fire ant bites were starting to itch.

The welcome rumble of a four-wheeler drew her attention before she could despair of the hike ahead. She expected to see Jared rushing to her rescue in typical federal agent fashion, so she was understandably surprised when she glanced up to find Zach Peabody instead. He looked as grim and annoyed to see her as ever. She'd never known a man to waste such classically good looks, all homegrown-lumberjack goodness and a rich swoop of auburn hair. God forbid the man smile every now and then.

"There you are," he grumbled as the engine of the four-wheeler cut off and he descended from his perch. "Mason sent me to come find you. He was afraid you'd gotten lost."

"That was sweet of him." Tess was too happy to know she wasn't walking back to care that Zach Peabody was her escort. Of the three Peabody brothers, he was the one who liked her the least—presumably because she'd once picked him out of a lineup and wouldn't hesitate to do so again, should the situation call for it. "And of you."

He grunted. "The last thing we need is the sheriff's whole force poking around up here because we lost you."

Tess sensed a threat in there but didn't take it to heart. She knew for a fact that Nicki had once been close to getting this man to turn on his brothers and report to the feds in exchange for immunity. A smart woman could do a lot with information like that. Tess might be out of shape and no closer to finding the source of the hemlock than before, but she *was* smart.

In fact, she had a smart plan to execute right now…

"How close are we to the Canadian border from here?" she asked in a tone as casually unconcerned as she could make it. "If we were to point north and head straight there, I mean?"

"You want me to take you to Canada? On a *four-wheeler*? Absolutely not."

It was all Tess could do not to roll her eyes. Honestly, Gertrude had ten times the intelligence of this man. There was a reason Mason ran the family business while Zach and Adam stuck to the literal heavy lifting.

"Of course I don't want you to take me to Canada," she said. She was about to find a place to climb up onto the four-wheeler when Zach took the guesswork out of it and hoisted her up. "I'm just curious, that's all. I've been meaning to put in an order for a bunch of Canadian candy, and I was wondering how quickly it can get here."

"Candy?" he echoed as he climbed up in front of her. He didn't start the engine right away, so Tess figured she at least had his attention.

"Well, that and potato chips," she said. "I don't know what they do to that All-Dressed kind to make them so delicious, but nothing we have in the United States comes close. Do you think I can buy it by the bag, or will I have to order a whole case? It's not that I'm against ordering in bulk, but if I *have* a hundred bags of chips, I'll *eat* a hundred bags of chips. The laws of nature demand it."

He grunted but not in an unkind way. "Fine. Make a list of all the crap you want, and I'll have one of the guys put a box together the next time he runs a logging shipment up north. *Women.*"

"Wait. What?" Tess knew she sounded surprised, but that was mostly just chagrin. This reluctant but generous concession wasn't going to help her plan to foster the smuggling of large amounts of cash over the border. "There's no need. I'm more than happy to just place an order somewhere and—"

He turned the key over and revved the engine into angry, vibrating life. "Whatever. It's not a big deal. To tell you the truth, I like those stupid little Coffee Crisps. Throw a few of those in your order for me, and we'll call it even."

Tess would have voiced further protest, but he propelled the vehicle forward so quickly that she had to wrap her arms around him or risk sliding off the back. She might have even reintroduced the subject once they returned to the logging camp, but she was too distracted to care. The moment Zach pulled to a stop and she slid off onto shaking, rattled legs, she saw a sight that startled a gasp out of her.

There, standing a few feet away and sporting a sweat-stained work shirt, was the young Black man from the bookstore. The one who'd asked her to sign a copy to his mother and then put it on the shelf for an even-more mysterious stranger to come back and find.

The one who almost certainly knew about Neptune Jones and what she was up to.

Chapter Fifteen

TESS BLINKED A FEW TIMES, CERTAIN SHE MUST HAVE CON-jured the young man out of thin air—or, at the very least, mistaken him for one of the other loggers. But no. The faster she moved her eyelids, the more he came into focus. She'd have recognized those swooped locs covering one eye anywhere.

"It's you!" she cried as she ran over to greet him. She half expected him to take one look at her and run off—or to at least show alarm at being caught—but all he did was stare. "Darcy. Your mom's name is Darcy. You left your book at my store."

"Uh…are you okay?"

"It's me," Tess insisted. "Tess Harrow. The author." She stabbed a finger at her own chest as if that would help clarify things.

"Congratulations?" he said again, this time with a flick of his one visible eye over her shoulder. "Am I supposed to do something with this lady, Zach?"

"You can try to ignore her, but it doesn't work. She's one of those bored housewives who's always peeking over the fence to see what's going on in someone else's yard."

Tess didn't appreciate this description at all. "You know

I'm standing right here?" she asked. "And that I'm not a housewife? I have a full-time job. Two of them, if you count the bookstore."

Zach made a big show of looking around the logging site, which was buzzing with dozens of men and women who had full-time jobs of their own. "Do you? Huh. My mistake."

Since Zach's sarcasm seemed heavy enough to linger, Tess returned her attention to the young man. "We had a whole conversation the other day at my bookstore. About serial killers and your mother."

"Uh…" The young man began backing away.

"No, no. Not like that. Just that you were looking for my book—the one about a serial killer—because you wanted it for your mom. You said she couldn't come to pick it up for herself because she doesn't like to travel."

"Don't worry about it, Jay," Zach said with a note of authority that made him sound almost like Mason. "I'll take care of her. Just make sure you get all the equipment cleaned off before you sign off this time, okay? If you let the mud cake on the tires overnight, it's like trying to scrape off concrete."

The young man—Jay—offered Zach a crooked grin. It was the *exact* same grin Tess had seen him flash that day at her bookstore. "Sure thing, boss man. You won't find a speck of mud anywhere. I promise."

Tess knew she'd been beaten and that for whatever reason, Jay had no intention of admitting he'd come to her bookstore, but she couldn't help asking one last question of him.

"Why'd you put it back on the shelf? Who were you leaving it for?"

Jay's eyes—both of them—met hers. He flipped his head in an expert move that gave her a brief flash of his full face. She realized why he wore his hair that way less than a second later. The eye hidden by his hair was lighter than the other by several shades of brown. He had heterochromia, and of such a highly visible nature that anyone who saw him once would be sure to recognize him a second time.

Including—*especially*—her.

"I don't know what you're talking about, lady, but if I were to spend almost thirty bucks on a book, you can bet your last dollar I'd have a pretty good reason for doing it."

Tess squeaked and tried to lunge forward to ask more questions—who was he, what did he want, and why had he let her see the telltale color of his eyes?—but Zach thrust up a hand to ward her back.

"Oh no, you don't. I'm not having you harass my new guy. Do you have any idea how hard it is to find skilled labor this late in the season?"

Jay loped off, presumably to clear the mud from the logging equipment, so Tess had to reconcile herself to hunting him down and asking her questions another day. "No, I don't," she admitted. "Tell me how hard it is."

Since the question had been uttered in a purely rhetorical spirit, Zach was annoyed to be called upon to answer.

"Hard enough that I'm not going to explain myself to you. Let's just say we had to bring that guy in all the way from Seattle—and he didn't come cheap."

At the mention of Seattle, Tess barely managed to subdue her gasp in time—but subdue it, she did. She might not have found the telltale hemlock that was used to kill Levi Parker, and she'd have to come up with a backup candy plan now, but she didn't regret her trip up here.

Mysterious Jay of the heterochromatic eyes was somehow tied up in all this. And unless she was very much mistaken, Mysterious Jay of the heterochromatic eyes wanted her to know it.

━━━━━━

"Here. I didn't get a chance to give this to you the day of your bookstore opening."

Tess and Jared were once again seated inside his truck, this time at the end of the drive leading up to her cabin. Jared had shown every inclination to make good their lie and take her out for a whirlwind date in Omak, but Neptune's dinner party was set to start in hour. Tess was going to be cutting it close to squeeze in a shower as it was. There was no way she was attending an event hosted by that woman with fire ants still crawling around in places best left unmentioned.

"Jared, you really didn't have to," Tess said as he pulled out a small box wrapped in extravagant gold paper. "To be honest, the bookstore was my own gift to myself."

"I know, but I wanted to." He shrugged. "It's not jewelry or anything, if that's what you're afraid of. Just something I thought you'd enjoy. I wanted your big day to feel special."

This was said in a voice so sweetly earnest that Tess had no choice but to rip into the package. Gifts weren't such a common thing in her life that she was willing to let this one pass her by. She lifted the lid off the box to reveal what looked like a miniature walkie-talkie with a looped cord coming off one end.

"Do...you have the other one?" she asked as she lifted it out. "Are we going to send secret signals late at night?"

He laughed and took the device from her hand, expertly fiddling with the controls before handing it back to her again. "No, but that sounds like fun. This one's only used to search for bugs."

Tess got the impression he wasn't talking about bugs of the six-legged variety. "Jared," she breathed. "It's not—"

"You can't tell anyone what it is or where you got it," he said, the words coming out in a rush of breath. "And you *definitely* can't let Nicki see. But you're the sort of woman who has everything, and I wanted to get you something different. Something special."

"Jared."

"If you don't like it, I can take it back," he said doubtfully. "I mean, I'll have to smuggle it into the field office, and I'm not sure—"

"Jared." She flung her arms around his neck this time so he wouldn't be in doubt about the meaning behind this repetition of his name. He smelled like a man who'd spent the better part of the day hoisting logs through the forest but not in a bad way. It was like falling into a cedar closet with a twentysomething on a hot summer day—not a bad gig, if you wanted it.

The problem was, Tess wasn't sure she did.

"I can't believe you stole me a bug detector," she said. "It's *perfect*. What does it pick up on? Hidden cameras? Audio devices? Satellites?"

"No satellites, I'm afraid, but it should get you anything with a radio frequency. It's the latest model, so we're talking a pinpoint in a warehouse." He grinned. "You like it?"

"Are you kidding? I *love* it."

She sat back and fiddled with the dials, unable to suppress her excitement. This was top-tier gift quality, right up there with an all-expenses-paid trip to Paris or a full set of Montblancs. Not that she'd ever received either of those things. For big occasions, her ex-husband had usually purchased her a last-minute gift certificate to some spa she'd never frequented before; for smaller ones, she'd been lucky to get anything at all. She still remembered the last Christmas they'd been together, when she'd spent weeks combing the city for a leather flight bag he'd had his eye on. In the end, she'd found one online and ended up paying twice what it was worth to have it shipped in time. All she'd gotten in return was a notebook that she was pretty sure had come from the bottom drawer of her own desk.

In fact, the only thing even remotely close to this kind of gift was the bear-spray belt from Sheriff Boyd on her birthday. It had been silly thing like the bug detector—given half in jest, half in earnest, and wholly with her own tastes in mind. She liked cool FBI devices and hated bears. She liked men who knew her well enough to choose such thoughtful gifts and hated that they made her feel so unsettled.

Life would have been so much easier if she could accept this thing Jared was offering her—romance without complications, admiration without strings—and move on with her life. For the past six months, his pursuit of her had been dogged and consistent, and even though she *tried* not to give him hope where there was none, the truth was impossible to ignore.

She liked him but not as much as she liked Victor.

Victor, who maintained a discreet and friendly distance. Victor, who refused to let his guard down by so much as an inch.

Victor, who was finally tossing all that aside...for Neptune.

Tess clasped the device to her chest, which suddenly felt too tight and painful for this conversation. "I'm going to run inside and test this out right now," she said, smiling warmly at Jared so he wouldn't feel slighted. "You should plant some bugs around town to test me. It'll be like geocaching, but with spy paraphernalia."

He laughed, but she could sense his disappointment. Moved by this—and by the fact that he'd gone out of his way to help her with the investigation today—she leaned up and pecked his cheek. It was a chaste kiss, barely more than a graze of her lips against his rough cheek, but he beamed as though she'd just proposed marriage.

"This was sweet, Jared. No one has ever stolen federal tech for me before."

"Yeah, well. Go on a real date with me, and maybe I'll see what I can do about finding some GPS trackers to plant around town."

With that, Tess slid out of the truck. She laughed and

waved, but with a slight air of trepidation. Jared *sounded* like he was kidding—and in no way, shape, or form did Tess condone the trading of romantic favors for ill-begotten gains—but there was something to be said for his approach.

Especially since Sheriff Boyd had never once tried to trade her for the same.

Chapter Sixteen

TESS AND HER ENTOURAGE ARRIVED AT THE SHERIFF'S house promptly at seven o'clock that evening, all four of them laden with bottles of leftover sparkling wine and something called a Niçoise salad that she was pretty sure would end up killing them all.

Gertrude had promised that the salad—which seemed to contain a hefty chunk of the remaining tuna as well as hard-boiled eggs, tomatoes, olives, and a variety of vegetables that had no business existing in the same meal, let alone the same dish—was an actual thing that people ate. Tess had her doubts, especially once she'd caught a whiff of it, but she was keeping them to herself. With enough sparkling wine, *anything* was palatable.

Even a meal at Victor Boyd's house hosted by Neptune Jones.

"Okay, does everyone remember the roles I've assigned them for tonight?" Tess asked as soon as Gertrude passed the salad off to Mumford with instructions for him to carry it straight to the fridge. She held up a hand to prevent her mom and daughter from barreling into the house after him. "I know it's asking a lot, but I refuse to have a full meal with that woman unless we get *something* out of it."

Gertrude barely managed to suppress the roll of her eyes, but Bernadette was buying into this chance at espionage with all the fervor of a Bond villain.

"Gertie is in charge of keeping everyone distracted so they don't notice when you slip into the guest room to take a peek around," Bee announced with a happy nod. "And I'm the lookout. If I see anyone about to creep up on you, I'll hoot like an owl."

"An owl will only work if we're all outside," Gertrude pointed out. "We'll need a different warning in case things move indoors."

"A cough?" Bee suggested.

"Too common."

"A shout?"

"Too obvious."

"Maybe I could just fall into a swoon" was her final suggestion.

Gertrude nodded her approval. "That'll do it. But you have to be really dramatic about it. The trick is to lock your knees so you go down hard."

As impressed as Tess was by this show of premeditation, she wasn't sure she wanted her mother doing anything that involved gravity. "Can't you just pretend to have a heart attack or something? You're the right age for it."

Bernadette's voice grew so tight it probably registered more to a dog's ears than a human's. "If you want me to help you illegally search through Sheriff Boyd's private residence, you'll take that back, young lady. I'm no such thing."

Since her mother had chosen to dress in her widow's

weeds once again, this time with a feathery black fascinator attached to a veil that covered her face, she looked very much the grand dame with a full sixty-five years at her back.

"Sure thing, Mom. You're a regular spring chicken." Since they were already standing out here too long, Tess turned to Gertrude and added, "For the record, I'm only going to take a quick look around. I won't steal anything of value, and I'll be sure to leave Neptune's belongings unmolested."

"Mom, you don't have to explain yourself to me."

"I'm just saying. This isn't about my personal feelings for Neptune. It's about murder."

"I know it is."

"Sheriff Boyd is a grown man capable of making his own decisions. And if that decision leads him to prefer an overpaid murder podcaster whose personality changes on a dime instead of me, then who am I to question him?"

Gertrude sighed and started moving toward the house. "Ohmigod, I wish she would just tell him how she feels already. This is starting to get ridiculous."

"I can hear you, Gertie!" Tess called to her retreating back.

"Good," the teenager returned. "You were meant to."

———————

Tess's opportunity came over dessert. Much to her surprise, Sven turned out to be an amazing chef. So amazing, in fact, that Tess didn't have to eat a single bite of that weird French salad, even though everyone claimed that Gertrude was well on her way to a Beard Award of her own.

"If you'll excuse me, I'm just going to go powder my nose," Tess said as she got up from the table laid out under the twinkling fairy lights and even-more twinkling night sky. As much as she hated to give Neptune credit for, well, anything, the woman had done an amazing job of turning Sheriff Boyd's neglected back patio into a dining experience that rivaled that of an Italian villa. Even the mosquitoes seemed to be cooperating, their usual buzzing annoyance stilled to a gentle hum.

Mumford held up the empty glass in front of him. "You should bring out another bottle of the sparkling wine when you come."

Neptune held hers up as well. "I second that plan."

As soon as Neptune spoke, Sheriff Boyd practically shot to his feet. "I'll get it. Hang on, Tess. Hold the door."

The last thing Tess wanted was for Sheriff Boyd to follow her inside, where he was sure to watch her movements with an eagle eye and a highly suspicious mind, but she didn't see any way around it. Her Royal Highness had requested wine, so it seemed Sheriff Boyd would move heaven and earth to ensure she had it.

"How'd it go with my mom this morning?" Tess asked by way of conversation. The house felt eerily silent after the conversational sparkle outside—a dinner party of people determined to please and be pleased, even though Tess wasn't sure any of them actually *liked* one another. "I asked her about it, but all she said was that she'd never been the sort to kiss and tell."

To her surprise, Sheriff Boyd laughed. He also leaned

on the doorjamb in a way that gave lie to his urgency to do Neptune's bidding. "That hasn't been my experience with the woman."

Tess answered with a laugh of her own. "She was a little *too* forthcoming about some of her Levi Parker details, wasn't she?"

"I like her. She reminds me a lot of your grandfather."

Tess found this statement surprising for a number of reasons. For one thing, she'd never heard Sheriff Boyd confess warm feelings toward *anyone*. For another, her curmudgeonly hermit of a grandfather and her lavishly indulgent parent couldn't be more different. In fact, their inability to get along had been a large part of the reason Tess had spent so little time in this town as a child. For the entirety of Tess's life, Bernadette Springer had required spa access, a daily infusion of vodka cocktails, and the general adulation of the masses. Melvin Harrow only needed four walls and the occasional sip of moonshine.

Sheriff Boyd must have sensed her incredulity, because he relaxed further, even going so far as to indulge in a grin. "I'm serious. I've never known two people so whip-smart… and so determined that no one find out about it. Your grandfather hid his intelligence in a cabin in the woods. Your mom hides hers in irreverence."

"Is that supposed to be a jab at me?" Tess couldn't help asking. "Because I don't hide anything at all?"

His grin fell. "You hide plenty."

"No, I don't. Ask me anything, and I'll tell you the truth. No elaboration, no varnish. Just words."

His eyes narrowed as he considered this challenge—for a challenge it undoubtedly was. There was too much history between them, and too much potential at a future, for him to fail to recognize what she was offering.

But he either *did* fail to recognize it or the murder investigation was taking up more of his time and emotional energy than Tess ever would.

"What's your mom doing here, Tess? I mean *really* doing here?"

"Huh?" She blinked. "What do you mean?"

He pushed himself off the doorjamb and approached her, not stopping until the toes of his cowboy boots touched hers. She was still staring at where they met her strappy espadrilles when he grabbed her upper arms and pushed his face down into hers. His eyes, always like a pair of black holes, seemed to swallow her whole.

"She gave no mention of visiting you ahead of time, did she? From what Gertie said, I got the impression she took you both by surprise. Has she given any indication of how long she plans to stay? Or what her intentions were before Levi Parker was found dead?"

That was a lot more than one question, and Tess found she didn't care for any of them. But she'd promised to tell the truth, and she intended to stick to it. She let those black holes suck her in.

"No, she didn't mention that she was paying us a visit, but that's not atypical for her. She's the sort who drops in for either five days or five months, depending on how the mood strikes her. She's made no mention of the length of her stay, but she's firm in stating that she didn't ask Levi to come here with her. From what I can gather, she was growing a little tired of him, and—" Tess cut herself off as soon as she realized the direction this conversation was taking. "Victor!"

He immediately shushed her. "Bring it down a notch. Do you want the whole party following us in here?"

No, she didn't. Technically, she didn't even want *him* following her in here, but there was no way she could let things stand now. "You think my mom has something to do with his death, don't you? A sweet old lady who—"

His snort stopped her short.

"Fine. A highly theatrical woman in the prime of her life who was—and I can guarantee this—in bed inside my cabin all night when Levi Parker was killed."

"Poisoning isn't always immediate, Tess."

"It's not what you think. Yes, she was tired of him, but that's just how she works. She casts off her discarded lovers like scarves, not like... like..."

"Cadavers?" he suggested.

"She's eccentric, not a murderer! Other than finding Levi tiresomely persistent, what possible reason could she have for wanting him dead? I find lots of men tiresomely persistent, but I don't *kill* them."

"No," he agreed, his expression perfectly bland. "But I've seen what else you do to them."

Tess felt her stomach tighten at his words but refused to let them get to her. This wasn't about whatever was going on between her and Sheriff Boyd—or between her and Jared

Wilson. This had Neptune's Flowerbomb Haute Couture all over it.

"That woman put you up to this, didn't she?" Tess demanded. "What did she tell you? That she followed my mom and Levi across the country? That she witnessed them having dinner and drinks a few times? So what? My mom has already admitted that."

"Tess…"

"It doesn't make any sense, Victor. Why would my mom wait until she was in Winthrop to do away with Levi? What possible motivation could she have for wanting her grand-daughter present to witness that kind of spectacle?" She didn't wait for answers. "I can't believe this is the turn your investigation is taking. First you let that woman into your house, free to poke around and plant her suspicions in every dark corner. Then you let that woman—"

"She has a name, you know."

"What?"

"You keep calling her *that woman* like she's an adulteress in a soap opera." Sheriff Boyd seemed inclined to be amused. "She has a name."

"I know she does. It's Darcy—a name she doesn't care to have said aloud and a name that happens to coincide with two mysterious strangers who stopped by my bookstore recently, one of whom also appears to be moonlighting as a lumberjack up at Mason's logging camp. That might not seem suspicious to you, but believe me when I say that the rest of us are starting to find it *very* interesting."

Tess had the satisfaction of seeing a flicker of surprise

cross Sheriff Boyd's face. It would have been too much to say he was *floored*, but it was clear he hadn't expected a counterattack.

"What do you mean, 'two mysterious strangers'?" he demanded. "Why is this the first I'm hearing about them?"

The answer to that should have been obvious. "Because you refuse to let me anywhere near this case. When would I have had the chance to tell you? You're so busy having Neptune—I'm sorry, *Darcy*—run your errands and examine your crime scene that there's no time for me to get a word in edgewise."

"She's not running my errands, Tess. Stop being ridiculous."

That word—*ridiculous*—did more to rile her up than the accusation that her mother might have murdered Levi Parker. As a mother, as an author, as a *woman*, she'd be the first to admit that she had her fair share of faults. She was stubborn and single-minded. She was terrible at cooking and even worse at meeting her deadlines. She was inclined to make snap judgments about people, and there were walls around her heart that she feared no one could break down— not even herself. But she resented the implication that any of that made her *ridiculous*.

"No?" she countered, so furious she was practically seeth-ing. "Then why did you send her to Seattle to follow some random lead for you?"

A low rumble escaped his throat, his own temper clearly starting to fray. "Is that what you think I did?"

She threw up her hands in frustration. "I don't know,

Victor. You tell me. I can't figure any of this out, and it's no wonder why. You do everything in your power to keep me away from your cases and out of your life."

"Tess."

She was close to tears and desperately hoping to hear the hoot of an owl or the sound of a heart attack taking place out on the back porch, but she was in it now. She might as well finish.

"I've tried to respect your boundaries—I really have. It hurts, obviously, and most days I feel like I'm bashing my head against a brick wall, but I know better than to push too hard. Otherwise, you might disappear for good." She dashed at her eyes with the back of her hand, annoyed to find it come away wet. "From now on, I'll bring all my theories and findings to Ivy. She's no more receptive to them than you are, but at least she can sift through them so you get the highlights. No matter what happens between us, I want this murderer brought to justice as much as you do."

Whatever Sheriff Boyd had to say to this outburst would forever remain a mystery. No sooner had she finished than Neptune called to him with a demand to know where the wine was. He looked pained at the request—even more pained when Tess used the distraction to slip off to the bathroom—but that was okay.

She might have made a *ridiculous* fool of herself, but she still had a guest room to ransack.

———

Naturally, the hoot of an owl *and* the sound of her mother suffering a heart attack hit Tess after exactly fifteen seconds of peeking inside the guest room.

Like the rest of the house, Neptune had taken over the guest room like a raccoon protecting its hoard of garbage treasure. Tess had no idea how the woman managed to live so nomadically, considering that she traveled with four suitcases stuffed to the brim with lacy underthings and a full rotating arsenal of her signature suits. Tess had barely managed to rifle through one of the piles scattered across the floor before she heard the signal calling off her search.

"For the love of everything, Mother," Tess muttered as she kicked the pile of clothes back into the haystack-like shape she'd found when she came in. "At least *try* to distract them."

"I think I'd better lie down for a spell," her mother declared in her most obvious and most audible Jackie O. voice. "I barely managed to duck and avoid getting hit by that owl in time. He came out of nowhere."

"I didn't see any owl," Mumford said.

"Me either," said Sven.

"I did." Gertrude's voice was loud and authoritative. "He was as big as your head. No, not yours, Sven. *Mumford's.*"

"Oh, my," put in Neptune. "As big as all that?"

Of everyone in attendance at the dinner party, only Sheriff Boyd didn't seem to have anything to contribute. Tess was still examining her possible exit routes when her mother's voice sounded again, closer this time.

"No, no. Not on the couch. My back aches just looking

at those springs. Isn't there a spare bed somewhere in here? The guest room, perhaps?"

Tess barely had time to dive under the bed before the entire party came ambling in. Neptune must have had the decency to be mildly ashamed of her habits, because Tess almost took the tip of her Aquazzura heel to the eye as she furtively kicked several piles underneath the bed. Tess had just managed to avoid Neptune's toe before she lost the battle. A stack of notebooks came flying for her face, one of the spirals catching her on the cheek as it passed by.

"Ouch," she muttered as the sharp slice of the metal grazed just below her eye. She clapped a hand over her mouth, but it was too late. The sound was too audible to be missed.

"Ouch!" moaned her mother in another of those Jackie O. bursts of inspiration. "It's spreading down my right arm now. I think you'd better call an ambulance."

"I think you mean your *left* arm, Grandma," Gertrude said pointedly. "That's how you know it's a heart attack."

"Look at you, love." The sound of a kiss being pressed onto Gertrude's head filled the room. "Since when do you know so much about emergency medical care?"

"Mom made me take a first aid class not long after we found that first dead body," Gertrude said, not without pride. "She wanted me to be able to save someone if we stumbled across another person in our pond."

"Did you still need to lie down, Ms. Springer, or have you seen everything you need?" came the sheriff's drawling voice. "Because I doubt Neptune appreciates us all barging into her personal space like this."

It was fortunate that Tess still had her hand over her mouth. Neptune's "personal space" was currently making her face bleed. She didn't know what kind of notebooks the woman carried around that had such coarse edges, but—

"Seen?" Bernadette echoed. "Why would I need to see anything? I'm having a *heart attack*."

"Yeah," Gertrude said. "After being attacked by an *owl*."

"Wait. Where's Tess?" Mumford added.

It was all Tess could do to keep quiet after that. Not because her co-conspirators were clearly not taking any of this seriously, but because she'd managed to find the notebook that had caused all the damage. The book itself looked ordinary, but one of the pages fell open to reveal a photo tucked inside.

It was an older picture, grainy in the way that came from a time back when film had to be processed, and slightly yellowed around the edges. And right in the middle stood Tess's mother.

She was tempted to fling the thing back where she'd gotten it, but there was no mistaking the image of Bernadette Springer—mostly because her mother was wearing one of the many iterations of her pink-tweed Chanel suit. In the picture, her arms were wrapped around the shoulders of two women. One of them Tess recognized as a friend from her mother's early days as a lawyer. If she remembered correctly, the two of them had been the only female attorneys at their firm up until the midnineties. The other woman, however, she couldn't recall ever seeing before.

This, in and of itself, wasn't of particular note, since Tess's life and her mother's had rarely intersected back then. In the days when Tess had been Gertrude's age, her mom had been largely absent. She'd rarely made it to parent-teacher conferences on time and had stocked the freezer with micro-wavable pizzas for one. Most days, the ghost of her perfume was the only real company Tess had, unless you counted the cleaning woman who sometimes stayed late to take advantage of their extensive and overpriced cable package.

But all three women looked so happy, so *carefree*, that it struck something deep inside her. Why did Neptune Jones have a photo that Tess had never seen before? And why had it been buried on the floor of Sheriff Boyd's guest room?

She practically vibrated with the urge to pop out and start demanding answers right then and there, but she had to wait until the sheriff sternly guided the party out of the room, leaving it in Bernadette's sole possession.

As a pair of masterminds seeking to clandestinely search Neptune's room, Tess and her family had fallen fearfully short of their goal. It was only a matter of seconds before Tess would need to climb out the window and pretend she'd been outside all along—and, if the bleeding on her face was any indication, somehow convince the others that she'd been attacked by the rogue owl along the way.

In those seconds, however, Tess managed to crawl out from under the bed with the photo clutched tightly in her hand.

"*There* you are, love," Bernadette said, showing no surprise to see her daughter or her current state of being. "What's that? Did you find what you were looking for?"

"That depends," Tess replied.

"On what?"

Tess opened and closed her mouth, trying to say the words that were trying their best to escape, but they wouldn't come. If her mother had *really* thrown herself wholeheartedly into this plan to search Neptune's room, then why had she interrupted before Tess got anywhere? And why was Sheriff Boyd so convinced that her mother's arrival in town was in some way dubious—and possibly tied up in Levi's murder?

She shoved the picture behind her back, suddenly loath to share the sole bit of evidence she'd managed to get her hands on. Until she knew what this picture was and why it was in Neptune Jones's keeping, she'd prefer to keep her suspicions to herself.

Not because she thought her mother was a murderer, but because she was starting to fear that Sheriff Boyd and Neptune Jones *did* think it. And if that was where this investigation was headed, then she needed to find a way to stop it before her mother's reputation—and, by extension, her own—were ruined any further.

"I'll tell you later," Tess lied as she flew to the window. "Give me two minutes to get back out there, and then you can finish your heart attack, okay?"

"No problem," Bernadette said with a cheer that seemed out of place, given the situation. "I'll give you five minutes just to be sure."

Tess was almost certain her mother would use that time to do a little ransacking of the room on her own, but she didn't say so. She felt pretty sure that Bernadette wouldn't find anything but piles of dirty clothes and the empty note-book from which the damning piece of evidence had already been removed.

Chapter Seventeen

THE NEXT DAY, TESS LOST NO TIME IN MAKING HER WAY to the one person in this town she trusted more than any other: Nicki Nickerson.

Even if Nicki hadn't been a federal agent, there was something altogether soothing about her common sense approach to processing information and putting it into perspective. If anyone would be able to talk Tess down, allay her fears, put her in a better frame of mind—

"Oh, dear. This is bad. This is *really* bad." The picture dropped from Nicki's hand and fluttered to the floor of the bookmobile, where it lay faceup, the three smiling women unconcerned at being so carelessly handled.

"Nicki!" Tess leaned down and scooped the picture back up, blowing off the dust and smoothing the edges. "This is the only copy I have. Be careful with it."

Nicki eyed her askance. "Are you sure it's the only copy?"

"Yes?"

She nodded once. "Then my advice is to burn it. Immediately."

Tess moved to the front of the bookmobile and pulled the lever that brought the doors to a swinging close. It was eight o'clock in the morning, so the chances of someone stopping by to peruse the shelves were low, but she wasn't taking any risks. Not anymore.

"Aren't you curious where it came from? And who's in the picture? This one in the middle is my mom, obviously, and the lady on the left was a friend of hers from her law firm back in the day, but I don't know who the third woman is. I tried to Google Lens it, but all it did was identify the tree behind them."

Nicki eyed her with misgiving, a look that made Tess feel like she was a dog about to be put down.

"What?" she demanded. "Is she famous or something?"

"You could say something like that." Nicki sighed and relaxed her posture a fraction. "Tess, don't you listen to *anything* your daughter says?"

"That child spent two hours last night telling poor Mumford about all her fan theories for that new anime show the kids are obsessed with. If you lived with that around the clock, you'd learn to tune her out too. There are only so many character ships I can take before my brain starts to melt."

Nicki's response to this was to pull out her phone and do a quick search. When she showed the screen to Tess, it was to reveal a much more updated picture of the unknown woman from the photo. She was older, obviously, but like Tess's mother, she'd aged gracefully. The laugh lines around her mouth indicated a life well lived, her eyes sparkling with a joy that Tess felt a sudden impulse to share.

"'Eudora Raphael. Painter and art gallery curator, famed for her highly stylized winterscapes of Upstate New York.'"

Tess paused from reading aloud to glance at her friend. "That sounds about right. My mom's always hanging around with artistic types."

"Keep going," Nicki said grimly.

"'Her body was found washed up on Harbor Island Park in Long Island. Although her murder remains unsolved, many believe it to be the work of—'" Tess dropped the phone like it was on fire. Fortunately, Nicki had been anticipating this reaction and caught it. *"Nicki!"*

"I told you. Burn that picture and don't look back." Nicki paused, apparently unaware of how close Tess was to passing out on the floor of the bookmobile. "Actually, now I *am* curious. Where did you get it? Was your mom carrying it around with her? I thought she was a lawyer. She should know better than to be caught with that kind of evidence."

Tess really *did* fall to the floor then, but it was more of a gentle giving out of her knees than a faint. She sank to one of the low stools, her muscles wobbling in a way she knew would come back to haunt her.

"I found it in Neptune's disgusting clothes pile," Tess said, her voice sounding as if from far away. "I swear, Nicki, that woman is worse than a teenager. Dirty underwear mixed in with important photos, her stuff thrown around like—"

Nicki snapped her fingers an inch away from Tess's nose. "Stop it. Focus. This doesn't prove anything except that your mom knew Eudora Raphael. So what? I bet lots of people knew her. Levi Parker obviously did."

Tess appreciated Nicki's attempt at comfort, but it was a clear case of too little, too late. "Yeah. He also murdered her and got away with it. If that's not a motive for my mom hunting him down and killing him, I don't know what is." She groaned and dropped her head to her hands. Now that Nicki had identified the mystery woman, the picture explained so much about this situation.

What was her mom doing with a man young enough to be her son?

Murder.

Why had she loaned him her hard-earned money and allowed him to follow her across the country?

Murder.

Why was she flitting about like a bereaved widow with nary a sign of actual remorse?

Murder.

"Oh, God." Tess glanced up to find Nicki wearing an anxious expression, her lower lip between her teeth and her brows furrowed tight. "Sheriff Boyd knows about this. I'm sure of it. He tried to warn me yesterday that my mom was up to no good—it's why I came to you instead of asking her directly."

Nicki shook her head. "No. If he knew about it, your mom would already be in custody."

"Not necessarily. This gives her motive but not opportunity. She was with me that night, remember? Only—" Tess groaned again, this time with a real edge to it. "Only Sheriff Boyd pointed out that poisons don't always go into effect immediately. I think he was warning me that he's going to have to bring her in. What am I going to do, Nicki? She's my *mom.*"

Nicki placed a pair of heavy hands on Tess's shoulders. "What you're going to do is continue acting naturally—and *burn this picture*. Think, Tess. If Sheriff Boyd knew about this picture's existence, it'd be in evidence right now, not floating around Neptune's room. You know how by the book that man is. For whatever reason, she hasn't shown it to him yet, so this is your chance to make it disappear. Unless she has another copy or some other proof of your mom's relationship to Eudora—"

Nicki cut herself off and tapped the back of the picture, where the words *Gallagher Library 1994* had been scrawled.

"Is this important? Something that might be able to prove your mom knew Eudora Raphael in more than just passing?"

Tess paused for a moment, thinking. The library sounded familiar, but she wasn't sure why until she pulled out her phone and looked it up. That confirmed her worst fears... right before heaping a few more on top of them.

"It's the law library at the University of Washington." Her voice faltered. "What do you want to bet that's where Neptune and her producer went the other day? She said she went to look up some records in Seattle but that it was closed until fall quarter. If she's building a case against my mom, she was probably looking for proof there."

"Oh." Nicki thumped down onto the stool next to Tess. She looked about as dejected as Tess felt. "Then I changed my mind. There's no need to burn any evidence. You're screwed."

Tess gave a bitter laugh. *Screwed* wasn't nearly a strong enough word for what she was facing. "Nicki, what am I supposed to do? Turn my mom in? Confess? Take Neptune out before she has a chance to ruin my family?"

"I don't know, Tess. This is above my paygrade. All I can say for sure is this: if your mom really *was* friends with this Eudora person, and she really *was* hunting Levi down to make him pay, I'm not sure I blame her." Nicki bumped Tess with her hip. "I'd take out a serial killer in the name of vengeance for you."

That was, without a doubt, the nicest thing anyone had ever said to Tess—especially coming from a woman she valued and would willingly seek her own vengeance over. In her wildest post-divorce dreams, she never imagined she'd find such an amazing female support system in such a short time.

"Aw, Nicki. That's so sweet." She felt herself tearing up and dashed quickly at her cheeks with the back of her hand. Now was decidedly not the time to grow morose. She had a murderer for a mother to deal with first. "But are you sure you couldn't just stop the serial killer *before* he gets to me?"

Nicki chuckled and slung an arm over Tess's shoulder. "I'll do my best, but you're not an easy woman to protect. For some strange reason, you always seem to be elbows-deep in a murder investigation. You and Neptune have a lot in common that way."

"Yeah, but she does it on purpose," Tess said, sighing. "What else have you discovered about her, by the way? I was hoping you'd have dug up some deep, dark secret that would get her out of my hair by now. I'd give good money to know how she got her hands on this picture."

"Was I supposed to be investigating her?" Nicki asked. She got up and stretched awkwardly, her tall frame and long arms difficult to accommodate in the undersized bookmobile. "I'm not sure what good it'll do. As far as I can tell, she's raking in millions of dollars with her podcast. She wouldn't risk murdering Levi Parker and jeopardizing all those sponsorships."

Tess knew that, but she'd still like it if the woman was found guilty of *something*. "Gertie tried to do a little digging, but there's only so much a teenager with an internet connection can do. How did you know Neptune's real name?"

"I didn't."

When Tess swiveled her head to stare at Nicki, the other woman only shrugged. "It came from somewhere above me in the federal chain. A guy in IT thought I might be interested because she was in town and I mentioned her in my report, that's all. I figured you could use the info more than me."

On any other day, Tess might have been willing to accept this at face value. She knew that Nicki was just one link in a massive chain trying to put a choke hold on Mason Peabody and his illegal operations, but the rest of her FBI team had always seemed like a nebulous thing, the mythical man behind the curtain.

On *this* day, however, she wanted answers.

"What guy in IT?" she demanded.

Nicki's eyes widened. "I don't know. Peter, Paul—I can't keep them all straight. He's been with the Bureau longer than I have, so don't start imagining he's some rogue spy sent to throw dust in your eyes. Why? Did it end up being helpful?"

Tess caught Nicki up as quickly as she could. She'd thought her tale would be a convoluted thing, requiring at least an hour to untangle, but the reality was much less detailed. And exciting. One book signed to a person named Darcy and another person named Darcy buying it was hardly the slam dunk it seemed.

"Don't look at me like that," Tess said as soon as she finished. "I know it sounds weird. It *is* weird. But I'm pretty sure the man who bought the signed book was the same one I saw talking to Sven on the street the other day. You should have your IT guy look into Sven while he's feeling helpful. I don't trust him."

"You're just saying that because he hit Gertie in the face."

Tess's only response to this was to stare at her friend until Nicki had no choice but to realize what she'd just said. "Okay, fine," she admitted with a grimace. "Hitting a teenager is grounds for suspicion. I'll email Peter/Paul and see what he has to say. But wouldn't you be better off contacting that hacker friend of yours? It seems like he'd be able to get you the answers you want faster—and much less legally."

"You mean Wingbat?" Tess furrowed her brow. It had been several months since she'd had a reason to contact Wingbat99, the whimsical name of a less-than-whimsical computer hacker who'd done some work for her in the past. She'd enjoyed her walk on the dark side with him and had even fallen prey to his socially engineered charm, but he was expensive—and he guaranteed payment by taking the funds directly out of her bank account. She'd had to switch banks twice already for fear he'd someday rob her of her life savings. "That's not the worst idea you've ever had, but he doesn't come cheap."

"Then it's a good thing you can afford it." Since it appeared that a patron was approaching the bookmobile, Nicki opened the door and gestured for Tess to hop out. "Your bookstore might not have much in the way of business, but the *New York Times* bestseller list just came out. Want to guess which number you are?"

Tess didn't have to guess. Her agent had sent her an excited text last night. As soon as Tess had seen it, it had taken all her self-control not to throw her phone in the pond.

"Lucky number thirteen," she said, grimacing. "The irony isn't lost on me."

Chapter Eighteen

THE LAST PERSON TESS EXPECTED TO VISIT THE BOOK-store later that afternoon was Edna St. Clair.

Tess had about a million other things she needed to do that day, and if there had been anyone else to watch the store, she'd have handed over the keys and taken herself off as fast as her feet would carry her. In descending order of importance, she wanted to tie her mother to a chair and interrogate her until she spilled everything, tie Sheriff Boyd to a chair and demand that he see reason where Neptune was concerned, and tie Neptune Jones to a chair just for fun. In fact, the longer she stood behind the counter of the store, painstakingly flipping through every copy of *Fury under the Floorboards* in hopes of shaking out another picture or a note that may have been hidden as part of Darcy-gate, the closer she was getting to putting Neptune at the top of her to-tie list.

And the worst part was, until Edna came cheerfully clanging through the door to the Paper Trail, she hadn't had a customer all day. This whole endeavor was starting to feel like a complete failure.

"Well." Edna stopped two feet inside the threshold, her owlish gaze taking in the warm buttercream walls and colorful racks of books. "I liked it better when it was your grandfather's ramshackle hardware store."

"Edna, you don't mean that." Tess set down the book she'd been searching. "Grandpa's hardware store was a dump. It had lead paint peeling off the walls and that weird, musty smell rotted into the wood."

Edna laughed. "It also had customers, which seems to be a thing you're lacking. Did you know that podcast lady set up a table in front of the deli to sell her autobiography?" She reached into the tote bag over her arm and pulled out three hardback copies. "I'm going to give them to my great-nieces and -nephews for Christmas. That'll teach them to not to send me thank-you cards."

Tess laughed, but she couldn't help feeling a sting of rejection too. "If you wanted crappy presents to send your loved ones, I have lots of tedious autobiographies in here," she said. "There's a whole shelf dedicated to YouTube celebrities."

"She's doing a *buy two, get one free* special," Edna countered.

"For *one* book? How many people need three copies of the same book?"

"And if you get them signed, you're automatically entered for a chance to appear in her podcast taping tomorrow afternoon. There's a line around the block."

Tess's only response to this was to drop her forehead to the checkout counter and leave it there. That woman was doing it to spite her—she was sure of it. Neptune could have just as easily set up her table inside the bookstore and made them both a lot of money, but that wasn't the point. Neptune Jones wasn't hand-selling copies of her book to the residents of a small rural town in Washington state for the money; she was doing it to prove a point.

Assuming the point was "I'm a hundred times more important to these people than you'll ever be," Tess was getting the message loud and clear.

"Buck up, missy." Edna slapped her hand on the counter next to Tess's ear. "As soon as you get around to solving this murder, she'll pack up and move on."

Tess glanced up, struck by this sound piece of wisdom.

Edna ruined it by immediately adding, "Although I don't see how you're going to solve anything, moping around this depressing place all day. Don't let anyone see you, or they'll think you've been defeated. Is that fancy journalist you hired still here? His friend was looking for him."

"His friend?" Tess asked. "What friend? He doesn't know anyone in town." The rest of Edna's statement sank in before she could follow this line of questioning. "And for the last time, I didn't *hire* Mumford Umberto. He's here of his own volition to do a feature piece on me."

Edna drummed her fingers on the countertop.

"Okay, so I may have helped him with his travel and accommodations, but he's the one who contacted me, not the other way around. He wanted to be here especially for my bookstore opening so he could—" Tess cut herself off, her eyes widening as she took stock of Edna standing in her full four-foot-eleven glory. "Edna! *He's* the one who contacted *me.*"

"Yes, yes. I heard you the first time. There's no need to shout."

"No, you don't understand." Tess forced herself to take a deep breath, hoping the infusion of oxygen would help clear the sudden whirling of her head. "He specifically requested to be here for my book release and store opening. I warned him that it would be chaotic and that I wouldn't be able to devote much time to his story, but he wouldn't take no for an answer—not even when the hotel booked up and he was forced to stay with me instead."

Tess wasn't sure where her thoughts were going, but she was prepared to follow them for as long as necessary. From the start of this thing, she'd thought it was odd that Levi had scored that corner suite at the hotel, his plans laid out so far in advance that he'd beaten dozens of visitors—including Mumford—to the lodging. There was no denying the truth of it: Levi's plans had been set in motion long before any of them had even thought to look for him.

And if Levi had planned things advance, then there had to be a trail that proved it—a trail other people might also be inclined to follow.

Especially a nosy reporter who refused to take any of Tess's hints to leave.

"At the time, I thought he just wanted to cover the bookstore opening." Tess shook her head, annoyed that none of this had occurred to her before. "I should've known there might be something more going on."

Edna cackled. "I take back what I said before. You are a fool. When it comes to greedy reporters, something more is *always* going on."

For once, Tess wasn't in a position to argue. She *was* a

fool, and if she hadn't been so blinded by Neptune and her own mother, she'd have done something about it by now.

"Edna, could you keep an eye on the store for me for a few minutes?"

"Well, I never." Edna gasped and clutched her hand to her chest as though Tess had just asked her to do a striptease. "You want me to work for you?"

"Not officially, no. I just need to check on something really quickly, and I'd rather not close down the whole store to do it." Tess had already grabbed her purse and was halfway to the door. "The cash register is the original brass one my grandfather used, so it should be right in your wheelhouse. Unless someone wants to pay by credit card, in which case—"

Edna interrupted her with a huff. "I charge twenty-five dollars an hour, and I want health benefits."

"Edna, all I need is for you to keep the place from burning down. I'll be gone five minutes, ten minutes tops."

"*With* dental." She smiled to showcase a row of pearly whites that Tess felt pretty certain she kept in a jar by the side of her bed every night. "It's nonnegotiable. In this climate, you're lucky to get me on such short notice."

Tess threw up her hands. She was pretty sure nothing that was being agreed upon here was legally binding, so she cast an apology to Future Tess, who'd be the one dealing with the fallout. *Present* Tess needed to get to the hotel to talk to the front desk clerk. Stat.

For the first time in days, the hotel wasn't a hotbed of activity. Since the crime scene had been cleared, the macabre interest in the corner suite had all but dissipated, and any visitors who were lingering on with visions of schadenfreude dancing in their heads were currently standing in Neptune's ridiculously long line. Tess knew that for a fact because she'd been forced to walk all two blocks of it in order to reach the hotel.

As soon as she stepped up to the front desk, she clanged the bell for service. The woman behind the counter, who was every bit as old as Edna and just as surly, turned with a heavy sigh.

"What now? If it's about the corner room, no one can—" She stopped as soon as she noticed who was standing on the other side of the desk. "Oh. It's you. The sheriff isn't here."

"I'm not looking for Sheriff Boyd."

The woman crossed her arms. Unlike Edna, who capered about on agile legs, Lorraine—as her name tag proclaimed— looked as though her legs were in danger of becoming rooted to the floor. Tess meant that literally; Lorraine was as tall as a tree, built like a tree, and had an exterior about as warm and welcoming as bark.

"I'm under strict orders not to let anyone upstairs," Lorraine said. "Especially you. 'No matter how much she begs or what she promises to give you,' he said."

Tess felt her smile stretch tightly across her face. She resented the implication that she begged or resorted to brib-ery in her pursuit of justice. At the very most, she *coaxed*.

"I don't want upstairs either," Tess said. "All I'm looking for is the date that Levi Parker booked his hotel room."

The tree didn't sway. "Why?"

"To check on something."

"What are you checking on?"

"Does it matter? It's not like it's private information. I could easily call up his credit card company and see when the charges went through, but it'll be a lot faster if you'd just tell me."

This was only partially a lie. No credit card company would reveal that information without a warrant, but as Nicki had pointed out earlier that morning, Tess had access to a hacker who'd be more than happy to hunt it down. For a fee, of course.

"Well, the sheriff didn't say anything about hotel room dates..." Lorraine began.

Tess saw her chance and pounced.

"You know how thorough and by the book Sheriff Boyd is," she said with what she hoped was a winning smile. "If he'd wanted that information to be kept secret, he'd have been sure to mention it."

Lorraine didn't look convinced, but she started pecking at the computer one slow keystroke at a time. It took all of Tess's self-control not to scream at her to hurry. The longer Edna sat alone in that store, the greater the likelihood it would no longer be standing when Tess returned. "Let's see here... Nope, not that one... Gosh darn this computer..."

"No hurry," Tess lied through tightly set teeth. "Some things are worth the wait."

"Here it is!" Lorraine slipped the readers dangling from the chain around her neck to the end of her nose and peered at the screen. "Levi Parker's room was booked almost exactly a month ago. July nineteenth. He paid in full for a week's lodging. Is that what you wanted to know?"

"I think so," Tess said. "Gimme a sec to check."

She pulled out her phone and checked her own records to find the original email from Mumford Umberto. Sure enough, it was dated for the twentieth—exactly one day after Levi had made concrete plans to be here.

In and of itself, the coincidence didn't mean anything. As Mumford himself had pointed out, such things could and did happen all the time. Lots of people had started booking rooms early since her bookstore opening and release-party plans had already been well underway by that time, and she'd encouraged people to make their arrangements in advance. But for Mumford to email her the day after Levi's travel plans had been secured was questionable in the highest degree.

"Almost as if he didn't come here for me at all," Tess breathed. "Almost as if I was just an excuse for him to get his hands on Levi Parker."

Tess wasn't sure what kind of lead she'd just stumbled on, but she didn't like the implication that Mumford had come here for reasons other than the article he claimed to be writing. She also didn't like what it meant for the cloud of suspicion her mother was currently living under. Not once in the past month had Bernadette mentioned coming for a visit or even being anywhere within Tess's vicinity, yet she'd insisted that Levi Parker had been following her across the country, not the other way around.

If Levi Parker had made advance plans to be here for

Tess's book signing, then it meant her mother had been the one doing the following. Call Tess paranoid, but that sounded an awful lot like something a murderer would do.

"There's no mention of him traveling with a guest, is there?" she asked, not expecting to find much in the way of answers but determined to try anyway. "Or of a woman named Bernadette Springer trying to book a room for the same dates?"

"Not Bernadette Springer, no. But we did have a cancellation around that same time."

"A cancellation?" Tess echoed.

"It normally wouldn't be flagged in our system, but this one was shut down for nonpayment. Apparently, the credit card the guy used didn't go through." Lorraine turned the screen toward Tess. She was pretty sure that sharing this information was breaking a few laws, and she was *definitely* sure that Sheriff Boyd would have a fit if he heard about it, but she was too fixed on the screen to care.

There, with the word *declined* across the top of the screen in bright red writing, was the name Mumford Umberto.

"Money troubles," Tess breathed. "I was right."

"You know this gentleman?" Lorraine asked.

Tess set her mouth in a firm line. "I thought I did—but apparently, I was wrong. What kind of journalist follows a murderer to a small town without the financial means to even book a hotel room for the duration of his stay?"

Lorraine frowned. "Am I supposed to answer that?"

No, she wasn't. Tess already had a good idea. She wasn't sure what Mumford was up to, but one thing was for sure:

his visit had very little to do with bestselling thriller author Tess Harrow.

⸻

When Tess returned to the bookstore, her thoughts in a daze, she found Edna standing on a step stool to reach the towering antique brass cash register as she rang up a customer.

"Let's see. That'll be $138.50. Did you want to round up the dollar amount for my tip jar?"

The customer handed her three fifties. "Sure. In fact, you can just keep the change and toss it all in there. You were really nice."

If Tess hadn't already been reeling from her realization that there had been a lot more advance plotting to this murder than any of them had guessed, this last bit would have knocked her flat. Not once, in all her interactions with Edna St. Clair, had she found the woman to be nice about anything.

"Like I said, don't think of it as self-help." Edna started stacking an enormous pile of books into a brown paper bag. "Think of it as an instruction guide to your brain. I'll get those other ones ordered and call you when they come in."

Tess watched as the customer cheerfully handed Edna the money and headed out the door. She continued watching as Edna picked up the phone and pressed the button indicating that someone had been on hold.

"Sorry about that. Another customer came in and needed help. You're lucky you called when you did. We're so busy

around here that we can't hold on to inventory for long."
Edna slipped her hand over the mouthpiece and cackled at
Tess. She winked and added, "It looks like we're sold out of
individual copies of *The Murderbot Diaries*, but you can buy
the whole set as a box. Should I put you down for all six?"

Tess almost choked as she watched Edna take the credit
card information over the phone and expertly ring up
another huge sale. She knew for a fact that they carried several individual copies of the first book in the series—it was
one of her favorites, so she'd been sure to stock up—and,
since Edna was looking at the exact same shelf she was, she
was pretty sure Edna knew it too.

"Edna, did you just *lie* to that customer?"

"I didn't lie," she said, affronted. "My eyes aren't what
they used to be. Is it my fault if I didn't see all the copies?
Look at how tiny the writing on the spine is." She paused and
added, "I also sold out your tray of lemon-blueberry scones
from the café. I told Mrs. Gray from the church book club
that they were calorie free. She plans to serve them up for
their meeting tonight."

"Edna!" Tess cried. "You can't just tell people anything
you want to get a sale. Gertrude makes those scones with
an ungodly amount of butter. What's Mrs. Gray going to do
when she finds out they have like a thousand calories each?"

Edna snorted. "She knows that already. She was just looking for an excuse to justify the three she ate on the way out
the door. I promised her some huckleberry ones for next
week, so you'd better put the ingredients on your shopping
list."

Tess eyed the older woman with a burgeoning sense of respect. "You really did that much business in the fifteen minutes I was gone?"

Edna tapped her watch face. "It was thirty-five minutes—and I round up, so don't try skimping me out of my money." As if afraid Tess might do just that, she clanged open the drawer to the cash register and pulled out the full twenty-five dollars. She added both it and the contents of the tip jar to her tote bag. "Was your errand all it was cracked up to be?"

"Yes and no. I got answers, but I don't like where they're headed." Tess stepped in front of the door to prevent Edna from making a quick escape. "When you came in here, you said something about a friend looking for Mumford. What friend were you talking about?"

"I can't remember," Edna said with a greedy look back at the cash register.

Tess crossed her arms and firmed her stance. "I'm not paying you to answer a simple question. Did you or did you not talk to a friend of Mumford's?"

"*Talking* is a strong way of putting it. I caught a man snooping out behind my begonias, and when I asked what he was doing, he said he was looking for Mumford."

Tess's arms came swinging back down. "A man was at your house looking for Mumford? What did he look like?"

"Tall and short. Wide and thin. He had a beard but not really."

"Edna!"

"Don't shoot the messenger. You asked."

As little information as Tess was able to get out of this description, she had a very good idea who they were talking about. Not-Darcy. *Again.*

"You didn't tell him anything, did you?" Tess asked.

Edna was as outraged by this question as if Tess had asked for the rights to her firstborn child. "Do you take me for a fool? Every single one of you would-be investigators has been poking around my begonias this week. He wanted to know if I had something called a Nest camera on my front door."

Since Tess was starting to suspect that both Mumford and this mystery man were more involved in Levi's murder than coincidence would allow, she found herself nodding along. Live footage of a murderer digging up poison would be a slam-dunk solution to a case that seemed to be leading nowhere. But Edna had already confirmed she didn't have any poisonous plants in her garden. And a Nest camera out front wouldn't catch much of anything except the activity from the street and the hotel across the way.

"And that's all he wanted?" she asked. "Just video footage and to talk to Mumford? He didn't ask you any questions about Levi Parker? Or mention my book?"

Edna's snort of derision was loud enough to give Tess a scare. "What's your book got to do with anything?"

Tess was debating how much to tell Edna about the succession of mysterious bookstore visitors when the decision was taken out of her hands. For once, the older woman was inclined to be accommodating.

"If you ask me, he was up to no good. He kept asking

me questions about the corner suite. And tuna fish, which I thought was a little fishy." Edna grinned. "Get it? Fishy?"

"Edna, are you serious?"

"There's no need to screech at me. I'm standing right here."

It had been Tess's intention to stick around the bookstore until Tommy's shift that afternoon, mulling over the facts of the case and trying to make sense of them, but she didn't see how that was possible now. She loved this bookstore, but it wasn't doing her any favors in the investigation department. Solving crimes had been hard enough when she could just keep pushing back her deadlines until she had a complete story to write down; solving them when she had a schedule to stick to and a cash register to mind was nearly impossible.

Tommy was proving to be a big help in the afternoons, but he wasn't the same as full-time help. What Tess needed was the freedom to come and go as she wanted, to pop in when the mood struck and pop out when it didn't. What Tess needed was—

She bit back a groan. "Edna."

"What now, girl?"

"If I were to take you on full-time, would you be willing to accept twenty dollars an hour? With a guaranteed thirty hours a week?"

Edna paused in the act of heading for the door, her interest snagged. She backtracked a few steps. "Guaranteed thirty hours, you say?"

"At the minimum, yes. Including some weekends and holidays."

"And you'll get me my health insurance? With dental?"

Tess was pretty sure her accountant was going to kill her for this, but she didn't see what other choice she had. If there was going to be murder popping up on a semi-regular basis around here, she couldn't be a mother and an author and a bookseller too. Something had to give.

"I can't promise it'll be *good* health insurance, but—"

"I take twenty-three different medications. I want them all covered."

Tess swallowed what little remained of her pride. "Fine. Yes. But you have to stop lying to the customers, or I'll get sued for false advertising." She paused for a beat. "And you have to start right now. Your replacement won't get here until three."

Edna's shout of mirth boded ill for the devil's bargain that had just been struck. "You have yourself a deal, Ms. Harrow. We'll get this business in the black in no time."

Chapter Nineteen

FOR ONCE IN TESS'S LIFE, FORTUNE FAVORED HER.

She found her mother at home with Gertrude, the two of them sitting on the back porch overlooking the pond, a picture of multigenerational rural bliss. When Tess had first envisioned living out here full-time, this was the exact picture she'd conjured up—of maternal bonding and long, lazy summer days in the fresh air.

It was such a calming sight that Tess paused to watch the pair. Her hip rested against the open doorway as a light breeze ruffled through the tangled strands of her hair.

"That was the year Tess almost failed tenth grade." Bernadette's voice carried as easily on the breeze as the scent of fresh ferns. "Did she ever tell you about that? The only reason they let her pass was because I bribed them with new equipment for the football team. I had to take on extra cases for a year to pay for it all."

"No way," Gertrude said eagerly.

"No way," Tess repeated, stepping firmly onto the back porch. So much for calm rural bliss. "Mom, I absolutely forbid you from telling Gertie that story."

Both her relatives turned to face her. Her mother was the first to speak.

"I can tell my granddaughter anything I want to," Bee said tartly. "Especially since it's the truth. The only thing I can't remember is how many term papers you ended up selling before you got caught and expelled."

"Mom!" Tess cried just as Gertrude did the same.

Gertrude grinned and added, "How many *did* you sell before you got caught? First the smoking, now academic fraud... I had no idea you were so cool when you were a kid."

Since the look on Gertrude's face contained more interest than judgment, Tess found herself answering more readily than she might have otherwise. "I only sold about a dozen, but they were excellent papers. I got caught because I forgot to change the spelling on Marguerite Bolson's paper. She was a terrible speller. I should've known better than to turn it in with all the I's and E's in the correct spots."

"I read a few of those papers. They *were* really good— collegiate-level stuff." Bee smiled at Tess over the top of Gertrude's head. "You always did have a way with words. I never told you at the time, but I was proud of you for your little side hustle. I raised you to be a go-getter for a reason. The world isn't always kind to women like us. We have to stick together, or we'll get eaten alive."

Tess's heart grew tight inside her chest. She thought of the photo tucked in her back pocket—of her mom standing with her dear friends, of a woman who'd died under mysterious causes and whose murderer had walked free—and wished there was some way to erase all memory of it.

Mostly because Tess *did* remember her mom bribing the school to ensure that she got no more than a few months of homeschooling and a slap on the wrist. She also remembered the long nights when her mother came home overworked and exhausted. At the time, she'd felt only the loneliness and abandonment of a mother who prioritized work over her daughter, but she knew better now.

Raising a strong-willed, fiercely intelligent daughter was no small feat. Especially on your own. Even more especially when you were trying to leave her a world that was better than the one you'd been forced to inhabit.

"What's brought you home so early?" Bernadette asked conversationally. "Don't tell me you've decided to close up the bookstore already."

"I hired some extra help," Tess said as she stepped out onto the porch and dropped into the Adirondack-style gliding rocker. It was her most extravagant purchase for this house, and she'd never once regretted it. The smooth wood and even smoother rocking motion did wonders in helping her relax. "I came back in hopes of hunting down Mumford and asking him a few questions. Is he here?"

"No, I haven't seen him since this morning," Bee said.

"I saw him at lunchtime, poking around the freezer, but that's it," Gertrude offered. "He kept muttering to himself and checking inside the boxes of food. I think he might be looking for more hidden money."

"He won't find anything in there but the vodka I keep for emergencies," Tess said with a roll of her eyes. She hesitated, wondering how much of her day's findings to reveal. She had no idea how much Mumford and the mystery man were tied up together and even less what either of them had to do with

Levi's murder, but one thing was for sure: her family's safety came first. "He can't stay here anymore, you guys. I'm going to have to ask him to find alternate accommodations. I'm not sure it's a good idea to have a man we barely know living under our roof while so much is going on."

Neither her mother nor Gertrude was slow to pick up on her real meaning.

"You think he murdered Levi?" Bee asked eagerly.

Gertrude shook her head. "He couldn't have. He didn't even arrive until the morning after Levi was found. The pilot confirmed it."

Tess leaned back against her chair with a sigh. "I'm not saying he's definitely the murderer, but I was talking to the clerk at the hotel today, and she said that he'd booked a room, only to have it canceled due to nonpayment. That's why he insisted on staying here. He couldn't afford anything else."

"Money *is* a powerful motive for murder," Bee agreed.

Gertrude still wasn't having it. Her brow and nose wrinkled together. "But how would killing Levi Parker make him any money? Grandma, you said yourself that Levi was always borrowing money from you. Wouldn't it make more sense for Mumford to murder you instead? Or, at the very least, to blackmail you?"

The laugh that escaped Bernadette's throat wouldn't have convinced a baby. "What on earth could he blackmail *me* for? The only thing I'm guilty of is reversing the patriarchy and dating a younger man."

Tess decided to test the waters. "According to Lorraine, he also tried booking his hotel room right after Levi did, almost a whole month ago. So whatever he's been planning has been in the works for quite some time."

The silence that fell over the collective group didn't seem particularly fruitful until Gertrude popped up out of her seat and turned to face her grandmother. "Grandma, didn't you say that Levi was the one who followed you here?"

Tess could have kissed her daughter for her impeccable sense of timing—and her unerring nose for facts. She'd cut to the heart of the matter without a moment's hesitation.

"Did I?" Bernadette asked vaguely. "Perhaps I did."

"If that's the case, then why did he book a hotel room a month ago?" The wrinkled shape in Gertrude's forehead deepened. "Grandma, did you know he'd be coming here? And not warn us about it ahead of time?"

Tess watched her mother closely for clues, but the Jackie O. mask slipped into place before she could gather anything concrete. With a titter and a tut, Bernadette was on her feet. "I don't know what you're talking about, and I'm far too exhausted to answer these questions right now. All this talk of my poor Levi has overset my nerves. Everyone seems to forget that I'm in mourning."

"Maybe you should pull out the black hat again," Tess said dryly.

The glare her mother cast on her could have withered stone. "Sarcasm will only get you so far in this life, Tess. At some point, you're going to have to show your actual human side—to me and to all the people you hold at arm's length that way."

Her mother swept off the porch and back into the house,

leaving behind a trail of her heavily floral signature scent. Gertrude watched her go with a puzzled expression.

"Mom, you don't think—"

"No, Gertie, I do not."

"But—"

"*No*, Gertie," Tess echoed, more firmly this time. "Don't go down that road. Nothing good will come of it. I'm sure Sheriff Boyd will find the murderer soon."

Her daughter cast her a sideways look, that narrow-eyed doubt so akin to Tess's own suspicions that she felt herself starting to sink. "Are you gonna tell him about this?" Gertie asked.

"I don't know yet," Tess replied with perfect honesty. "But I'm starting to fear I may have no other choice."

———————

Tess waited around the cabin for another hour in hopes that Mumford would make an appearance. Her mother and Gertrude had headed into town to see if anything exciting was happening, but Tess was determined to get that man out of her house before nightfall. She even sat down at her desk with the intention to write, but she was having a difficult time getting her newest story started. What she *wanted* to write about—an evil murderer set loose only to be cut down by an elderly woman seeking vengeance for the death of her friend—seemed too much like a confession of murder to be put into words. And what she *could* write about—an evil murderer set loose only to be cut down by an as-yet-unknown culprit—was already being covered ad nauseam in Neptune's podcast.

At least, that was the excuse Tess told herself as she settled in with her headphones and the entirety of *Murder, at Last* queued up on her phone. According to the podcast website, there were a total of twenty-six hour-long episodes dedicated to the story, so catching up would take some time.

As soon as she pushed Play, Neptune's velvety voice started crooning through the headphones.

"To the outside world, Levi Parker is everything a romance-novel hero should be. Tall. Good-looking. A Clark Gable for the modern era. Unfortunately, his charm is secondary only to his penchant for elderly widows...so he can *murder* them."

Tess groaned and fought the urge to throw her phone across the room. If this was what $20 million a year sounded like, she wanted her agent to renegotiate her audiobook deals.

"I first met Mr. Parker in line at a Starbucks. I ordered my usual—a bone-dry cappuccino—while he opted for a frothy, whimsical concoction that looked like a milkshake in caffeinated disguise. 'It's my first day out of prison,' he apologized, his teeth flashing like a row of Chiclets gum squares. 'I've been dreaming of one of these for months.'"

Tess snorted to herself. "*Chiclets gum squares* was the best simile she could come up with? Amateur."

"'Prison?' I asked him. It was the one and only time the two of us would speak. 'Are you dangerous? Should I be afraid?' To this day, his answer still sends a shiver down my spine. 'I'd never hurt anything as beautiful as you,' he said. 'I only break those who have already been broken. That way you know exactly where the bones will crack.'"

Tess seriously doubted that this exchange had taken place—no one introduced themselves with a reference to prison, and they *definitely* didn't start talking about cracking bones in the same breath—but she found herself getting swept up into the narrative. All these years, she'd been telling her stories through the perspective of a grizzled veteran detective who saw the world through jaded eyes. Neptune's self-professed naivete held an undeniable allure.

In fact, the longer Tess sat there listening, the more that allure took hold—along with an idea she'd never before allowed herself to consider.

There was no denying that the words weren't flowing out of Tess's fingers and into the typewriter as well as they used to. In the early days of her career, she'd been so enamored of writing and of the recalcitrant Detective Gabriel Gonzales that it had been a sheer pleasure to sit down every morning with a blank page and a head full of ideas. Lately, however, every word had to be wrested out of her as if by force. Jaded experience could only carry a detective—and the author who'd created him—so far. At some point, she needed a fresh start. She needed her naivete back.

"I need to kill off Detective Gonzales."

As soon as the words left Tess's mouth, a knock sounded on the front door. She gasped—more in reaction to her own realization than the visitor—and tugged the headphones out of her ears. She was so distracted that she didn't even check who was paying her a visit before calling out, "Come in."

The door pushed open to reveal a familiar auburn head. Since she'd had very little dealing with Adam as of late—and because Mason wouldn't be caught dead in a faded flannel with the sleeves cut off—she was quick to detect which Peabody triplet was paying her a visit.

"Oh. Zach. It's you."

He stepped the rest of the way into the cabin, a large box under one arm and a look of interest in his gaze as he swept it around the room. His brows raised in surprise as he took it all in.

"I haven't been inside here since your grandfather asked me to help him root out a nest of raccoons a few years back," he said. "It looks...different."

Since that *different* was tiptoeing perilously close to an insult, Tess was quick to counterattack. "Was that before or after you took to blast fishing in his pond without permission? I can never remember."

Zach's face fell into a glower. "I already apologized for that."

Tess was pretty sure he hadn't—and that wild horses wouldn't drag an apology out of him now—so she nodded at the box under his arm. "Is that for me?"

"Yeah. It's your delivery from Canada."

It took Tess a moment to recall what he was talking about. When she finally did, it was with a squeal and a greedy hand out for the box. "Ooh, my Canadian candy? Already? You didn't have to bring it all this way yourself."

"Yeah, well. I was making a trip into town anyway." He tossed the box onto the large wooden table that her grandfather had built. "The guy we sent up there added a whole bunch of stuff that wasn't on your list. You can just toss out anything you don't want."

Tess grabbed a letter opener and slid it across the tape covering the top of the box. The piles of candy inside far exceeded her request. In addition to her Coffee Crisps, there were Crunchies, Caramilks, Maltesers, bags of Old Dutch chips, and more flavors of Kit Kat than she ever knew existed. "Oh, wow. This is great. How much do I owe you?"

Zach rolled an uncomfortable shoulder before plucking a few of the Coffee Crisps and tucking them into his shirt pocket. "Don't worry about it. We have connections."

"You have…junk food connections? Are you sure you want to admit that out in the open?"

This wrung a reluctant chuckle out of him, more grunt than laugh. "Whatever. Mason says to keep you happy. If this is what makes you happy…"

Tess greedily tugged the box closer. She wasn't sure she cared for Mason's motives, but she wasn't one to turn down free candy. "It does. At least pass my thanks along. Whoever you sent up to Canada for this knows his stuff."

"I'll let Jay know." Zach turned to leave, but his mention of the young man's name caused her to fling up a hand.

"Wait—you sent the new guy? The one from Seattle?" She thought but didn't add, *The one who's pretending he didn't come to my store and buy a book for Darcy?*

"It's not a big deal. He ran a shipment of logs across the border for us yesterday." Zach tilted his head toward the door. "Can I go now? Some of us have work to do."

Tess nodded and walked him out. She was eager to ask questions but not at the risk of exposing her interest in Jay. "In my defense, I'm also working," she said as she nodded to the couch, where her phone was still playing the podcast, the tinny sound of Neptune's voice buzzing through the headphones.

"Is that what you call work?" Zach huffed and trotted down the steps. "Must be tough to be you."

Tess closed the door behind him, sorry but not sorry to see him go. The moment the coast was clear, she ripped into a Coffee Crisp—and, okay, a green tea–flavored Kit Kat to wash it down. She was contemplating the caloric impact of a third candy bar when she caught sight of a piece of paper tucked under the bottom flap of the cardboard box. Assuming it was an invoice or receipt, she plucked it out and crumpled it up. She might have tossed it out too, only the letters *inthrop* caught her interest.

"It couldn't be," she said through a mouthful of chocolate. She smoothed the paper flat and read it three times before she remembered to chew. Even then, she struggled to swallow. Her throat was suddenly drier than the Sahara.

The secret note—for it could be called little else—had been written in all capital letters, their blocky perfection untraceable. Whoever had written it didn't want her to know who they were, and for good reason. The information was suspicious in the highest degree.

6/22–7/30 HOTEL PALAZZO, SAN DIEGO, CA
7/31–8/13 LUXOR SUITES, MANHATTAN, NY

8/14–8/21 MAIN STREET STATION, WINTHROP, WA
8/21–??? TAVERN SQUARE, VANCOUVER, BC

Tess wasn't slow to pick up on the chain of cities listed in the note. They were identical to the ones her mother had outlined as those that she and Levi had visited together over the last few months—with the exception of Vancouver, where Tess could only presume Levi had been headed next.

"He was headed to Canada after this?" Tess wondered aloud. And, because it seemed like the more important question: "Why is this in my box of candy?"

The answer to that came as easily as if someone had whispered the answer in her ear. Jay had left it here for her, of course. She flipped the note over to find all the confirmation she needed.

DIDN'T YOU GET MY LAST NOTE??

Tess sucked in a sharp breath before blowing it out again, wishing that someone—Nicki, Ivy, *Victor*—was here to help her untangle this. The part that stood out with more clarity than all the rest was that Jay was now unquestionably the man who'd come into her store and bought the book. He'd left it behind on purpose and with a message in it: a message for her, a message about Levi Parker, a message that the nondescript man had come into the store and taken before she'd had a chance to find it.

Equally clear was that Jay wanted her to know about Levi's travel plans. With a sinking heart, Tess realized that there was only one person who could either confirm or deny his future hotel booking at Tavern Square.

"*Mother,*" Tess muttered.

There was nothing else she could do. The confrontation with her parent had to happen, and it had to happen now. Carefully flattening the paper and tucking it into her purse, Tess headed out the door.

Chapter Twenty

Tess wasn't sure how she ended up sitting in her car in the sheriff's office parking lot, but she had a strong suspicion it was cowardice. Her whole life, she'd been proud of her strength as a daughter and as a mother, as one in a long line of women who weren't afraid to stand up for what was right.

Unfortunately, that strength didn't carry over to sitting down with Bernadette Springer and demanding answers. She *wanted* to—she really did—but what was the point? Her mom would flit about and avoid saying anything incriminating, her lawyer instincts and flair for drama combining as one. She'd turn the tables and accuse Tess of being histrionic—or worse, meddling.

Which was why, when the passenger door to her Jeep was yanked open and Sheriff Boyd slid into the seat next to her, she could only feel relief.

"Is there a reason you're sitting here and staring down my deputies every time one of them exits the building?" he demanded without preamble. "Because I've had three of them turn around and come back inside. Apparently, they fear for their lives."

Tess laughed, though it was mostly to cover her sudden

relief. She'd wanted to see Sheriff Boyd much more than she was willing to admit to herself.

"Your deputies don't seem to have much in the way of courage," she said. "What do they think I plan to do? Kill them off in my next book?"

"Either that or run them over with your Jeep. Please don't. I have enough to do without you taking out half my force." He paused. "Seriously, Tess. I don't have time for a chat right now. Is this important?"

She tried not to let the question sting, but she felt the lash of it all the same. "Of course it's important. I wouldn't be here otherwise."

His dubiously raised eyebrow was a clear sign of battle, but Tess ignored it. She wouldn't let him provoke her. Not when his patience and understanding were more necessary than ever. With a sigh, she reached into her pocket and extracted the photograph of her mother.

"If you're looking for a motive in order to pin this murder on my mom, I've got it for you." She held out the photo, feeling every inch the traitor she was. "One of the women in this picture is an old friend from my mom's first law firm. The other one…"

She didn't bother to complete the sentence. This picture was already worth its requisite thousand words—it didn't need her feeble attempts to add more. Instead of snatching at it, as Tess had expected Sheriff Boyd to do, his brow puckered. He glanced down at the picture and back up at Tess's face, a searching intensity in his gaze.

"Where did you get this? Did your mother have it?"

"Did my mother carry around incriminating evidence in a place where I could easily access it?" Tess snorted. "No. She's a handful, but she's not stupid."

"Then where?" Instead of waiting for an answer, he lowered his voice and added, "For once in your life, I need you to be frank with me. Where did this photo come from, and how long have you had it?"

"For the record, I've never once lied to you. I sometimes *omit* things, and I don't send you a detailed itinerary of my every move around town, but I'm not a liar. And don't forget that I'm the one bringing this photo to you. *Not* because I want to see my mom locked up and behind bars for the rest of her life, but because there's a lot more at play here than you realize."

"Tess," he said, his teeth gritted. "For God's sake, no more speeches. Where did this come from?"

"I found it in your house. More specifically, in the guest room, where Neptune is currently sleeping. It was buried underneath a pile of her disgusting clothes, and if that doesn't tell you how unfit she is to be your investigative wingman, then I don't know what else will. Who hides evidence in their underwear? Invest in a safe, for crying out loud. Or at least a hollowed-out Bible. Cross contamination is no joke."

A sound somewhere between a curse and a laugh escaped Sheriff Boyd's lips. "I knew you three were up to something. An owl, indeed."

"I thought my mom ended up going with the heart attack."

The sound was definitely more laugh than curse this

time. "You're lucky Neptune doesn't know you well enough to suspect a trap the moment her back is turned." He plucked at the button of one of his shirt pockets and extracted a neatly folded evidence bag. As casually as if bagging up his restaurant leftovers, he took the picture and slipped it inside. "I don't know how she got it out of the hotel room, but thank you. It was a risk to let her in my crime scene, but I thought I had my eyes on her the whole time."

"What? Wait. *What?*" Tess was strongly inclined to take the picture back—by force, if necessary. "This came from Levi's hotel room? He was carrying around a picture of my mom with one of his murder victims? He knew she was after him?"

The sheriff didn't answer her. With maddening calm, he rested back against the seat, his posture more relaxed than she'd seen it in a long time. "The thing I can't seem to figure out is whether *he* was the one who originally sought out your mother in Sedona, or if *she's* the one who's been doing the hunting all along."

Tess could only blink, her mind in a whirl.

"Based on Levi's MO for the other murders, he's more of an opportunist than a plotter. There's no connection between the three victims, and all signs point to him having met them in random hotel bars. To me, that says your mom is more likely to be the one chasing him." He sighed. "Then again, she's had plenty of opportunities to do away with him over the past few months. Why did she wait until she got to Winthrop to kill him? Home-territory advantage? Because it gave her access to you?"

"To me?" Tess echoed. Every word out of the sheriff's mouth seemed to be driving her deeper and deeper into a state of delirium. Her mother was the primary suspect? And had been this whole time? "How would being near me help her plot a murder?"

The answer came as soon as the question escaped her lips. *Because I'm a thriller writer with several books containing detailed body-disposal methods. Because there's a huge patch of forest behind my cabin where a body could feasibly be hidden. Because I'm friends with the local sheriff, who might be counted on to look the other way when an evil man is killed under his watch.*

"Victor, I would never do that," Tess said. Of everything, this seemed the most important part to make clear. "I'm a lot of things, but an accessory to murder isn't one of them."

He rolled his head toward her, his gaze difficult to read. "Are you sure about that? Even if your mother's life was at stake?"

The very thought of that question coming from his lips—and now, of all times—filled Tess with a sudden pulse of rage. "I literally just handed over a piece of evidence of my own free will. Knowing that it made her look guilty, knowing that she's somehow implicated in all this. Do you really think so little of me?"

He flushed, acknowledging the injustice of this question, but that didn't stop him from flinging an accusation back at her. "It doesn't matter what I think," he said. "You don't believe she's the murderer."

"Of course I don't. She's a sixty-five-year-old narcissist

who's about as subtle as a neon bat signal." Even though Tess's words were harsh, her tone was resigned. As much as she hated to admit it, the facts were lining up against her mother at an alarming rate. "Fine. I might as well tell you the rest."

Sheriff Boyd's gaze was sharp. "The rest of what?"

"Remember that time Gertie found a hundred grand hiding underneath a fish?"

"Tess," he warned, his gaze more like a razor's edge now. "What did you do?"

"Nothing illegal, so you can stop looking at me like that. And both Nicki and Jared knew about my plans, so it was practically an FBI-sanctioned plot." She pulled out the hand-written note and added it to the heap of evidence starting to pile up in the sheriff's lap. "I asked Mason and Zach to grab me a shipment of Canadian candy—partly because I wanted to see if they'd try to sneak money over the border that way but mostly because it's delicious. Here. Have a Coffee Crisp. They're my favorite."

He didn't take the proffered candy bar. He was still turning the note over in his hand, a bemused expression on his face.

"I didn't get any surprise money this time, but I did get that note. I also know for a fact that Levi booked his stay at the hotel here a month in advance, so my guess is that my mom was the one doing the following."

"How do you know that Levi booked his stay here a month ahead of time?" Sheriff Boyd asked.

Tess saw no reason to lie. "The same way you do. By

asking around." She tapped a finger on the note. "I also called that hotel in Vancouver to check on Levi's reservation, and they confirmed. He was planning on heading to Canada after this. Fleeing the country, no doubt."

The sheriff's grunt contained neither censure nor approval. "What was in the first note?"

"The first note?" Tess echoed.

"On the back, where it asks if you got the first note. What did it say?"

Tess leaned back against her seat with a sigh. She'd hoped that unburdening herself to Victor would help clarify things—if only in her own mind—but she felt as though she were slipping deeper and deeper into a muddied pit.

"I don't know. I never got it. It was left for me in a signed copy of *Fury under the Floorboards*, but a mystery man bought the book before I could get to it—a mystery man who Edna says was snooping around her house, looking for Mumford and Nest-camera footage. If it helps, the guy who wrote this note is currently working up at Peabody Timber under the name of Jay. He won't admit it, but I promise it's him."

"Are you serious?"

"I know none of it makes sense. That's why I'm talking to you." She turned her head to look at him, taking an odd sort of comfort in the grim set of his jaw. "You wanted me to be up-front for a change, so I am. For some strange reason, everything seems to tie back to my bookstore and to some-one named Darcy."

The sheriff groaned. "If this is about Neptune again, so help me—"

Tess slipped her hand over Sheriff Boyd's and squeezed. "It's not. Not directly, I mean. I'm not going to pretend I trust her or even like her all that much, but I'm not singling her out because of my personal feelings."

His fingers twitched under hers. "Your personal feelings?"

She was careful not to meet his gaze. "If you want to let her into your crime scene to steal evidence and incriminating photos of my mom, it's none of my business. If having her stuff scattered all over your house makes you happy, it's not my place to object. You've made that abundantly clear."

"Tess…"

For some reason, her throat suddenly grew tight and thick. "It's fine. I'm fine. Just be careful how much you trust her, okay? She's only in this for the story. She and Mumford both."

"Mumford? Your reporter?" the sheriff asked. It might have been Tess's imagination, but she thought his voice sounded as strained as hers. "What does he have to do with anything?"

"He has money troubles," Tess admitted. "And I'm starting to think he's not here for a feature about me at all—in fact, I think he knew Levi was going to be here long before the rest of us did. I was going to ask him to move out of the cabin today, but he hasn't been back. If he puts up a fight, I may need to call on you to help forcibly eject him."

The sheriff opened his mouth before closing it again. There were probably a thousand questions burning on his lips, but there was no use asking them. Tess didn't know any more about what was going on around here than he did.

"You said the guy's name is Jay?" he asked instead. "Up at Peabody Timber?"

This focus on the tangible—on the one fact that Tess had been able to bring to the table—made her feel a sudden rush of pride. And something else, but she wasn't in a position to examine what that was. Not while Victor was sitting so close to her, the air heavy with unspoken sentiment. "Yeah. He's Black and in his early twenties, and wears his hair over one eye to hide his heterochromia. You can't miss him."

"I'll head up there myself to question him."

Tess nodded down at the photo in his hand. "And that?"

He followed the line of her gaze with a frown. "It's evidence, obviously. Neptune should have never taken it."

"She's going to pin this on my mom, isn't she? She needs an ending for her podcast, and this one is perfect. Murder in exchange for murder. An old woman seeking vengeance for her friend."

"She's certainly going to try," he said, with such simplicity that it sent a shiver down her spine. Mostly because it *was* the perfect ending. Her mother had motive and opportunity, and now that Neptune had seen the proof with her own eyes, there was no taking it back again.

"Can't you at least arrest her for tampering with your crime scene?" Tess asked. It seemed unfair for Neptune to get away with this. Tess had done several questionable things in the pursuit of justice, but she'd never stolen evidence. She wouldn't dare. Sheriff Boyd would have her handcuffed and in the back of his squad car within seconds.

"I might. I'm still weighing my options. She's a lot harder to get rid of than you'd think."

Tess turned to stare at him. "Get rid of? You mean you don't want her in your house?"

"Of course I don't want her in my house, Tess," he said, his voice teetering on the edge of something sharp. "I don't want her anywhere near this blasted case. But she rolled into town before I could stop her and has more connections than a member of the royal family. Damage control is the best I can hope for."

"I don't understand," Tess said, her heart lifting despite her determination to keep it in check. He didn't like Neptune? He wasn't falling under her well-tailored, velvety-voiced spell? "You invited her onto your crime scene. You drank Wild Turkey with her."

He chuffed, careful not to look at Tess as he chose his next words. The space between their bodies seemed to pulse with something that was more than physical. "What other choice did I have? Haven't you listened to her podcast at all? She has the power to completely destroy your mother's life—and by extension, yours."

Tess's head suddenly felt full—of emotions and thoughts, of a rush of blood strong enough to send her reeling. "Wait. You're doing this for my mom? For *me*?"

He released a laugh so bitter that it only contributed to the feeling that the world was suddenly, inexplicably, *gloriously* upside down.

"Yes, Tess. I'm doing it for you. Do you think I *want* her snooping around my crime scene and stealing case photos? Do you really imagine I'd prefer drinking desk bourbon with a stranger over going to the party that you and Gertrude worked so hard to put together?" He pulled his hand out from under hers and turned to face her, a strange and wild glint in his eyes. "I don't know how involved your mom is in all this, but it's not looking good. I had a bad feeling about it the night I questioned Levi in the bar, and that feeling has only grown with time. I'm doing what I can to minimize damages, but there's only so much I can ameliorate a woman like Neptune by pretending to agree to an exchange of information."

"Victor," Tess breathed, her chest so tight it felt as though she'd never draw a full breath again.

"And it'd be a lot easier if you *didn't* antagonize her every chance you get," he added, sighing. "Or spend all your free time running around with—"

But he cut himself off there with a self-conscious look and a long, shaking breath, the unspoken name of Jared hanging in the air between them. It would have been a good time to clear that air, especially regarding Tess's not-feelings as far as Jared was concerned, but intuition told her this wasn't the time. If these things Victor was saying were really true—that he'd been playing Neptune from the start; that he was only doing what lay in his power to protect Bernadette, Tess, and Gertrude from the slander of thirty-five million podcast listeners—then she owed him a lot more than a quick parking lot apology.

She cast him a playful look instead—the easy way out, yes, but also the only way they were going to get to the bottom of this case before it was too late.

"So what you're saying is, Neptune is a total pain in your backside?" she asked.

He looked so relieved that he actually laughed out loud. "That's what you're getting out of this?"

"She's a terrible houseguest who committed misdemeanor tampering her first day here?"

"Sure, Tess. If that's what gets you through the day."

"Oh, it does. You have no idea how much I needed to hear you admit that." She paused. The time to get serious was back. "You probably should at least run a criminal record check on her though. Her *real* name, not the fake one. Darcy Jones."

"I already intend to."

"Her producer too," Tess added. "Even if she doesn't have a record, Sven probably does. Did I tell you that he punched Gertie in the face?"

Sheriff Boyd shot up in his seat like an arrow. "The devil he did!"

Tess felt a warm glow of satisfaction—not that her child had been maimed, obviously, but that the sheriff was as outraged as if his own daughter had been the one under attack. "Oh, he did, all right. He claims it was an accident in the heat of the moment, but whose first reaction to anything is to hit a child?"

The sheriff shifted closer to her. "Is she okay?"

"Yeah. You know Gertie—she's the most resilient person on the face of the planet. She can survive anything." Honesty compelled her to add, "Except maybe the news that her grandmother is a murderer."

"Tess, I'm doing the best I can, but—"

"I know," Tess said. And she *did* know that now—she really did.

Unfortunately, she also knew that no matter how much Sheriff Boyd wanted to protect her, he'd have no choice but to arrest Bernadette if that was where the evidence took him. He was a man of honor, which meant he'd stop at nothing to bring Levi Parker's murderer to justice even though the world was better off without him.

She reached across the console, aiming for the sheriff's hand to offer a reassuring and strictly friendly pat, but he moved at the last minute. She grabbed his thigh instead—a strong, sinewy thigh that grew taut the moment she touched it.

And then she didn't pull back right away. She had no idea what made her do it—whether mortification held her fast or if the surprising warmth sucked her in—but she stayed in place. So did he.

"Thank you, Victor," she said, her voice thick.

He didn't move except to swallow. "For what?"

"I don't know," she admitted. "For going to such lengths for my family. For caring about my daughter." *For holding on to that untouched painting as though it were something worth having.*

He pulled away before that last one could escape. With a swift, practiced movement, he swung the door open and slid out of the seat. Tess was afraid she'd scared him away for good, but he popped his head back in before he made it more than a step.

"Caring has never been the problem, Tess," he said, his voice so soft she had to strain to make it out. "You know that as well as I do."

Chapter Twenty-One

IT WASN'T UNTIL AROUND MIDNIGHT THAT TESS STARTED to *really* worry about Mumford—and even then, her concern was foisted on her by forces outside her control.

"It was Grandma. In the dining room. With the lead pipe." Gertrude reached greedily for the envelope in the middle of the board game and opened the flap. With a crow of triumph, she scattered the cards across the table. "That's three in a row for me. You guys are terrible at this."

"What we are is tired," Tess countered. The cuckoo clock above her head had chimed the eleven o'clock hour while Gertrude had hunted them down across the Clue board. "And old."

"And macabre," Ivy said as she stretched herself up from the table. "Monopoly would have been just as much fun, but without all the murderous undertones."

Much to Tess's surprise, the deputy had shown up at the cabin less than an hour after that conversation in the Jeep with Sheriff Boyd. She liked to think that Ivy's professed reason—to escort Mumford out, should he prove himself difficult to dislodge—was the real one and that the sheriff had only the Harrow household's safety in mind. A niggling feeling in the back of *her* mind, however, kept reminding her that his much more likely reasoning was to keep an eye on Bernadette. He didn't want his prime suspect slipping off to Canada in the dead of night.

"I don't know when I've enjoyed myself more." Bernadette planted a kiss on Gertrude's forehead. "Who knew murder could be so much fun?"

Before Tess could hiss at her mother to be a little *less* obvious, the older woman laughed.

"It was a joke, Tess, so don't eat me. Though I will say that the longer I go without Levi Parker in my life, the happier I am to have gotten rid of him. I feel positively girlish these days."

As this was starting to sound perilously close to a confession of murder, Tess was quick to usher her mom out of the room and toward bed. Tess's good-night was hastily uttered, and she'd have been lying if she didn't say she felt a certain amount of relief to have the door closed with her mother locked behind it.

"Bed, Gertie," Tess said in an attempt to forestall the inevitable.

It didn't work.

"But, Mom. Mumford hasn't returned yet. I want to be here when you accuse him of murder."

"For the last time, I'm not accusing him of murder," she said, more for Ivy's benefit than her daughter's. "I just don't trust his motivations anymore, that's all. When you have an impressionable young child to protect—"

Both Ivy and Gertrude laughed out loud. Tess would have kept going, but she was too weary to keep up the pretense. She fell into her chair in a slump.

"Fine. I don't like him, and I don't like how nosy he's getting about things that don't concern him. He's supposed to be here to take notes about how I take my coffee and what my writing schedule looks like, not—"

Ivy snorted again, this time with real humor. "I've got fifty bucks that says you haven't touched that typewriter since the moment that dead body showed up in the hotel. You never write when there's murder going on."

This was true, but she could hardly be blamed for it. Only officers of the law and—apparently—murder podcasters could keep their nose to the grindstone when so much mystery was in the air. She was about to open her mouth to defend herself when the squawk of Ivy's radio cut through the air.

"Deputy Bell, we've got a possible 10-100 out on Kliner Way."

Even if Tess hadn't already memorized the police-scanner codes for the state of Washington, the speed with which Ivy reached for the radio at her hip would have told her everything she needed to know about a 10-100.

It meant a body. Usually, a dead one.

"That's not good," Ivy responded. "Where's the sheriff?"

"Already en route. How quickly can you get out there?"

Ivy cast a wary look at Tess. "I'm not supposed to leave the Harrow residence until I've personally escorted Mr. Umberto from the premises. Sheriff Boyd's orders."

That made Tess feel a lot better about the sheriff's reasoning for sending Ivy out here but not great about the safety of her family. If Mumford really *was* dangerous, then she was a fool for letting him stay out here as long as she had. It was a wonder they hadn't all been found dead in their beds. Or futon, as the case may be.

The radio squawked again. "Yeah, um, I don't think that's going to be a problem. You should probably get moving."

"Wait." Tess reached for the radio before Ivy had a chance to respond. The reaction was more instinctive than anything else, her sudden spike of adrenaline chasing away all thoughts of being polite or following police protocol. She pushed the receiver button and spoke directly into the mouthpiece. "Are you saying what I think you're saying?"

"Sheriff Boyd hasn't called it yet, but early reports are saying the body belongs to your Mr. Umberto," the voice on the other end said. "And it's not looking too good for him."

―――――――

It took every ounce of Tess's control not to accompany Ivy out to Kliner Way. She was desperate to confirm for herself whether or not the dead body that had been found belonged to Mumford, and she was almost certain that Neptune Jones would be there to wring out every last second of drama for her podcast, but she also knew that Sheriff Boyd wouldn't thank her for her interference.

After everything he'd said and done for her, she owed him that much. For once in her life, she planned to do the sensible thing and go to bed. Gertrude and her mother were already deep in the dreamless sleep of the innocent—or the innocent until proven guilty—so the wisest course of action was to follow suit.

Unfortunately, sleep had other ideas. No matter how many times Tess thumped the futon to burrow out a comfortable spot, she felt every lump. They lodged underneath her like jelly beans rolling around the floor of her bookstore.

"Fine," she said to no one in particular. "I give up."

She puttered into the kitchen to make herself a cup of instant coffee, her mind bubbling over almost as fast as the electric kettle. While it was true that she'd felt no strong affection for Mumford Umberto, she *was* responsible for his presence here in town. He'd come on a flight she'd arranged, was staying at her cabin, and had been sticking his nose into *her* business. Those things might not stack up to much in legal terms, but Tess felt each one piling up like a stone on her chest. For all she knew, he had a wife and kids stashed somewhere—a wife and kids who'd be devastated by his loss, whose lives would be irrevocably changed now that he was no longer in it.

She blamed these feelings of guilt almost as much as her restlessness for why she tiptoed to the door of Gertrude's bedroom and slipped into the dark interior. Unlike Neptune, Mumford was a painstakingly neat houseguest. His suitcase stood upright underneath Gertrude's favorite *Nightwave* poster, the bed perfectly made, and no sign of dirty clothes anywhere. In fact, if Tess wanted to snoop around, she'd have to pry open the suitcase—a thing she was pretty sure Sheriff Boyd would dislike, should Mumford turn out to be another poisoning victim.

She was staring so hard at the suitcase—her good angel and impish devil warring on either shoulder—that she didn't notice the dark blur of movement right away. She heard it first: a low susurration like the legs of a tracksuit rubbing together. Next came a prickling sensation on the back of her neck, warning her that she wasn't alone. By the time she caught sight of the dark figure unzipping itself from the wall and pouncing toward her, it was too late. Her scream was held in check by a large, hot gloved hand pressed over her mouth as the intruder grabbed her from behind.

Tess knew of several self-defense moves to get her out of just such a predicament, but she didn't have a chance to put any of them into action. The man—for his strength and tall-ish size indicated that he couldn't be anything else—brought his mouth low to her ear and crooned words of comfort.

"I'm not here to hurt you, I swear. Please. I just wanted to drop off... I thought you could use... Oh God." At this, he emitted a low, pained groan. Since Tess had been rather obedient up until this point, she saw no reason for that sound until a sob escaped him. "I can't stay. It's too dangerous. They'll come for me next—I know it."

He released Tess so suddenly that she sank to the ground. Only then did she notice Gertrude's wide-open window and the fluttering of her paisley curtains—mostly because the man pulled away, darted a panicked look around, and dove out of the window. Tess toyed with the idea of chasing after him, but there was no need. Despite the black cap pulled low over his eyes and the dark hoodie he wore to mask his movements, she'd have recognized him anywhere.

"Or *not* recognized him anywhere," she muttered.

There was no doubt in her mind that he was the same

nondescript man she'd seen on the street talking to Sven, the same one Edna had confronted for skulking around her house. There was something so familiarly unfamiliar about him—like he was a man she'd seen a thousand times before and would see a thousand more times before she died, and without ever knowing his name.

He also seemed to know about Mumford's death long before information on it had been made public. It was the only explanation for what he'd been doing inside this room—or why he'd acted as though he was a hair trigger away from joining Mumford in the grave.

Tess flipped on the lights and immediately began scouring for clues. She was afraid she'd have to break into Mumford's suitcase whether Sheriff Boyd liked it or not, but she had the good sense to explore the corner where the man had been hiding himself. Sure enough, a copy of *Fury under the Floorboards* sat pristine and untouched on the bedside table. She was pretty sure Mumford hadn't purchased it, since her publisher had sent him an advance reader copy back when the plans for his interview had first been underway, and she doubted he'd have been willing to shell out the thirty bucks necessary for a signed copy.

With shaking hands, she grabbed the book and flipped open the cover. She wasn't at all surprised to find her own name scrawled there, along with the message to Darcy with a wish for all her murder hopes and dreams to come true.

"So he *was* the man my mom saw," Tess breathed. "The one who came to the store and requested the exact copy left by Jay."

She ran her fingers over the words, surprised only by how unsurprised she was. Everything kept coming back to the bookstore and Darcy. And, she thought grimly, to *her*.

She continued fluttering through the pages, not expecting to find much. However, once she reached page 99, she noticed a bit of writing along the page's edge. And not just any writing either. This was in all capital letters.

THE TUNA IS NO HERRING.

"The tuna is no herring?" Tess echoed blankly. She continued moving through the pages, but they were free of anything but printed type. Only page 99 contained the cryptic message, though it didn't take a genius to decipher it.

It was the first note—the one that had been referred to in her box of Canadian candy and the one that she'd been supposed to see long before now. The tuna obviously referred to the fish that had hidden the hundred grand, and herrings were well-known in the thriller writing world as a device to throw the audience off the scent of the real killer.

From there, the meaning was clear: instead of a ploy used by Peabody Timber to smuggle and wash their illicit cash, the money was somehow connected to the murders. Tess was more than happy to consider this possibility and would have gladly turned her nose onto the scent of this trail instead.

Only Jay had visited the bookstore *before* they'd discovered that fish. For that book to have been purchased, written in, and returned to the shelf hours ahead of time could only mean one thing: Jay had known it was coming in. Jay may have even been the one to send it.

In other words, Jay had some serious explaining to do.

Chapter Twenty-Two

THE DEAD MAN WAS, IN FACT, MUMFORD UMBERTO.

"Before you ask, Tess—no, it wasn't hemlock, and no, we don't have any suspects at this time." For once, Sheriff Boyd must have woken up on the conciliatory side of the bed, because he was waiting for her at the door to the sheriff's office when she arrived the next morning.

Well, to say he was waiting for *her* might have been a stretch since Kendra was right on her heels, but Tess wasn't about to cavil over the details. She handed the sheriff a cup of coffee with the ubiquitous four sugars and three tablespoons of cream, sensing that he probably hadn't been to sleep at all last night. The shadow on his jaw, which had skipped five o'clock and headed straight for midnight, proved it.

"That's not why I'm here," Tess said with a friendly nod to Kendra. So far, the sheriff's sister had yet to say anything, but that was pretty standard as far as that woman was concerned. "I mean, if you want to clue me in on the details, I'm not going to turn you down, but I actually wanted to know what you learned from Jay."

"Jay?" he echoed blankly. A bustle of movement from the sidewalk behind Tess spurred him into action. He pushed open the door and gestured for the two of them to follow him inside. "You mean that new kid at Peabody Timber you wanted me to talk to?"

"Yeah, that one. I finally got his first note."

Tess was pretty sure that mysterious notes and bookstore intrigue were low on the sheriff's priority list right now, but he gave her his full attention in a way that she could only consider flattering. "Really? Where was it?"

"That's where things start to get weird," Tess confessed.

A low chuckle escaped from Kendra. "*Start* to?" She didn't wait for an answer, opting instead to roll her eyes toward her brother in a clear bid for his attention. "I'll leave and let you two get to this obviously important business, but I wanted to let you know that I took care of that thing we discussed."

Sheriff Boyd nodded. "Good. Thank you."

The meddler inside Tess couldn't resist. "What thing?"

"Kendra is doing a little investigative work for me— strictly off book, you understand, so don't go telling the world that Detective Gonzales recruited his long-lost sister to dig into the things that he doesn't have the time to do himself. It has nothing to do with this case."

"Victor, I would never," Tess said, but with a laugh on her lips. That was something she totally *would* do, if the idea about killing her detective off and starting with a fresh new sleuth hadn't taken such strong possession of her mind. "But if you wanted help, you know I'd be more than happy to provide it."

He cast her such a pained look that she didn't press the issue. After bidding Kendra a quick farewell, she turned the conversation back to the note. Even quicker, she outlined the events of the night before, including the nondescript man's break-in and the book he'd left her. Sheriff Boyd absorbed it all without batting an eyelash, which just went to show how strange this whole case had become.

"You brought the book with you?" Sheriff Boyd asked, his hand outstretched.

"Naturally." She reached into her bag and extracted it. "The note about the fish is on page ninety-nine. You have my note about the hotels, so I can't confirm that the handwriting is the same, but it looks like Jay's work to me. You talked to him yesterday, right?"

He flicked his gaze over the message and back up to Tess. "No. There's no record of anyone matching that description working there."

"What? How is that possible?"

"According to Mason Peabody, they haven't brought anyone new on since they hired Jared last spring."

Tess opened her mouth and closed it again, unable to accept this. "But Zach mentioned him by name. And everyone working there saw him. Ask Jared."

"Don't worry. I intend to." The sheriff's mouth drew into a flat line. "But I'm afraid it might have to wait. Tess, this thing with Mumford—"

She winced. "I know. It's awful. How did he die?"

It was obvious that Sheriff Boyd didn't want to tell her, but this was the sort of news that got around quickly. "Stabbed."

"Stabbed?" Tess echoed. That didn't sound at all like the same murderer who had done Levi Parker in. That had been all premeditation and careful plotting, the application of a poison that could have taken anywhere from a few minutes to a few hours to go into effect. This felt different. *Desperate.*

A feeling of deep foreboding suddenly flashed through her. "Not stabbed with a hatpin, right?"

The look the sheriff leveled on her could have cut, carved, and demolished stone. "Of course not. Do you have any idea how hard it would be to kill someone with a hatpin?"

Tess was too relieved to hear this to argue about the facts—which, according to her research, had shown that the expert jab of a hatpin through the eardrum could, in fact, do away with a pesky victim.

"It was just a thought," she murmured. "But about this man in Gertie's room last night…"

The sheriff stood and waited for Tess to gather the words necessary to make this next part clear. Considering how much he likely had on his plate right now, his patience carried extra weight.

"He was scared, Victor. Terrified."

He arched a single brow. "Like he'd just killed a man and was worried about getting caught?"

Tess shook her head. That hadn't been the sense she'd gotten from the nondescript man at all. "No. Like he'd just *seen* a man get killed and was worried about falling prey to the same fate. What if he was telling the truth when he told Edna he was a friend of Mumford's—or an assistant of some kind? That would explain why he was poking around her house." A thought occurred to her, causing her whole body to turn stiff. "And why he came in and bought that signed copy of my book. Mumford was one of the first people to know about how Jay put it back on the shelf. He probably hoped to get his hands on it to see what the big mystery was, only he didn't want me to know how curious he was. Or why."

The sheriff nodded once. Instead of arguing or questioning her logic, he seemed to accept this theory at face value—a great thing for Tess's ego but not so great for her mounting sense of fear.

"I'll put an APB out for a man matching your mystery visitor's description, but I doubt it'll lead anywhere. In the meantime…"

Tess held her breath and waited to hear what advice Sheriff Boyd had to give her in a situation like this one.

When he spoke, it was to confirm her worst fears: "In the meantime, keep an eye on your mother."

"Victor! You don't honestly think she stabbed Mumford in cold blood last night, do you?"

"No, I don't," he said grimly. "That's why you should keep an eye on her. We wouldn't want anything terrible happening to her next."

━━━━━━━━━━

Since Tess had already driven all the way into town, she decided to pay a quick visit to the bookmobile—and to the woman behind the wheel—before she headed home. Nicki was expecting her.

"Well, this is certainly turning into something, isn't it?" the librarian said by way of greeting. She slid the bookmobile doors open and ushered Tess inside. "Another dead man with your fingerprints all over him."

"Not my *literal* fingerprints," Tess protested. "I never physically touched either Levi or Mumford."

Nicki gave an airy wave of her hand. "You say tomato, I say there's a second corpse suspiciously tied to you and your family. Did you just come from the sheriff's office?"

Tess grimaced. "Is it that obvious?"

Nicki's shrewd gaze raked over her from top to bottom. "A little bit, yeah. Let me guess—he yelled at you for poking your nose where it doesn't belong again, didn't he?"

Tess fell onto one of the footstools with a slump. "I wish. Instead of yelling, he heard what I had to say before warning me to keep an eye on my mom. For once, my evidence might actually end up being useful. I had a late-night visit from a man who may have witnessed the murder."

"Well, well. Wonders never cease."

The note of humor in Nicki's voice caused Tess to glance up sharply. "What's that supposed to mean?"

"You tell me. You're the one who seems to be at the center of all this. I've never known anyone to attract trouble the way you do, Tess. It's like you're cosmically cursed."

Tess wished she could disagree with this, but it was true. For once in her life, she wished she *wasn't* at the heart and center of this particular investigation, but it wasn't as if she had much of a choice in the matter. True, she could have refused to let Neptune goad her, closed her eyes and ears to the drama that was unfolding around her, but what about all the rest? It wasn't as if she'd *asked* someone to use her books to send strange messages about fish and people named Darcy.

"I'm starting to feel cursed," Tess admitted. "Did you ever hear back from your Peter/Paul IT guy on where he got that information about Neptune's real name, by the way? No matter how hard I try to shake the feeling, I'm almost sure that information is somehow at the center of all this."

"You mean, you're almost sure that *Neptune* is somehow at the center of all this," Nicki countered, but not unkindly. "And it's the weirdest thing. He called this morning to ask me what I was talking about. He claims he has no idea what email I referred to."

Tess felt her heart thump. "What? How is that possible?"

"That was *my* first question, so I had him pull up my account and read the message for himself. Only it wasn't there."

The thumping of her heart grew more pronounced. "What do you mean, it wasn't there? You deleted it?"

"No. I mean, there was no record of it being there in the first place. No message, no deleted draft, no electronic evidence of its existence at all. If I hadn't read the email with my own two eyes, I wouldn't believe it was possible." She paused. "But I *did* read it, and I know it was there."

"Nicki!"

The librarian grimaced. "I know. The Bureau is *pissed*. My email account is suspended while they tear it apart looking for how it might have happened. There's a chance it's a glitch, but that wouldn't explain why someone sent it to me in the first place. Whoever was responsible wanted you to have that information, and they knew I was the best way of getting it in your hands."

"Nicki!" Tess exclaimed again.

"Don't worry. It's not the end of national security as we know it. These things happen sometimes. Even the FBI isn't completely impervious to hackers." As soon as the word *hackers* left her lips, Nicki turned to Tess. Her expression wasn't alarmed or worried—it was annoyed, and Tess knew exactly why. "Tess, please tell me this isn't what I think it is."

"Wingbat99," Tess said with a sigh. There was no use denying it; this had her hacker contact written all over it. The mystery and the playfulness of it—the unnecessary cloak-and-dagger that would end up costing her a lot more than just money.

"You really think he's involved in this?"

"I *know* he is," Tess said. In fact, she'd have come to this realization last night if she hadn't been so distracted by dead bodies and men breaking into her home. "The note in the book was written on page ninety-nine on purpose. This whole time, he wanted me to know it was him. He wanted me to know he's here in Winthrop."

"He's in Winthrop?" Nicki demanded. *"Now?"*

"Not officially, no." Tess thought about how Jay didn't actually exist—not according to the Peabodys, anyway—and grabbed her purse. "But he shouldn't be hard for me to track down."

Chapter Twenty-Three

WINGBAT99—JAY, OR WHATEVER NAME HE WANTED TO go by—was, in fact, quite difficult to track down. Thanks to Sheriff Boyd's dire warning that her mother could very well be in danger of murder, Tess was hesitant to leave the older woman's side. Add in a teenager who also needed careful watching and a cabin that no longer felt safe enough to hold them, and this was the result: Tess, sitting in a packed Jeep at the bus station, with one finger in her ear as she tried to hear Wingbat's voice over what had to be the worst connection known to mankind.

"Are you in a cave or something?" Tess asked as the crackling of terrible reception ebbed and flowed in her ear. "I can barely hear you."

"I'll tell you my location for ten million dollars, and not a penny less."

Tess shouted out her indignation, but the sound was quickly muffled by her mother's voice from the back seat. "Why don't you put him on speakerphone, love? I can't make out what he's saying."

"Yeah, Mom," Gertrude piped up as she fiddled with a few of the dials on the radio. "Send him through the Bluetooth so we can all hear."

"No, don't—" Tess began, but it was too late. Gertrude had already worked her magic and connected the phone. The crackling was so loud that it sounded like they were sitting in the middle of a bonfire. "Gertie, turn that off right now! I'm trying to have an important conversation."

"Is that your daughter?" Wingbat asked when the static abruptly turned off. "I've been dying to talk to her. What's it like having a famous almost-murderer for a mother? Do they make fun of you at school, or does it give you a certain amount of street cred?"

"Definitely the first one," Gertrude said before Tess could make a motion to silence her. "Especially since everyone knows she's good friends with the local sheriff. No one invites me to parties because they're afraid I'm going to narc on them."

"Gertie, that's not true!" Tess protested. "You went to Timmy's birthday party only a few weeks ago."

Gertrude rolled her eyes with so much force that Tess was pretty sure Wingbat could hear them moving. "He's two years younger than me, and we played laser tag. That is *not* the kind of party I should be going to at my age."

"She has a point," Bernadette said. "You can't keep her a child forever, Tess. She'll need to start forging her own path soon."

"She's *fifteen*," Tess said. "I don't have any immediate plans to kick her out and feed her to the wolves. I hope she'll always know she can count on a roof over her head."

"Aw, thanks, Mom," Gertrude said, only half sarcastic.

"That's more than I ever got out of my mom," Wingbat agreed cheerfully. "I *could* always go live with her if I wanted to, but she's a doomsday prepper, so I'd have to sleep on her extra cases of powdered eggs. Last I checked, she was up to about thirty-five."

The mention of Wingbat's mother yanked Tess's thoughts back on track. "Are you talking about your mom *Darcy*?" she asked.

His rich chuckle sounded. Now that Tess was paying attention—and since she'd already connected the heteroch-romatic dots—she wondered how she could have missed it. He sounded *exactly* like Jay.

"Okay, so that one was a tiny lie. It was for your own pro-tection. I *could* tell you her real name, but then I'd have to kill you."

Gertrude snickered.

"Is that a 'no' on the ten million, by the way?" Wingbat asked. "I'm fully prepared to disclose my whereabouts for such a sum."

"Don't you dare touch my bank accounts," Tess warned. "I could easily hand this information over to Sheriff Boyd and let him deal with you, but I wanted to give you a chance to explain yourself first."

"That's very nice of you. Let's see… I was always a bright child, especially when it came to technology. I took apart my first transistor radio when I was just two years old. To hear my mom tell the tale, it's because of the heavy metals the U.S. government drops on us from chemtrails, but—"

"Not the explanation for how you came to be a hacker," Tess said, half laughing. "The explanation for what you're doing here and how you're tied up in all this."

"All this?" he inquired politely. "I'm currently working on a number of projects. You'll have to be more specific."

Tess was pretty sure what she needed was to get him in a room for a stern talking-to, but she was willing to play along for now. "Fine," she said. "What do you know about the murder of Levi Parker?"

He didn't hesitate to answer. "Not a lot, to be honest. I'm not much of a podcast guy myself, but I've seen some of the chatter on the conspiracy boards. From everything I can make out, it sounds like he got what he deserved. I'd put good money on him being the one responsible for those three old-lady murders. Your mom was lucky to get out of that relationship alive."

"Well, I never—" Bee began, but Tess cut her off.

"Save it, Mom." Louder, she added, "You might as well tell me the rest, Wingbat. I'm onto you. You knew that Neptune's real name is Darcy, and you wanted to make sure I got that information by having me sign the book over to her and then infiltrating the FBI so the message would get passed along through Nicki."

"Whoa, really?" Gertrude breathed.

"Yes, really," Tess said, a terse note in her voice. Now that she'd seen for herself that Wingbat was only a young man— almost a kid, really—her mom powers were starting to come out in full force. "He also knew about the money being sent to me via the fish long before anyone else did. You called it *a herring*. Why? What's that supposed to mean?"

"Honestly, Tess," Wingbat scoffed. "If I have to explain the intricacies of mystery writing to you, this is going to be a long conversation."

Both Gertrude's and Bernadette's snickers spurred Tess to keep going. "That doesn't even include the information you sent me about Levi's travel schedule both before and after this trip to Winthrop. You wanted me to know exactly where he was staying."

"No, I didn't," Wingbat said. "Why would I care about Levi Parker's travel plans? I'm not in the business of tracking murderers. That's your line, not mine."

Her mother's voice sounded a little faint. "What's this about Levi's travel plans?"

Too late, Tess remembered that she hadn't yet confronted her mom about how deep her suspicions ran—or how much of a figure Bernadette Springer played in them. She cast a quick glance over her shoulder to find that her mom looked, for the first time, like the grieving widow she was pretending to be.

"Wingbat sent me a list of all the hotels that Levi's been staying at," she explained in a brusque, emotionless tone. Allowing any sign of her feelings to show would only give her mother carte blanche to fall into hysterics. "First San Diego and then New York, before moving on to Winthrop." She hesitated over the last part. "And up next, of course, Canada."

The pallor of her mother's skin didn't change. "He was going to *Canada*?"

Tess blinked. "You didn't know that? You weren't going with him?"

"No, Tess. I've told you a hundred times already. I wasn't going anywhere with him. He just kept popping up. In fact, that's why I came to—" She bit down on her lip to prevent herself from saying more. In a show of touching solidarity, Gertrude reached into the back and took her grandmother's hand.

"This is all very interesting, of course, but I'm a busy man," Wingbat interrupted. "I don't know if you noticed, but I kind of have a new job."

Tess marshaled her thoughts back into a semblance of order. "About that," she said. "What's the deal? Mason and Zach are pretending like you don't exist."

Wingbat chuckled. "That's because I don't. Not officially, anyway. Now, if you'll excuse me—"

"Wait!" Tess's voice took on a panicked edge. She wasn't even close to getting all the answers she needed out of Wingbat, and she had the sinking suspicion that he wouldn't be so eager to pick up the phone the next time she called to demand information. "At least tell me how you're involved in all this. What do you know? What are you hiding?"

"I know more than you ever will, but I'm not hiding anything. In fact, I've been more than generous when it comes to revealing my client's personal information." He chuckled again. "*Think*, Tess. A man like Levi Parker is of zero interest to me. He died with a total of sixteen dollars to his name and several outstanding parking tickets, not to mention the heavy losses he recently took on some horse betting. I never work with anyone whose bank account is running that dry. I have a quality of life to maintain."

Tess suddenly felt dizzy. All that thinking was starting to lead to some very suspicious answers, but she wasn't sure she could voice them while her entire family sat in the Jeep with her.

"It was nice to meet you, Gertrude," Wingbat said. "If you ever need someone to take care of that trust fund for you, be sure to look me up. Or, you know, send a Wingbat signal. We're practically neighbors now."

The call ended with a burst of static before cutting off altogether. Gertrude showed every sign of wanting to discuss the revelations shared by Tess's hacker-for-hire—particularly that bit about the trust fund that neither Tess nor her mother had mentioned to her yet—but Bernadette spoke up before she could start her chatter.

"Canada," Bee said, extending the vowels so that it sounded more like a question than a statement. "*Canada*. That jerk never said anything about fleeing the country. After all those months together, all that time I spent—"

She cut herself off before she revealed anything incriminatory. At least, anything *more* incriminatory.

"Is he allowed to flee the country?" Gertrude asked in the silence that followed. "If he was still alive, I mean. Isn't it, like, illegal to cross the border if you're a criminal?"

Bee answered mechanically, her legal training kicking in over the top of her emotions. "They won't let you in if you have a felony on your record, but Levi was never formally charged with anything. He was free to go wherever he wanted."

"Huh. I guess he *was* making a run for it." Gertrude turned to peer at her grandmother. "You really didn't know, Grandma?"

"Of course not," she said. "Why do you think I came to this godforsaken town? I figured it was the one place he wouldn't follow me. I mean—*Winthrop*? And if he did, who in their right mind spends any length of time here? I figured a few weeks of sitting around and scratching spider bites, and even the most dedicated murdering gold-digger would get tired and move on. No offense, Tess."

"None taken," Tess murmured before she realized just what her mother had said. When she did, she turned around so suddenly that she felt a painful twinge up her neck. "Mom!"

Her mom was careful not to meet her eyes. She began playing with a leather strap on the back of the seat instead. "What? I didn't want to put it in such bald words, but you brought it on yourself. I've never known anyone as stubborn and persistent in her pursuit of the truth—and don't forget, I spent thirty years sitting across the courtroom from some of the state's best prosecutors."

"You knew Levi Parker was a murderer," Tess accused.

"Of course I did. The whole world knows it."

"You went to Sedona on purpose to use yourself as bait to set a trap."

"Well, really, Tess. Why else would I go to the desert? Do you have any idea how long it took me to get the sand out of my clothes after that trip? Not to mention the crevices of my—"

"Ew, Grandma," Gertrude protested, but she'd picked up on the thread of the conversation and was more than happy to tug at it. "Were you trying to entrap him or something? Get a confession on tape? That's so cool. Like a honey trap. Seducing bad men for the good of the world."

Tess didn't miss the way her mom started striking the leather strap against her palm—or how quickly the playful air in the Jeep dissipated.

"Not for the good of the world, Gertie," Tess said. She lowered her voice as soft as she could get it and still be heard over the sound of that steady thwap-thwap. "For her friend. The one that Levi took for all she was worth before killing her and dumping her body off Long Island."

The thwapping sound stopped at once.

"So you know it all, huh?" Bee asked. "I was hoping that part would escape your notice."

"Wait. What am I missing?" Gertrude looked back and forth between them, a heavy line bisecting her brow. Tess could almost see the wheels turning as her daughter replayed the many episodes of *Murder, at Last* she had memorized. "What friend are you talking about? Not…Eudora Raphael?"

Tess winced to hear the woman's name spoken aloud, but her mother rose nobly to the challenge.

"Yes, pet. Eudora Raphael, though I knew her first as Doris Ploughty. You can understand why she changed her name. No one wants to buy paintings from a woman called Doris Ploughty. She might as well have baked apple pies and sold them on a roadside stand."

Gertrude wasn't buying that descent into irreverence any more than Tess was. The girl immediately unbuckled her seat belt and crawled into the back to sit as near to her grandmother as possible without being in her lap.

"You should've said something, Grandma," Gertrude said, her voice tight. "We might have been able to help."

Bee's smile was sad but warm as she took Gertrude's hand in hers and patted it. "That's sweet, but I'm long past needing a shoulder to cry on."

"Not with *that*," Gertrude said, *tsk*ing lightly. "With your plan to take Levi Parker out. That's what you did, right? Hemlock in his whiskey? Where did you get it? How much did you give him? Do you still have some I can see?"

"I didn't kill him," Bernadette protested feebly. "Honestly, Gertie. It wasn't me."

"You can tell us, Grandma. We won't rat you out—not even to Sheriff Boyd. Will we, Mom?"

"No, Gertie-pie," Tess agreed. "We won't rat Grandma out. Not because we're criminals by association, but because she's telling the truth. She didn't kill him. I suspect she *wanted* to and that she planned to do exactly that in New York or San Diego, but somewhere along the way, she lost her taste for vengeance."

"It was San Diego," Bee agreed a little sadly. "I thought it would be easy. I ground up some sleeping pills in his dinner one night and lured him out onto the balcony off my hotel suite, but I found that when push came to shove— literally—I couldn't do it."

Gertrude cast a wide-eyed look up to the front of the Jeep, but Tess only shook her head. Her mother probably needed to get this out—and the less they interrupted, the more cathartic it would be.

"There I was, standing right behind him, my hands on his back. He was already slurring his speech and stumbling around, and several people down at the bar had seen him kick back enough whiskey to make his fall look natural. I'd have gotten away with it for sure. No one would think to accuse a woman in a pink Chanel suit. It isn't *seemly*."

Tess could only shake her head. Only Bernadette Springer would think that dressing like Jackie O. would get her off for murder.

"That's all there is, really. Once I knew that I couldn't go through with it, I tried my best to get rid of him, but he kept following me. Always demanding more money, more access to my accounts, more information on where I kept the deeds to my real estate holdings." Bee shook her head in warning before Tess could speak. "There's no need to chastise me, Tess. I know it was risky, but I thought I was being careful. I felt sure I'd be able to shake him in New York, but he must have heard about your book-release party and figured I'd come here next."

"So he really *was* going to kill you here?" Gertrude asked, her voice small. "If someone hadn't killed him first, I mean."

Bernadette shook her head, her mouth a grim line. "Things hadn't gotten that far yet. There was no way he'd bump me off until he had his hands on my money. In fact, I think he enjoyed that I didn't make things easy on him. It was as if he knew I was onto him…but he still wanted to see if he could take me for all I was worth. I suspect he liked the chase almost as much as—if not more than—the money itself."

"He did," Tess said. "He was."

"What?"

"He *did* like the chase, and he *was* onto you." Tess grabbed her phone and pulled up the photo of Bee and Eudora standing in front of the law library, which she'd been careful to snap before handing the evidence over to Sheriff Boyd. "This was found in his luggage, along with a full dossier of our family history. He knew that you'd been friends with Eudora. It's only a small leap from there to assume that he knew all the rest too."

Bernadette was only given a quick glance at the phone before Gertrude snatched it away from her. Tess tried to stop her daughter, but the teen was both quick and determined.

"Grandma!" Gertrude cried, her face crumpling. "Poor Eudora. Poor *you*."

Those four words were all that were necessary to release the torrent of emotions that Bernadette had been striving so hard to keep at bay. Her look of anguish was as genuine as one could get.

So, too, was her determination to push it aside for her granddaughter's sake. Gertrude's head was buried in Bee's shoulder, so the girl didn't see the way those emotions played across her grandmother's face, but Tess caught every glimmer. Her mother was shocked and sad and full of remorse—and wholly concerned with protecting Gertrude from each one.

"Shh, pet. It's okay. I'm okay." She ran a soothing hand over Gertrude's hair. "*I* might not have been able to kill Levi, but someone else stepped in and did it for me. He can't hurt anyone else ever again."

At that, all the dizzying implications of the phone call with Wingbat came rushing back to Tess. Not just of his playful assumption that she knew more about this case than she really did but also his equally playful admission about his client list.

Mostly because she didn't doubt that every single word he'd said was true. He *had* known about the fish in the cooler. He *had* tried to warn her that it was somehow connected with Levi's murder. And he *had* sent her a list of hotels that coincided neatly with Levi's travels.

He was also good enough at his job that he wouldn't bother working with anyone who couldn't pay—and pay handsomely—for his services. Tess didn't love forking over the cash every time she called him up, but she could withstand the burden.

And so could a certain someone whose podcast made $20 million a year.

"Not you too, Tess," her mother said with a glance at Tess's suddenly frozen expression. "There's no need to look at me like that. I'll be okay. You forget that Eudora's death happened over a year ago. It stings—I'm not sure it'll ever stop doing that—but I'm not as heartbroken as I once was. I expect that's why I couldn't kill him in the end. I needed the red-hot rage of those early days, not the simmering burn of regret that came after."

"It's not that," Tess murmured.

"Then why do you look like you've just stumbled on another murder?"

Because she hadn't stumbled on a murder—she'd stumbled on a murderer. Rather, she'd just confirmed everything she'd suspected since the moment Neptune had breezed into this town.

"The first day Neptune was here, do you know what she said to me?" Tess didn't wait for an answer. "She said that she'd just missed running into Levi in the hotel bar. That most of time, she was hot enough on his trail to request the room next to his, but the hotel was full because of my book event."

"So?" Bernadette said. "What does that have to do with the price of eggs?"

"Don't you see, Mom? The list of hotels Wingbat sent me wasn't about Levi's travel plans or even yours. It was Neptune's itinerary. *Neptune's* movements."

"You think Neptune was fleeing to Canada? What on earth for?"

"I don't know, but that's what Wingbat was trying to tell me just now. That Neptune's the one we should be watching. Only—" She cut herself off and pressed her hands against her temples, her eyes squeezed shut as she tried to force all the pieces into place.

"What is it?" Gertrude asked. "What's wrong?"

Tess popped her eyes open again. "Only I called that hotel in Vancouver to confirm that Levi Parker had a reservation. He did. I distinctly remember it."

Gertrude squeaked. "Mom!"

"Which can only mean one thing," Tess said, her voice dangerously near a squeak of her own. "The two of them were traveling together. They've been traveling together this whole time."

Chapter Twenty-Four

TESS POUNCED ON IVY THE MOMENT THE DEPUTY GOT off from work that evening.

"I need you to tell me where Sheriff Boyd is with the background check on Darcy Jones," she said as soon as the familiar tight bun and solid shoulders appeared in the dark alley outside the sheriff's office.

Instead of answering, Ivy whirled around, a hand on her hip as she reached for her gun. "For the love of everything, Tess! You can't sneak up on me when there's a literal murderer roaming the streets. I could have shot you."

"You wouldn't have," Tess said with a nod down at Ivy's hand, which hovered over the holster but had yet to touch the thumb release on the pivot guard. "Sheriff Boyd has you too well-trained. No one on his force would dare to shoot first and ask questions later."

Ivy narrowed her eyes. "Yeah, but I could still take you out with a well-aimed punch or two."

"That's probably true," Tess agreed. "So it's a good thing you recognized my voice. Would you please stop being dramatic and answer me? I'd go in and ask him myself, but I don't want to bother him unless he's pulled it up already. Do you know if he ran it yet?"

"Tess, you aren't an investigator in this case. In fact, you aren't anything in this case except a material witness. I can't just hand over stuff like that because we're friends."

That was all Tess needed to hear. "So he *has* run it," she said. She nodded decisively and prepared to push past Ivy. "Thanks, Ivy. I'll go talk to him myself."

A strong hand on her shoulder prevented her from making it more than a step. "It won't do you any good," Ivy said. Even though her hand was firm, her voice was not. "No one by the name of Neptune Jones exists in the database. As for Darcy Jones, there are about fifteen hundred of them, but none of them pull up anything dangerous or related to your murder-podcaster nemesis."

Tess took exception to the last part of this. "She's not my nemesis."

"Oh, I'm sorry. My mistake. The woman who *isn't* your nemesis but who causes you to lie awake at night, gnashing your teeth in jealousy and rage."

Tess took exception to this too, but Ivy kept her from saying so with a laugh. "Tess, you might be good at writing fictional stories, but everything in your real life is an open book. The whole town knows you can't stand the sight of her."

"Yeah, because she's going around and murdering people in cold blood," Tess countered. She was tempted to reveal her newest suspicions to Ivy—about Neptune and Levi potentially traveling side by side, about how Wingbat might even be able to prove it—but she wasn't ready yet. There were still so many unanswered questions to clear up first. "But I can't say I'm surprised about her name coming up empty. If this is her first foray into murder, she wouldn't be flagged in any systems."

Ivy practically rolled her eyes. "Murder isn't the only reason people are in the system, you know. One of your Darcy Joneses had been fingerprinted because she's a public school teacher. Another one was in the foster-care system as a kid. A third had like twelve DUIs. You'd be surprised how easy most people are to track. Once you've been stamped and inserted into the government database, you stay there forever."

"Now you're just giving conspiracy theorists fodder for their delusions," Tess said, but with a nagging feeling that she was missing something. "I don't suppose anything came back on Sven?"

"Just a DUI of his own from a few years back. Nothing indicating he has a predisposition for attacking teenage girls or going on murdering sprees in small towns."

Tess was disappointed by this, but she could hardly pretend to be surprised. A murder-podcast producer with a long track record of crime probably didn't make for good PR.

"Thanks for keeping me updated," she said. "I don't suppose there are any leads on poor Mumford's killer? Or the mystery man who broke into my house?"

Ivy's grimace told Tess everything she needed to know about those particular questions.

"Okay, fine. I'll stop poking my nose in where it doesn't belong. Only…" Tess felt her face pucker as she trailed off. The truth was, she wasn't so sure her nose *didn't* belong. When your houseguest was stabbed on a dark rural lane, coolers of fish were sent to you with money hidden inside, and your own personal hacker paid a visit and not-very-helpfully left a trail of notes behind, how could you avoid being involved?

"Only what, Tess?" Ivy asked.

Tess shook her head. "Only I get the feeling the answer is right here. I just can't figure out why it's so hard to see."

———

Tess drifted off to sleep under the crooning, dulcet tones of—yes, she was willing to admit it—her nemesis.

She lay in Gertrude's bed with her headphones on and the fourth episode of *Murder, at Last* queued up on her phone. Gertrude had wanted to sleep in here herself tonight, but Tess's mind still danced with visions of late-night break-ins, so she'd taken the teenager's bed for herself.

Since it was the first time she'd been on an actual mattress in over a week, it was understandable that she was sinking deeper and deeper into the bed, her mind and body relaxing as one as Neptune lulled her into a state of rest.

"One of the hardest things about a job like mine is maintaining a boundary between my quarry and myself," Neptune said in a purposefully thoughtful tone. "It's the same phenomenon that happens between kidnapping victims and their kidnappers—a sort of Stockholm syndrome that grips the heart and won't let go. On a moral level, I know that Levi Parker is a bad man—a dangerous man. On a personal level, I can't help but feel for his plight."

Tess jolted up in bed, one of the headphones slipping out. She rammed it back in so fast that it caused a twinge of pain. Was Neptune going to admit to actually *liking* Levi Parker?

"Take his childhood, for example," Neptune continued. "Had he grown up among a loving, middle-class family, it would be hard to develop sympathy for him. But knowing that he struggled to find a foothold in the system—a child abandoned by the parents who were supposed to love him unconditionally—it's easy to see where his pain may have originated."

"That's it," Tess breathed. She was fully awake now, adrenaline pumping through her system so fast that it was like drinking a triple espresso followed by half a dozen Red Bulls. "That's the piece I've been missing."

She swung her legs over the side of the bed, once again recalling everything Neptune had told her on day one—the confessions of guilt that Tess had been too distracted to hear. Not just about how Neptune always stayed in the hotel room next to Levi but also about how Levi had grown up a foster kid, each of his murders a ploy to get back at the foster mother who'd wronged him.

"Darcy Jones," she said aloud. Ivy herself had confirmed it just a few hours earlier. "Not an elementary school teacher, and not a woman with a dozen DUIs, but a kid who'd grown up in foster care."

As far as Tess was concerned, that sealed the deal. Neptune Jones and Levi Parker weren't just a murder podcaster and the murderer she was chasing—they were friends. *Childhood* friends. Tess was almost certain that if Ivy pulled up the record for Darcy Jones from the foster-care history and crossed it with that of Levi Parker, there'd be an overlap. That was why Neptune had been so upset when Tess and Gertrude discovered her real name. As someone who regularly stuck her nose into other people's business, Neptune knew it was only a matter of time before Tess dug deep enough to discover the link.

Only… Tess's brow wrinkled as she considered the bigger picture. Neptune and Levi sharing a deeper connection answered quite a few of her questions, but it raised almost as many back up again. Why would Neptune have murdered her childhood friend using a highly painful and toxic poison? How did the hundred-thousand-dollar fish fit into the story? And what on *earth* was Neptune doing cozying up to Sheriff Boyd if she had so much to hide?

Tess threw back the covers, uncertain about everything except for one glaring course of action.

"Neptune Jones isn't going to spend any more nights under Sheriff Boyd's roof while I'm alive to prevent her," she said aloud. "Especially since I know how to prove she's up to something."

———

The nice thing about being friends with a hardworking county sheriff currently sitting on two unsolved murders was that he was up and out of the house well before dawn. Tess knew that for a fact because she'd been crouched in a shrubbery at the end of the road leading up to his house since four o'clock that morning.

Sleep had been impossible with so many thoughts rattling around in her brain, so Tess had grabbed the supplies she needed and headed out as soon as she could. The note she'd left for her mom and Gertrude was sure to spark outrage, but it wasn't as if what she was about to do was dangerous.

Was it legal? Technically not.

Was it ethical? Tess was willing to admit that her plan fell into a gray area, but morality didn't count when there was a murderer on the loose.

Was it practical? Abso-freaking-lutely. Especially since Tess had been itching to put her bug detector to use since the moment Jared had put it in her hot little hands.

The only problem now was getting Neptune and Sven out of the house before her legs started cramping up. Good thing she had a plan for that too. Grabbing her phone, she dialed the only other person she felt sure would be up at this hour.

Ivy picked up on the first ring. "Tess, do you have any idea what time it is right now?"

"Yes, and don't try to pretend you aren't up and dressed already. If I know Sheriff Boyd—and I do—he's got a meeting scheduled for his entire team any minute now. He likes to brief you guys before the journalists and vultures have had their first cup of coffee."

Ivy's sniff of annoyance confirmed everything Tess had just said. "Don't forget the annoying authors who refuse to leave the professionals to do their work. They're usually asleep until noon."

"I haven't slept that late since I was in college," Tess

protested. "Besides, you're going to thank me for this one—I promise. Is there a way you can lure Neptune out of the sheriff's house for me?"

Tess could hear Ivy's sharp intake of breath as clearly as if the woman was crouched in the bush next to her. "Tess, what are you about to do?"

"Nothing dangerous, so you can stop sounding like a junkyard dog. I just need to slip into the sheriff's house for one quick thing—"

"That's it. I'm calling him to come get you right now. Don't move."

"Ivy, *please*." The determination in Tess's voice must have come through because the deputy paused. She also seemed to be waiting for an explanation, so Tess had no choice but to give her one. "Okay, so remember that thing you said yesterday about how one of the Darcy Joneses you came across grew up in the foster system?"

"Yeah. So do literally half a million kids every year. Talk about searching for a needle in a haystack."

"I don't need a haystack. I already know where the needle's being kept." She switched her cell phone to her hand and tried adjusting her position so that not *all* her blood was cut off from her toes. "You're the only other person in this town who hasn't listened to those stupid podcasts, so I'll fill in the details for you. Levi Parker was also a foster kid—a thing Neptune mentions several times in her podcast and said to me like five minutes after I met her. She's kind of obsessed with that plotline."

"Apparently, she's not the only one," Ivy muttered.

"I'm serious. I have a hunch that their relationship went a lot deeper than she let on. How else would she always know to be one step behind him, showing up in every city mere hours after he did? Because he told her, obviously. For all I know, they picked the destinations out together."

"Tess…" Ivy said, but with less warning and more piqued interest in her voice.

Tess pressed her advantage. She wasn't sure how much longer she'd have it. "And if you'd listened to the podcast, you'd know she has a weird affection for him. Like, in one breath, she outlines all the horrible things he did while he was alive, and in the next, she talks about how his smile lights up a room. It's super weird."

"Or it's compelling fiction."

"Yeah. Compelling fiction that nets her somewhere in the vicinity of twenty million dollars a year. Early on in this investigation, I thought for sure that she wouldn't have harmed Levi Parker because he was her cash cow—the thing keeping her podcast going and putting money in her pocket." She paused just long enough to draw a breath. "But what if he wasn't just her cash cow? What if he was her *pet* cow?"

"Are pet cows a thing?"

"Okay, it's a bad metaphor, but you know what I mean. Maybe the reason her podcast is so successful is because she has just enough inside information on Levi and his activities to place her one step above everyone else." Now that Tess was on a roll, it was getting harder to keep hiding in this stupid bush. With every word, she found herself getting more caught up in how perfectly everything was coming together. "And maybe—just maybe—all this stuff with my mom was a way for her and Levi to set a trap for an even better story and higher ratings. Think about it, Ivy. She needed some kind of ending to her podcast. Levi meeting my mom must have seemed like a stroke of good luck. My mom had motive to murder him—I'm sure the sheriff has showed you that photograph by now—and Winthrop was the perfect setting. Not only because of my mom's ties to me, a well-known author who's been steeped in several murders of her own lately, but because we're a hop, skip, and a jump from Canada. I bet she's taking her mad millions and disappearing into the void. It's what I'd do if I was a murderer in need of a quick getaway."

The pause that greeted this amazing conclusion swelled Tess with pride. Ivy was obviously floored. She was flabbergasted. She was—

"Yeah, but then why did she kill poor Mumford?" Ivy asked. "He was annoying, yes, but he wasn't *dangerous*. It hardly seems worth the effort."

Instead of being cowed by this, enlightenment hit Tess in a burst of brilliance. "Because he knew about Neptune and Levi, obviously. I don't know why I didn't think of it before. He and the mystery man were working together—not to do a story on me but on *them*. That's why the mystery man was snooping around Edna's house the other day. She told me he wanted to know if she had a Nest camera on her front door."

"I wouldn't believe a word out of Edna's mouth, if I were you."

This was a thing Tess would normally agree wholeheartedly with, but it was a strange thing to make up—especially since Edna barely knew what a Nest camera was. "Yeah, but it makes sense. Her house is across the street from the hotel and has a perfect view of the corner suite. Mumford probably wanted some sort of proof that Neptune was sneaking into Levi's room. And I've been feeling for quite a few days now that he wasn't the least bit interested in my story. Only in Levi Parker, the recent murder, and the fish money."

Ivy groaned. "That fish money is going to end up being the death of this case—and of me."

"It won't be the death of you," Tess promised. "But unless I'm very much mistaken, it *was* the death of Mumford."

And there it was, the final part of the puzzle clicking neatly into place. Tess had known for a while now that Mumford had been having money problems and that he'd been poking around her freezer in hopes of finding another hundred grand lying around. Unless you believed in the power of supreme coincidence—a thing Mumford had, by his own admission, been strongly against—you wouldn't waste your time that way.

Unless, of course, you had a *reason* to assume more money would be found hiding in a freezer. Because you were expecting it. Because the first batch, so rudely intercepted by a teenager, was supposed to have been yours.

"Tess you're just rambling now. Do I need to send an ambulance to come get you? Are you accidentally hiding in a patch of poison oak?"

"I'm serious about this, Ivy," Tess insisted, though she did take a peek around her to look for poison oak all the same.

Like hemlock, it was known to spring up in these parts. "If you were a financially struggling journalist on the cusp of breaking a huge scandal—say, the clandestine affair between a murder podcaster and the man she's hunting—would you be content with one paltry little article?"

"If it's my literal job? Yes."

If Tess had been in a standing position, she would have stamped her foot in protest. "You would not! Especially not if the murder podcaster was a zillionaire. If you were thorough—and for all his faults, Mumford *was* that—you'd look into the possibility of blackmail to go along with it."

Tess was pretty sure that also explained how Wingbat was so up to snuff on all the fish-money details. If Neptune really was a client of his, he'd know all her financial dealings. By his own confession—and as had been proven in his regular dealings with Tess—poking around private bank accounts was something of a hobby of his. Wingbat would have known all about the hundred-thousand-dollar payout being smuggled to a blackmailer—and that the tuna fish, tied up as it was in Levi and Neptune's business, was indeed no herring.

Money-laundering scheme, indeed. Mumford had almost pulled the wool over her eyes on that one.

Tess paused as signs of movement started appearing at the sheriff's front door. "Hang on a sec, Ivy. I might not need you to call up Neptune and get her out of the house after all. I think they're finally leaving."

"Tess, you can't go inside that house." Ivy spoke in her most official police deputy voice, but it had little power to drown out the excitement pounding through Tess's veins. "If even a fraction of the things you're saying are true—"

"They are. Look and see if the foster home where Darcy Jones grew up is the same one that housed Levi. That should be a good start." The bobbing heads of Neptune and Sven appeared in the doorway. They were talking excitedly about something as they filed out to the waiting van. "I'm just going to do a quick sweep of the sheriff's house for bugs."

"For *bugs*?"

"It's not as weird as it sounds," Tess explained. "You know that Sheriff Boyd invited Neptune to his house to keep close tabs on her, right? To control the flow of information to protect my mom?"

"Tess…"

"Well, I think Neptune might be returning the favor. Jared once mentioned that her van is filled with high-tech equipment, but not the kind you'd need to record a podcast. It's more expensive than that—more advanced. I think he may have been onto something."

"Why do I get the feeling this isn't going to end well?"

"Because you're a pessimist, obviously." Tess switched the phone to her other ear. "I'll be super quick, Ivy, I promise. I'm just going to do a quick sweep to see if I'm right about Neptune. I'll head straight into town when I'm done."

"Tess, don't—" Ivy began again, but Tess hung up on her. For one, she didn't particularly want to be talked out of this plan. For another, the van was starting up and heading down the drive. She didn't want to lose any time as she hightailed it inside, her gift from Jared clutched in hand. She'd find the bugs and prove without a doubt that Neptune Jones was up to no good.

"Then the whole world will finally see that she's not all she's cracked up to be."

Chapter Twenty-Five

SHERIFF BOYD'S HOUSE WAS CRAWLING WITH BUGS.

To be more precise, his house was *planted* with bugs, but Tess knew better than to let a prime piece of imagery slip through her fingers. The moment she slid through a window—the one to Neptune's guest room, unlocked and completely open for any enterprising criminal to get in—she turned on the bug detector as Jared had shown her. It lit up like a portable Christmas tree.

There was one behind the television. One in the toaster. Two in hallway lamps. If that wasn't bad—and invasive—enough, Tess also found one in the bathroom fan and one in the little reading light next to Sheriff Boyd's bed. The bathroom one was gross on several levels, but it was the one in Victor's bedroom that really disgusted Tess.

She'd tiptoed inside the room on hesitant feet, a strange hush coming over her as she invaded the sheriff's private domain. It was the only room in the house that wasn't bedecked in floral decor from the nineties, but it wasn't the Spartan bachelor pad she'd been expecting either. It was neat and tidy, as expected, but a floating bookcase took up the entirety of one wall, a well-worn leather club chair in the corner next to it. Several houseplants, all of which were thriving in ways that would do Edna St. Clair proud, stood near the floor-to-ceiling windows, which were bare of curtains. Instead, the glass was clear and open to the forest, with light filtering in and making everything seem welcoming and warm.

"I can't believe that woman had the audacity to put a bug in his *bedroom*," Tess muttered as she switched off the detector and slipped it back in her pocket. She didn't touch the reading lamp or the listening device attached to it, careful to leave everything exactly as she'd found it. Sheriff Boyd would want to bag it all as evidence.

Of wrongdoing. Of spying. Of *murder*.

A wave of nausea came over Tess as the full realization of what she'd just uncovered hit her. For almost two weeks now, Sheriff Boyd had been harboring a literal killer inside his home. He'd done it to protect Tess and her family, to keep them safe from the winds of suspicion for as long as possible—and the whole time, he'd been putting himself at risk while he did it.

"The stupid man has no idea what kind of danger he's in," Tess said as she slipped back into the living room and tried to figure out her next step. To call this in, obviously, but also to put an end to this ridiculous push and pull between her and Victor. He might not be ready to take this thing of theirs to the next level, but *she* was. And it was high time he heard it from her own lips.

That was when she saw it.

"What the—"

The adrenaline-fueled hammering of Tess's heart

suddenly turned pitter-patter. She drew closer to the bay window in the living room, certain her eyes must be playing tricks on her.

"He wouldn't. He isn't."

But he would, and he was. Amid all the upheaval of his murderous houseguests and elbows-deep in a double homicide that would rock his small town forever, Victor had taken up a hobby. And not just any hobby—he was painting.

The handmade wooden easel that sat in the window was small enough to belong to a child, but it had been propped up on a set of *World Book Encyclopedias*, so it was within easy reach of a man who stood almost six languid feet tall. The pots of paint were arrayed in recycled baby-food jars— where had he gotten those?—each one neatly labeled and sealed. All of that was interesting, of course, but not nearly as much as the canvas that sat half dabbled in swipes of blue and green.

Tess recognized it at once as a paint-by-number kit of the mountains and aurora borealis. A painting that could—in the right and willing hands—be beautiful.

"He found it," she said, her words barely audible to her own ears. "He found it and he's *painting* it."

Tess had no idea how long she'd been standing there, all the implications of that painting sinking slowly in, but it was too long. That much she realized as soon as she heard the creaking of a door and the sound of a smooth footstep behind her. Too late, she recalled what she was doing here—and why. This wasn't a grand romantic gesture between friends. It wasn't even a friendly bout of breaking and entering.

She was gathering evidence against a murderer...and the murderer wasn't likely to let her walk out of here without a fight.

"You shouldn't have said anything," a low voice growled from behind her. "The bugs are still on. I could hear every word."

Tess had just enough time to whirl around and catch sight of the voice's owner before a sack was thrust unceremoniously over her head and she was dragged, kicking and screaming, out the door.

Chapter Twenty-Six

IF NEPTUNE JONES THOUGHT SHE COULD KILL TESS NOW that she knew Sheriff Boyd was working on that painting, she was a much stupider woman than Tess had first assumed.

"You might as well tell your boss that I won't go down easily," Tess said the moment the sack was lifted from her head and her mouth freed from the gag that had kept her silent this whole time. Her hands were still tied behind her back, her body wedged in a small space in the back of the white van stuffed so full of boxes and bags of electronic equipment that there was barely room for her, but her mouth was working fine.

It was dry, obviously, but it worked.

"I told Ivy Bell exactly where I was and exactly what I was doing, so you won't get away with this for long," Tess added, lest her captor think she was exaggerating. "I even told her that I was looking for the bugs, so she knows they're in the house."

Sven looked down at her with such a look of distaste that she feared she may have made a mistake. But then he laughed and shook his head, his mouth twisted in a smile that made her skin crawl.

"You're lying. You didn't tell anyone where you were.

And even if you did—" He had her cell phone between his forefinger and thumb. Dropping it to the ground, he drove his heel into the screen and ground it to cracked dust. "They won't be able to find you in time."

At that, Tess admitted to a slight quaver of fear. While she found it highly unlikely that Neptune and Sven would get away with her murder as well as the deaths of Levi and Mumford, she didn't trust them not to take her out in a blaze of glory just for the heck of it. For all she knew, Neptune would want a recording in case she took up podcasting in prison.

"It's no use," she said in an effort to buy herself some time. Since Ivy really did know what Tess had been up to—and since she'd surely confirmed the background-check findings by now—there was a good chance *someone* would start looking for her. "There's no way Neptune can pin this one on my mom. I'll admit that the plan to frame my mom for murdering Levi was a good one, but taking out Mumford was a mistake."

She caught Sven's gaze and, in an act of iron will, held it.

"Murdering me will be a mistake too," she said. "You can tell Neptune I said that. I'll wait."

Sven's grin twisted harder. "You really don't get what's happening, do you? Even after all this time."

Something unsettling started revolving through Tess's stomach. "I might be hazy on a few of the details," she admitted, "but I know most of it. About how Neptune and Levi grew up together. About how they were in a relationship. About how they were fleeing to Canada together after

Mumford found out the truth and started blackmailing them."

Sven's expression was so flat that the unsettled feeling turned hard. It was like a weight pressing down on every single one of Tess's internal organs.

"Ohh," she breathed as realization almost knocked the wind right out her. "That's it, isn't it? She was going to Canada with Levi."

"Don't say another word, or I'm putting the gag back in your mouth. And this time, I'm spitting on it first."

Tess grimaced as he loaded up a particularly nasty ball of phlegm and dislodged it into the gag, but nothing could prevent the words from escaping her mouth. Not now. Not when so much more than just her life was at stake.

"But you can't go to Canada, can you?" she said. "That's what this whole thing is about. Because of your DUI. That's the one non-felony crime they won't let you in for. We looked it up."

His words became a snarled growl. "Has anyone ever told you that you talk too much?"

Everyone, all the time—and she wasn't about to stop now. "Levi and Neptune were going to cross the border without you. Whatever plans their future held, wherever they were going next…you weren't invited to be a part of it. So you killed Levi using hemlock poison. A woman's method. An *old* woman's method."

He held the gag up menacingly. "I'm warning you, lady— this is going into your mouth now."

Since he made no move toward her, Tess recognized this

for the bluff it was. For the first time in—she was guessing—a long time, Sven wasn't just the man behind the curtain. Tess had seen how hard he worked: packing up equipment and directing the podcast, always shuffling behind Neptune with a clipboard in hand. A life constantly on the move, following in Neptune's dirty-clothes-ridden path as she trailed Levi around the country, had to be a trial. A *well-paid* trial, obviously, but that would have been coming to an end soon.

"You killed Levi and made Neptune think my mom did it. But then Mumford didn't get his blackmail money underneath the fish because my daughter found it first. So he was applying pressure. He stepped over the line."

"You know who else is stepping over the line right now?" Sven warned.

Tess glanced around quickly, trying to take stock of her surroundings. From all she could make out, they were on a forest-access road somewhere. It was an ideal place for murdering an innocent woman and dumping her body. Tess acknowledged a growing fear that she might not make it out of this thing alive. Only...

She puckered her brow, interest in Sven's motivations and movements temporarily replacing her worry. Understanding a murderer's steps was a key part of writing a good thriller, and something about all this didn't make sense.

"What?" he demanded, seeing her expression. "What's that face for?"

She slowly shook her head, trying to puzzle out his end game. "I get that you plan to kill me out here, but I don't understand how you think you won't be arrested. When I go missing, Sheriff Boyd will hunt you down to the ends of the earth. He won't let you get away with this. You know it, I know it, and—"

A thump from the back of the van caught Tess's attention.

"Sven…" Tess's heart leaped into her throat. He noticed and laughed in a way that could only be described as diabolical.

"That sheriff of yours won't have to hunt down the killer," he said. "He'll have one handed to him. Not alive, obviously, but that won't matter. You already laid the groundwork for me."

The thump sounded again, and this time, Tess was able to place exactly where it was coming from. A large black box marked "Speakers" was starting to pound and shake. Tess had done enough research about live human burial to recognize that pounding as a foot kicking frantically against the sides.

"Sven?" Tess asked, drawing his name out until it contained at least six syllables. "Is Neptune inside that box?"

"I guess you really are as smart as they say. It's almost a pity I have to do this." He shrugged as though what came next was a matter of complete indifference to him. "At least it'll provide a neat ending to the podcast. In a bloody showdown, the murder podcaster takes out the famous thriller writer…and the famous thriller writer takes out the murder podcaster in the process. Neptune herself couldn't have done better."

A muffled protest from inside the box indicated that Neptune had heard every word of this—and that she took strong exception to it.

Sven untied Tess's hands from behind her back, but not before pulling a gun from the back of his pants and making sure Tess knew he wasn't afraid to use it.

"You'd better pop it open and get her out," he said, waving the gun way too close to her face for comfort. "The sooner you two get this over with, the sooner I can leave this god-forsaken town."

Tess glanced at the wooden box with a frown. "Pop it open...how? It looks like you nailed her in there."

"I did." He gestured toward a crowbar sitting on top of a toolbox. "That should do the trick... But don't try anything funny. I'm twice your size, and I have no problems making this as painful as possible for you both." He released his sinister laugh again and added, "Besides, I'd hate to have to make your poor little teenager bleed again."

Tess's hands shook as she grabbed the tool in question and started to work the nails that held the box shut. It felt eerily similar to popping open a coffin, though the repeated thumps and murmurs from inside ensured her that Neptune was very much alive—and not at all pleased to have woken up this way.

The moment the lid started to lift off, Neptune pushed from the inside. Her hands and feet were bound, and there was a gag over her mouth, but there was no mistaking her look of displeasure—or the fact that she made captivity look ridiculously good. Tess had no idea how she'd managed to smudge her makeup just enough to give her the perfect smoky eye or how the sheen of fearful sweat on her body gave her such a glow, but it felt disastrously unfair.

"Go ahead and untie her," Sven said, standing back and holding the gun level. He held up one of his hands, which had a white bandage wrapped around it. "But watch out. She's a biter."

"Good for her," Tess said as she started working the knots. Neptune's chest heaved as Tess freed first her feet and then her hands, but she didn't struggle until they both stepped out of the van. Tess was relieved to be back on solid ground again, but as soon as the gag fell from Neptune's mouth, she spat angrily at Sven.

"You are officially the *worst* podcast producer I've ever had," she said, sneering. "And don't forget I started in a basement with that guy who talked to ghosts."

"Oh, dear," Tess murmured. It was an inadequate statement to cover the current situation, but it was either that or "We're both going to die a gruesome and horrible death, and there's nothing we can do to stop it."

Neptune turned her sneer on Tess. "Did he tell you what this is about? His grand plan to take all my fame and money for himself? As if my lawyers will let him lay a finger on my podcast after I'm gone. If you so much as touch my bank accounts or the *Murder, at Last* rights contract, they'll be all over you."

"Um…that's not really what's happening here," Tess pointed out, but she may as well have stayed silent for all the attention Neptune paid her.

Neptune spat again. Tess had no idea how she was making so much saliva; the gag in her own mouth had pretty much wiped her out for the next few hours. "The salary I paid you was more than generous. You could have asked for a raise instead of resorting to murder."

Sven's face was growing increasingly redder the longer Neptune spouted her venom at him, so Tess felt it was time to intervene. There was no need to make their deaths *more* painful than they needed to be.

"I'm pretty sure this has less to do with money and more to do with the fact that you were planning on leaving the country with your old-lady-murdering lover," Tess said, an air of apology hanging about her. "Also, that Mumford Umberto was going to expose your entire story to the world so that you'd lose all credibility in the eyes of the podcasting world. They'd have probably stripped you of your Podcast Awards—you and Sven both. It's hard to recover from something like that."

Neptune reared back, her eyes wide. Her foot hit a rock, and she stumbled, but neither Tess nor Sven made a move to help her.

"Wait. You know all that?" Her head swiveled back and forth between them, but Tess felt the accusation was meant more for her than for Sven.

"Sorry," Tess said with a shrug. "Solving crimes is kind of my thing. The weirder, the more likely I am to get it right. Ask Sheriff Boyd."

"No one is asking Sheriff Boyd anything," Sven muttered. He used the gun to gesture toward the side of the road. "Now, both of you get over there and act like Neptune is about to shoot Tess in the back."

Neither Tess nor Neptune complied with this demand.

Tess, because she didn't relish the idea of taking a bullet when her back was turned. Neptune, because she looked as though she was about to cry.

"That's why you shoved me inside a box?" Neptune asked. Her face started to crumple, her lower lip wobbling in a way that reminded Tess of Gertrude when she'd been a little girl. "You're going to make me shoot Tess in the back? *You're* the one who killed my poor Levi?"

Tess barely managed to stop herself from rolling her eyes. How this woman was considered the authority on all things murder and criminal investigation was beyond her. At this point, Gertrude was more aware of the situation than Neptune was.

"He shoved you inside that box because he's going to kill you," Tess explained, a bitter note in her voice. "But only after he makes you kill me first. He's going to stage it so it looks like you've been behind everything this whole time— Levi's death, Mumford's death, *my* death. It's the only way he's walking away from this thing a free man. My mom is no longer a viable suspect, and everyone else who might have done it is dead. It's either you or him."

"But—"

"Enough of this," Sven said. "It's time."

Neptune keened on such a sharp note that it felt like fingernails raking across Tess's spine. "You can't do this, Sven. *Please.* You can have the podcast money—all of it, every last penny. We'll kill Tess together, stage it so it looks like she's the one who did it. I could sell it as the ending to this story. You know I could, especially when it comes to the sheriff. All

I have to do is cozy up to him and tell him a sob story about how she wanted vengeance for her mother's friend. He'll believe me, Sven—you know he will."

Tess expected Sven to treat this as the desperate piece of nonsense it was, but he turned to Neptune with an interested tilt to his head. "Go on," he said.

"Wait. What?" Tess tried to intervene, but he flung up a hand to stop her.

"What about Mumford?" he said. "How do we explain that?"

"Easy. We'll pin it on his accomplice, the one who tried shaking you down by the van the other day. We can't be the first people they've tried to blackmail. We can pretend I paid Mumford the hundred grand—for the second time—and that his accomplice decided to keep it all for himself."

Sven used the barrel of the gun to scratch his jaw. "I dunno, Neptune. Two separate, unconnected murders happening at the same time? Isn't that kind of coincidental?"

"Yeah, but that's why it works!" Neptune clasped her hands in front of her. "Coincidences happen all the time in real life—you know that, Sven. It's only in podcasts where everything has to neatly tie up. People expect it to read like some dime-store crime thriller."

Tess almost laughed out loud at how much Mumford would have appreciated this particular approach. She was only stopped by the realization that Neptune was rapidly winning Sven over to her side. In another minute or so, Tess was going to find herself facing two killers instead of one.

"It's the perfect ending," Neptune added. She had Sven's

full attention now, the two of them drawing closer together as their plotting became more intricately woven. "With both Levi's murder and Mumford's murder accounted for, all that's left is to get rid of Tess. We could make it look like a car accident—oh! Or suicide. She was so racked with guilt over killing Levi that she decided to end her life with a literal bang. We could even just make her disappear. People do that in places like this. Bears, Bigfoot... Who knows what woods like these hold?"

As far as Tess was concerned, that was the last straw. She'd already tackled Bigfoot in this forest once, thank you very much. She wasn't about to do it a second time.

The crowbar was still within reach. If she stretched carefully, she could get her hands on it without either Sven or Neptune noticing her movements.

"And you'll really give me the podcast money?" Sven asked. "You won't back out of our deal afterward?"

Neptune made the motion of an X over her chest. "Cross my heart. I'll need to keep a little for myself—to keep up appearances, you understand—but it's more than any one person can spend in a lifetime. I'd rather be alive and broke than dead with all the riches in the world."

This eminently sensible point of view did little to make Tess soften toward the woman. She'd just managed to get her fingers wrapped around the base of the crowbar when her foot caught on a pebble. The soft scuffling sound wasn't much, but it did draw Sven's attention. As soon as his head started turning in Tess's direction, Neptune spoke again.

"You deserve a reward for putting up with me all these

years," she said, drawing closer with a sad smile. "I know I haven't always been the best boss, but I couldn't have done any of this without you. You're a good podcast producer, Sven. Whatever else happens here today, I want you to know that. It's been an honor and a privilege to work with you."

Tess didn't wait to hear more. With the crowbar now firmly in hand, she lifted it as high as it would go before swinging it at Sven's head with a weighty thump.

He went down a lot easier than Tess expected. Crumpling like a paper bag, he fell in an inert heap at her feet, dust billowing out in a puff like smoke. Tess's breath came just as quickly, adrenaline forcing her to clutch at the crowbar so tight that she could feel her fingers starting to cramp.

Still. That didn't stop her. She pounced forward again, this time with the crowbar aimed like a baseball bat.

"Now it's your turn," she said as she moved toward Neptune.

"What? Why?" Neptune turned and darted around to the front of the van. "I just saved your life."

Tess slowed her footsteps, but she didn't let go of the crowbar. "What are you talking about? You were trying to convince Sven to disappear me into the woods forever."

"I wasn't! I was *distracting* him for you. It took you long enough to pick up on it." Neptune *tsk*ed. "If you'd ever listened to my podcast, you'd know that this was how that serial killer from Tennessee was caught a few years back. The only way to bring a greedy man down is to feed him exactly what he wants to hear."

Tess crept closer. "And if you'd ever read one of *my* books, you'd know that Detective Gonzales never negotiates with kidnappers. They can't be trusted. The only way to take one of them out is by force."

Neptune snorted. "Yeah, but that's fiction. Make believe. I report facts."

Tess snorted right back. "Oh, yeah? *Facts?* Is that what you'd call sleeping with a murderer you're actively podcasting about? And then trying to pin his murder on a sweet old lady whose only real crime was trying to defend her friend's death?"

"I know how it sounds." All the color drained from Neptune's face, and her shoulders slumped. "And it looks even worse. But I really did think your mother was the murderer, Tess. All the signs pointed to her. She's been following us around for months, and as soon as Levi realized who she was from that picture, he planned to—"

"Ha! So you admit he was going to try and kill her."

"No! We were going to escape to Canada before Levi had a chance to take her out. That's the God's honest truth." Neptune swallowed. "I could control Levi, I swear. Whatever he did before, however much he hurt people, he always behaved as long as he had me by his side. Even when we were kids, he listened to me. I just needed to get him away somewhere he could be safe—somewhere we both could be."

"Nice try," Tess growled, but Neptune shrieked and raised her hands.

"I can prove it," Neptune added, her desperation rooted so deeply that Tess was having a hard time holding on to her anger. "I have this hacker, a guy who can do untraceable things with money like you wouldn't believe. I'll call him up, get him to show you what he's done. I hired him to set up all kinds of foreign accounts so Levi and I could make a quick getaway. He comes highly recommended in certain circles."

Tess almost laughed out loud. "Like I'd trust a word out of Wingbat99's mouth."

Neptune's hands came down. "Wait. You know Wingbat?"

Tess thought about telling the truth—that Wingbat was the one who'd put her onto Neptune's trail in the first place; that for all his lawbreaking charm, he was, in a weird way, her friend—but Sven was showing alarming signs of coming to. Tess was also loath to rat the hacker out. That seemed like a surefire way to get her bank accounts drained.

Instead, she leveled Neptune with a disdainful stare. "You aren't the only one who needs occasional access to back channels you don't want flagged by the government." She paused and added, "Or the only one who has enough money to pay for it."

Neptune didn't respond.

"Here." Since Tess was tired of doing all the work, she handed Neptune the crowbar. "I don't think I can do it again now that the immediate danger is over. No matter how many times I go through this, I can't get over the way skulls crunch when you hit them."

She had a few more arguments in her arsenal, but there was no need to pull them out. The adrenaline and anger that had helped fuel Tess's first blow were still coursing strongly through Neptune. Tess had to glance away as the other woman knocked Sven out for a second time.

"Now what?" Neptune asked as she stood over the

unconscious heap of her podcast producer. "I don't think we can lift him into the back of the van, but we can hardly leave him here while we go for help."

Tess heaved a sigh. For a woman who prided herself on her ingenuity and bravery in the face of danger, Neptune was annoyingly unprepared to deal with the realities of a hostage situation. Crouching down, Tess patted around Sven's pockets until she found the flat rectangle of his phone.

"Now, you tie Sven up with some of those electrical cords in the back of his van while I call Sheriff Boyd," she said. Almost as an afterthought, she added, "But make sure you gag him first. Use the one he spit his phlegm all over. He deserves it."

As Tess dialed the sheriff's number and Neptune carried out her orders, she could have almost sworn that the other woman watched her with a burgeoning sense of respect.

"You're...weirdly good at this," Neptune said. "Have you ever considered switching to podcasts? People love suspenseful tales when they're told from a first-person point of view."

"I know they do," Tess said, her mind only half on the scene around her. She was thinking of her own Detective Gonzales, who was getting too old and too tired for all this murdering nonsense. If she couldn't find it in her heart to kill him, she could at least let him retire. There came a time in every crime solver's life when they wanted to *stop* getting stuffed in the back of vans and facing down danger at every turn.

Sometimes, they just wanted to settle down and take up a hobby. Like podcasting. Or macramé.

Or painting by number.

Chapter Twenty-Seven

"DO YOU HAVE ANY IDEA HOW DANGEROUS IT WAS TO GO snooping around my house with zero backup and no clear plan of action?" Sheriff Boyd stared at Tess from across his desk, his hair practically standing up on end and a look of contorted fury on his face. "You could have been killed. You almost *were* killed."

"Technically, I told Ivy what I had planned," Tess pointed out. Her own hair was looking none too calm right now, but her expression was perfectly serene. That was mostly because Sven was safely behind bars—and so was Neptune Jones. Even though Tess felt fairly certain the woman's fleet of attorneys would get her out of this mess with little more than a slap on the wrist and a zillion-dollar podcast deal, Sheriff Boyd had slipped on a pair of handcuffs and read her Miranda rights just as though she'd been any common criminal.

True, Neptune's mug shot was likely to turn out better than a highly filtered Instagram photo, but Tess had found the whole process deeply satisfactory.

"Besides, after everything you did for me and my family, I wanted to give you something in return," Tess added. She grabbed a stale caramel candy from the sheriff's desk—the ones he kept there just for her—and popped it into her mouth. "Behold. I brought you proof, a confessed murderer, and a tidy solution all at once."

"*Tidy?*" Sheriff Boyd practically roared. "You call this *tidy*?"

"It's not my fault the whole story ended up being so convoluted. I don't do the crimes. I just solve them." She paused. "But it should be easy to prosecute, right? Now that Mumford's mystery accomplice turned himself in and all?"

The sheriff gave up on playing Bad Cop and fell into his chair in a slump. The exhaustion and worry of the past few hours hadn't done the bags under his eyes any favors, and the scratchy growth along his jaw had reached peak scruff.

"His version of events will help, yes. We were lucky he developed a conscience at the last minute and came in to ask for help." Lest Tess get the wrong impression and think Sheriff Boyd was actually *grateful* for all her hard work, he glared and added, "We'll need his testimony to make up for the fact that I'll have to cover up when and how you acquired federal bug-detecting tech and then broke into a county sheriff's house to use it."

Ah, yes. Tess was afraid they'd be getting around to that part.

"Would you believe me if I said I bought it online?" she ventured.

"Tess…"

She held up her hands in mock surrender. "You can get almost anything on the internet nowadays, I swear. Even hemlock, which is where I assume Sven bought the poison to take Levi Parker out."

"Tess," he said again, this time with a touch of real weariness about the corners of his mouth. "Was it Jared or Nicki who gave it to you?"

Tess had no desire to answer that question—and not just because she didn't want to get Jared in trouble. To admit that he'd given her an illegal but highly thoughtful gift would be to admit that she'd accepted it. That she'd *liked* it.

"I plead the fifth," she said.

The sheriff looked away. "Blast that man," he muttered. When he glanced back at Tess, it was with an air of resigned dejection. "I wish you'd tell me what Jared Wilson has that I don't. I know he's younger and better-looking than I am, that he has a flashier job and is carrying a lot less emotional baggage—you know what? I see it now. Forget I asked."

"Victor!" Tess shot up like a bolt. This was so similar to her own conversation with Kendra that she could almost believe that *he* was the one who'd been listening in through all those bugs.

"You should probably give the device back to him," he said with a shake of his head. "If not for your sake, then for his. He could get into real trouble messing around with stuff like that."

Reaching into the bottom drawer of his desk, he pulled out the infamous bottle of Wild Turkey and unscrewed the cap. After pouring a liberal amount into his coffee cup and handing it to Tess, he held the bottle up in a mock toast.

"I'd drink to your happiness together, but I'm not sure I can. Should we drink to another successfully solved case instead?"

Tess reached out and pulled the bottle from his hands so fast that she spilled at least three shots' worth all over his desk. "What's the matter with you? You're on the clock right now."

"I know. And if the paperwork this case has saddled me with is any indication, I'll continue being on the clock until next year. If anything calls for day drinking, it's that." He sighed and raked a hand through his hair. "Well, that and the fact that I'm trying to get up the nerve to say something I'm not sure you'll like hearing."

"Victor!" Tess cried again, this time leaning so far over the desk that she was almost nose-to-nose with him. Her heart was pounding hard enough to keep time, but that didn't stop her from staring the sheriff—*her* sheriff—straight in the eye. "Before you say anything, I need you to tell me where you got that aurora borealis painting in your house."

If she'd hoped to catch him off guard with her sudden turn of conversation, she was bound for disappointment.

"That's what I had Kendra hunting down for me," he said, his gaze equally straight. "It's not exactly the same as the one I had when I was a kid, but it's close. I'm a little rusty after all these years, but I like the way it's shaping up. I think I might actually be able to make something of it."

"She told you about our conversation?"

He rolled one shoulder. "Among other things, yes. Most notably that if I didn't want to lose out on the best thing that's ever happened to this town—and to me—I needed to stop hiding behind my job and actually do something about it." A rueful smile touched his lips. "I'll admit that she had more in mind than this, but it's the best I can do. I'm *trying*, Tess, but it's been a long time. Too long. I'd really like it if you'd be willing to help me fix that."

Tess wasn't sure how she managed to drop the bottle and bunch her hand in the front of Victor's shirt without spilling more of the bourbon all over the place, but she did. She also wasn't entirely sure what she planned to do once she dragged him across the distance, but fortunately for her, Victor wasn't as out of practice as he claimed to be. His mouth was on hers at once, his lips moving with so much ferocity that all the pain of the gag that had been recently stuffed in her mouth came roaring back.

"Oh. Ouch." She winced and touched tenderly at the sides of her lips. "Sorry. I'm still a little sore. Kidnapping and all that."

"No, I'm sorry. I shouldn't have done that."

Tess opened her mouth to cry out—he'd started it, he couldn't backtrack now, she'd kiss him until her lips bled if that was what it was going to take to finally get through to him—but he stopped her with a chuckle.

"I just meant while I'm supposed to be taking your statement," he said. This time when he smiled, it was with a tenderness that made Tess's heart stop. "But if you'd like me to do it again later—"

"Yes. Yes, *please*."

He ducked his head with a quick, blushing gesture. "In that case, I believe I still owe you a few stories about my old Seattle days, don't I?"

This coming on top of that kiss and that confession—of

the heady realization that this thing between them was *finally* happening—was almost too much. Tess squeaked.

"I mean, you technically didn't hold up your end of the bargain in the slightest." His words were back to their customary drawl, but Tess wasn't fooled. With that particular light in his eyes, she'd never be put off by that drawl again. "You put your fingers all over my investigation at literally every turn—"

"I didn't! Your investigation was the one putting its fingers on me."

He coughed and continued unabated. "—snooped around my house uninvited on more than one occasion—"

"To *save* you. I knew something was up with Neptune from the start."

"—put yourself directly in harm's way and did your best to drive me into an early grave with worry—"

That one gave her pause. "No. Really? You worried about me?"

"—but if it'll make you happy to hear about my past, then I'll tell you." He reached out and touched her hand. It was just a fleeting press of his fingers, but it told Tess everything she needed to know. "I want to make you happy, Tess. It's the only thing I've wanted for quite some time now."

A feeling of such warmth flooded through her that it was a wonder she didn't combust on the spot.

"I'd like you to do that too," she said, feeling suddenly shy. As that was a feeling that didn't come over her very often, she delighted in the new, heady, downright *girlish* sensation of it. "Maybe you could invite me over for dinner again? I hate to give Neptune credit for, well, anything, but your patio is kind of amazing now. I'd love a chance to sit out there without all the espionage getting in the way."

"Inviting yourself over already? That sounds like the Tess I know." His chuckle was so rich that Tess felt herself responding in kind. "Is tomorrow too soon?"

If the sudden fluttering in her stomach was any indication, the answer to that was a resounding no.

"Not at all," she said. "I'd invite myself over tonight if I didn't feel ready to collapse as it is."

"Don't let that stop you," he said, his voice growing oddly rough. "I'd be happy to catch you."

Their eyes met and held, the two of them suspended in a moment that contained as much promise as it did memory, as much friendship as it did heat. They could have remained that way much longer too, only the sound of a bustle near the front of the station drew their attention.

"I wouldn't go in there just yet," they heard Ivy's too-loud, too-obvious voice say. "The sheriff and Tess are, ah, hashing out some final details. It's a little intense for my tastes—and definitely yours."

Tess felt pretty sure this was the most understated euphemism of all time, but that didn't stop the sound of footsteps rushing through the door and toward Victor's desk. Tess's heart sank as soon as she saw who the visitors were. Nicki was always a welcome sight, but Jared's presence made things a little awkward—especially since he took one look at them and guessed what kind of *intensity* Ivy had been referring to.

Jared opened his mouth and closed it again, his expression so pained that it took all Tess's self-control not to jump to her feet and start consoling him. For one thing, she doubted Victor would appreciate her attempts to soothe the younger man's feelings when his own where still so raw. For another, it seemed there were more important issues at play.

"Tess, you'd better get on the phone and get me a sit-down meeting with your hacker," Nicki said in a tone that was harder and flatter than any she'd heard from her friend before. "Immediately."

Tess looked first at Nicki and then at Jared, her brow furrowed as she tried to figure out what she was missing. Even though Wingbat had almost certainly had a hand in Neptune's activities as of late, she didn't think he'd done anything that necessitated federal intervention.

"It doesn't exactly work like that," Tess said apologetically. "I can let him know you're interested, but he decides when and how things work. Since he has all the power, he makes all the rules—he's very Gen Z about the whole thing. Just ask Gertie. She's the same way."

"This is serious, Tess." Since this remark came from Jared rather than Nicki, and because he sounded sterner than Tess had ever heard him before, she gave a start of surprise. "I've asked every single person up at the logging camp, but no one will admit he was up there. I saw him. I talked to him. I *know* they're lying to me."

This came as no surprise to Tess. Wingbat/Jay was better at disappearing than that batch of murder cupcakes Gertrude had made for Tess's book-release party. He wouldn't surface again until he wanted to…and even then, it was touch and go whether or not he'd let Tess know when he did.

"And worse, we now know why." Nicki turned to glare at Tess. "The Peabodys are onto Jared being a fed. They've been aware of who he is this whole time."

Victor coughed in a way that left no room for doubt. "No offense to your undercover skills, Wilson, but does that really come as a surprise? I always thought it odd that they were so willing to bring a stranger on."

"You're right," Jared admitted, his eyes darting from Victor to Tess and back again. "But what we didn't expect was that they'd get around me by turning all their money-laundering operations digital."

Tess almost squealed as she realized what Jared and Nicki were saying. "You mean, I was right this whole time? The tuna fish was a front?"

"No, that really was part of Mumford's blackmail scheme." Nicki turned her lips so far down that Tess felt a quaver of fear. "But ever since you and Neptune roped Wingbat into Winthrop affairs, he's been sniffing around, looking for another way in. Somewhere along the way, he got the idea to reach out to Mason Peabody with an offer to expand his enterprise. We have reason to believe he's now overseeing the entire money-laundering operation."

"Wait. Really?"

"Yes, really." Nicki and Jared shared a glance that boded ill for what came next. Tess found herself reaching for Victor's hand without thinking about it. "And as soon as you've recovered from this latest murder nonsense, you—Tess Harrow—are hereby ordered to help the feds catch him."

Epilogue

THE SECOND OFFICIAL OPENING OF THE PAPER TRAIL turned out to be a much bigger success than the first.

Tess wished she could pretend that the massive turnout had more to do with the rampant success of her latest Detective Gonzales novel—not to mention the several lovely Yelp reviews that Tess suspected Edna was posting under fake accounts in her spare time—but she knew the truth the moment the doors swung open and the crowd started pouring in.

They were bloodthirsty monsters, every last one of them. Worse—they were diehard *Murder, at Last* fans.

"Is this where Neptune Jones and Levi Parker met under cover of night?" asked a woman with a massive fanny pack and a camera the size of her head.

"Do you still have the rope marks from where Neptune Jones's producer tied you up?" asked another woman, showing no remorse at grabbing Tess's sleeves and trying to push them up.

"Can we buy the book that has the note revealing Neptune Jones's secret identity?" This last question came from a man in a three-piece suit and an honest-to-goodness monocle screwed up in one eye. "Money is no object. I'll pay whatever you ask."

"As far as I know, Neptune and Levi only met in hotel rooms," Tess said, resigned. She sighed and held out the platter of murder cupcakes—Gertrude's newest recipe, and already adding a strain to her waistband. "The rope marks faded away weeks ago—and no, you can't buy that particular copy of *Fury under the Floorboards* because it's been booked as evidence. However, I do have several signed copies ready to go if you'd like to buy a normal copy."

The fans looked disappointed at these matter-of-fact responses to their questions, but they all happily took a cupcake. They also got the macabre show they were after in the form of a veiled figure appearing in the doorway to the back room.

"Ignore my daughter. She's a woman of no sensibility. To her, death is merely a tale to be told, a story that can be scribbled down on paper and forgotten."

Tess's snort of derision was lost in the sudden gasp as the crowd recognized Bernadette Springer in her full widow's weeds. She carried an ancient Bible in one hand and a string of rosary beads in the other. Tess was pretty sure her mom hadn't gone anywhere near a rosary bead since her girlhood days of being educated in a strict Catholic school, but that didn't seem to matter. The overall effect was, to put it bluntly, *effecting*.

"You're the woman Levi Parker was going to kill next!"

"You barely escaped with your life!"

"You were going to murder him to seek vengeance for the death of Eudora Raphael!"

Their attention turned away from Tess on a dime—and she, for one, was glad to see them go.

"Don't take it to heart, Tess," a low, rumbling voice said near her ear. "The Neptune drama will die down eventually, especially once her trial is over. They'll be back to being Detective Gonzales fans in no time."

"To be honest, my mother can have them," Tess said, gratefully dropping her head on Victor's shoulder. She liked how strong and solid it felt—and how much like a place where she belonged. They were still working out exactly what a relationship between the two of them looked like, but the overall picture was shaping up almost as well as Victor's painting of the northern lights. "Did you hear that Neptune had her lawyers reach out to my mom about a doing a possible *Murder, at Last* spin-off together? I'm terrified she's going to agree."

They stood back and watched as the woman with the fanny pack handed Gertrude her camera and requested a photo. Gertrude, always happy to oblige, took up the role of photographer almost as well as she'd handled the catering.

"Think of it this way," Victor said as he grabbed one of the murder cupcakes and swallowed half of it in one bite. "If your mom's working on a podcast, she won't keep staying with you much longer. That has to count for something."

Tess sniffed. To tell the truth, she was getting kind of used to having her mom around. She took up too much space in the cabin and refused to give Tess her bed back, but Tess could recognize how good it was for Gertrude to have her grandmother around.

"Excuse me." A tall man in a trench coat approached and shyly held out a copy of *Fury under the Floorboards*. "You're Tess Harrow, right? Would you mind signing my—"

He glanced over at Sheriff Boyd and let out a whoosh of air.

"Holy crap. You're Detective Gonzales, aren't you? He's real? You're real?" The man almost dropped his book in his excitement. "I had no idea he was based on an actual person, and I'm just about the biggest Tess Harrow fan there is."

Instead of releasing the pained groan Tess felt sure was coming, Victor offered the man a lopsided grin. "It's supposed to be a secret, so don't tell anyone. I can sign your copy too, if you want."

To Tess's delight, the man eagerly accepted this offer. As soon as Tess finished scrawling her name across the title page, Victor lifted the pen and signed Detective Gonzales's name, complete with his fictional badge number of 102003.

"This is the best thing that's ever happened to me," the man said, clutching the book to his chest like it was his firstborn child. "The book club at home is never going to believe it."

Tess waved the man off before turning to Victor with an arched brow. "So you're admitting it now, huh? Does this mean you'll come with me on my next book tour?"

"Not a chance." He crossed his arms and aimed for a scowl, but he fell disastrously short of this goal. "But it would be nice if you gave Gonzales something to look forward to in the next book. A promotion, maybe, or a lengthy vacation. After all the paperwork you've caused the poor detective, he deserves it."

Tess laughed and let herself relax—*really relax*—for the first time in what felt like forever. Her life wasn't likely to be easy for the next few months, what with a rogue hacker to track down, the FBI hounding her for information, her mom walking around with visions of podcast fame twinkling in her eyes, and Gertrude's driver's test coming up, but this was one area she had covered.

"Don't you worry," she said as she grabbed the other half of the murder cupcake from his hand and shoved it into her mouth. "I have big plans for Detective Gonzales. I wasn't sure how to tell you, but you might as well hear it now."

"Tess," Victor warned. "Why are you looking at me like that? What are you going to do to my detective doppelgänger?"

"Oh, nothing," Tess said, continuing to look at Victor in exactly the same way as before—with mischief and happiness and maybe a smidgen of infatuation. "But I got my editor's approval just this morning. My next Detective Gonzales book will be the last one ever."

"Tess!"

"That's right, Victor. I'm killing you off, and there's nothing you can do to stop me."

Keep reading for an excerpt from
the second book in Tamara Berry's
By the Book Mysteries series

ON SPINE
OF
DEATH

Chapter One

Tess knew the exact moment the blood started
dripping down her hands.

The frigid air of the cellar where she was trapped had
long since caused her skin to grow numb. She couldn't feel
the sharp slices of the zip ties digging into her wrists or the
thick trickle of blood moving down her fingers, but that
didn't matter. As soon as her veins opened up, the enormous,
mangy rat in the corner would lift his nose, twitch his whis-
kers, and come in for a taste.

"Rats!" Tess cried. "I'm going to get eaten by rats!"

Since she'd long since slobbered her way out of the duct
tape across her lips, her shout came through loud and clear.

"I'm not kidding," she added, her voice wavering frantically. "He's the size of a terrier. Let me out of here!"

The rustle of approaching footsteps was accompanied by a thump as the cellar door above her head swung open. Tess winced at the sudden brightness of the outside world, which didn't abate even when a head popped down through the hole to block most of the light.

"Ohmigod, Mom. People on the street are starting to ask questions. What's wrong with you?"

Tess felt no relief at the sound of her daughter's voice—or at the sight of the pitch-black, chin-length bob hanging down over her head. "What's wrong with me is that I'm about to be attacked by a rabid animal with a taste for my blood."

"How do you know he's rabid?"

"I don't. But that won't matter to the people at the hospital. Unless we manage to catch him and bring him in to be tested, they'll make me get all thirty rabies shots either way. It's protocol."

Gertrude, who was fifteen going on fifty, wasn't moved by this picture. "Then say it."

Tess screwed up her face and did her best to ignore the squeal of her rodential nemesis crawling closer. "No."

"Mom, you made me promise. I can't let you go you unless you say it."

"I won't."

"Fine. Then I'm getting back to work. Herb is letting me use the sledgehammer."

"A sledgehammer?" she echoed. "To do *what*?"

From upside down, Gertrude's grin looked like a

grimace. "We're taking out that old brick wall near the back of the store. You never told me that demolition could be so much fun. He says if we can't get the bricks out this way, we'll have to bring out the big guns."

The head started to disappear before Tess could decide whether or not to ask what *big guns* entailed. In the two weeks since renovations on her grandfather's old hardware store had started, she'd learned it was best not to ask too many questions. Questions led to long-winded tales of asbestos, lead, radon, and other construction horrors that would cost—by Herb's estimation—tens of thousands of dollars to repair.

"Make sure you wear a construction hat," Tess warned.

"Yes, Mom."

"And those cute steel-tipped boots we bought you."

"Stop calling them cute. They're not cute. They're *functional*."

"Fine. Wear your ugly and useful boots. And if you get anywhere near a rusty nail—"

"I'm leaving now," Gertrude interrupted with a snort of disgust. "These bricks aren't going to smash themselves."

In a moment of panic—and, she was willing to admit, desperation—Tess called out once more.

"No! Wait. Leave the trapdoor open a crack. It smells damp down here. I think I can taste mold spores starting to take root on my tongue."

This didn't move Tess's daughter any more than the threat of rat attacks or rabies had. "That's not how mold spores work." Gertrude said and paused. "Well?"

Tess heaved a sigh. "Fine. Go ahead and abandon me. I'll

just stay down here to make a meal for the creepy-crawlies of the world."

"Okay," Gertrude said cheerfully. "Let me know if you change your mind, *Magdalene*."

Tess watched as her daughter closed the trapdoor, once again plunging her into a world of darkness and mold. *Magdalene* was Tess's safe word, but there was no way she was saying it. By her estimation, she'd only been down in the cellar below the hardware store for about an hour. To call it quits after such a lackluster attempt at escape would only prove her daughter right. *And* Ivy *and* Sheriff Boyd *and* everyone else who'd said there was no way Tess could do it.

Take one woman, bound at the wrists by zip ties, and attach her to a chair. Duct tape her mouth, leave her without any tools, and shove her into a convenient hole. Mix and let rest.

"But I wasn't counting on rats," Tess muttered as she started to once again saw her wrists against a sharp edge at the back of the chair. "No one said anything about rats."

Even as she spoke, she knew that the woman in her book—code name Magdalene—would be encountering rats inside her prison. Tess Harrow, renowned thriller writer, was something of a legend when it came to using real-life incidents to fuel her fiction. Her last book, *Fury in the Forest*, had been based on her own experience of finding a dead body in the pond behind the rustic cabin she now called home. The book was already in its sixth printing and showed no signs of flagging.

As she continued sawing, more frantically now, the first

band of the zip tie gave way. Tess shouted in triumph, even though the action caused the second band to dig deeper into her flesh. She was going to have some serious zip-tie burn after this, and there was still a good chance that rat would take a bite from one of her fingers, but it was worth it. She'd been *sure* it was possible for a fortysomething, slightly overweight divorcée to escape from the deep underbelly of the criminal world. Not *quickly*, obviously, and not with anything approaching finesse, but those things could be glossed over in the retelling.

"That'll show my editor," Tess said as she began sawing at her hands anew. "You don't have to be Keanu Reeves to escape from a tight spot. With a little persistence, anyone can—"

BOOM!

At the sudden rattling of her prison walls, Tess gave a start of surprise, but she refused to let it derail her. If she knew her daughter—and she did—Gertrude was taking to the sledgehammer like a teenager to, well, a sledgehammer. The steady trickle of dirt from above her head was vaguely alarming, but no more so than any of the other horrors down here.

Tess had no idea what her grandfather had used this cellar for, but there was no denying the creep factor. When they'd first uncovered it from below the ancient linoleum floor they'd peeled up, Tess had half expected it to contain the bodies of her grandfather's enemies. Instead, she'd found a burst of inspiration.

Which, when you thought about it, was just as good.

"Keep it quiet up there!" she called, but without any expectation of being answered. Her shoulders were starting to burn, and the trickle of dirt was starting to turn into a torrent, but she could feel the last of the plastic giving way.

Or rather, she *would* have, if the world hadn't suddenly started shaking around her.

BOOM! BOOM!

"Seriously, you guys! If you're not careful, I'm going to be—"

Her next words died—and were buried—on her lips. So was the rest of her. Amid the avalanche of debris, rocks, and dirt that opened up on top of her, Tess lost her ability to do anything but scream.

And even that was taken away from her before too long.

Being buried alive would do that to a woman. Especially once she realized that dirt wasn't the only thing falling from the ceiling. With a last, desperate gasp of air, Tess found herself being showered with what looked—and felt—like human bones.

She didn't know whether it worse to die of a femur to the head or a lungful of damp, loamy soil, but it didn't matter. As her chair tipped and fell—with her arms still strapped to it—she lost all track of everything except how it felt to be six feet under.

Chapter Two

"I THINK WE SHOULD LEAVE HER TIED UP."

Tess glared from her position on the ground, her hands still bound behind her and the taste of earthworms in her mouth. "Very funny, Sheriff Boyd. If you don't get me out of this cellar right now—"

"You're right." The tall, well-built frame of the sheriff's head deputy, Ivy Bell, crouched next to Tess. "We need to photograph and catalog this evidence before we move her. Hold still, Tess. It'll only take half an hour."

"*Half an hour?*" Tess echoed, but she might as well have not spoken for all the attention the two officers paid her. They were loving this, she knew—she could tell from the slow, methodical way they moved through the rubble that used to be the cellar. *And* from the way Ivy kept telling Tess to smile and say cheese for the camera.

"Relax. These bones are at least thirty years old," Sheriff Boyd drawled. "They can't hurt you."

From her angle on the ground, Tess could only make out the sheriff's scuffed cowboy boots and jeans-clad lower legs, but that didn't matter. She knew down to the dark, silken strands of his hair and the quirk of a cleft palate scar above his lip how he looked. And *not*, as some people might think, because she was particularly interested in him as a person. It was just that he happened to be the spitting image of the fictional detective who'd gotten Magdalene trapped in a cellar in the first place.

Detective Gonzales, who only existed inside the imagination of Tess Harrow and the several million people who'd read her books, would never leave a woman tied up so he could collect evidence. He might be a hard-boiled man of the law, but he was also a *gentleman*.

"They're human, that's for sure," Ivy said as the camera flashed. "I'm guessing they were buried underneath the floorboards, but all that sledgehammering must have dislodged them."

"You say that like I wanted this to happen," Tess said. She tried to wriggle her way out from underneath a humerus, but Ivy commanded her to lie still. Tess continued, "It might surprise the two of you to discover that I don't *like* finding dead bodies everywhere I turn. Nor do I enjoy having several feet of dirt fall on top of me. I could have suffocated."

Since she'd been nowhere near suffocation—and since both Ivy and Sheriff Boyd knew it—her protests were largely ignored.

"I told you it was too dangerous to start construction on the hardware store without first checking the foundation," Sheriff Boyd said. "My exact words were, and I quote, 'You're likely to bring the whole roof down.'"

"The roof is fine. It's the floor that didn't make it," said Tess.

Ivy released a low whistle as she dropped the last of her evidence markers and snapped a few shots. "And a good thing, too, or we might never have found this poor sap." She paused. "Check out the marks on this rib, Victor. That's a hatchet job if I ever saw one."

Tess called on the last of her strength and thrust her bound wrists against the splintered edge of her chair. To her surprise—and relief—it worked. The plastic, already strained and ground down, gave way. With a cry of thanks, she yanked her hands out of their bonds and twisted her body to examine the bones in question.

Since the bones were literally on top of her, it didn't take long for Tess to see what the sheriff and Ivy were talking about. The bones had been entombed in the floor of her grandfather's hardware store for so long that they no longer held any horror—or any flesh. Tess reached for a scapula only to have her hand smacked away.

"Don't you dare." Ivy spoke with a sharp reprimand that reminded Tess of a schoolteacher. "Those aren't for you."

"I wasn't going to stick it in my pocket and take it home," Tess protested, but she was careful to give Ivy a wide berth as she flexed her fingers to get the circulation flowing back to them. As she'd suspected, her wrists were raw, and there was dried blood crusted on her fingernails like nail polish. Those were small considerations when compared to the fact that she was standing in the scattered remains of an actual human being. "Who do you think it is? And why was he buried in the floor?"

When neither Sheriff Boyd nor Ivy answered right away, Tess held up both hands.

"Nuh uh. I know what you're thinking, but my grandfather

didn't do this. He was a curmudgeonly hermit, but he wasn't a *murderer*." Since it seemed important to point out, she added, "And even if he was, he'd know better than to bury his victim in his own hardware store. That's the fastest way to a jail sentence that I've ever heard of."

"Who's going to jail, and how often can I come visit?" a voice called from above.

All of Tess's interest in the mortal remains of their mystery skeleton vanished at once. Gertrude had been through enough murder and intrigue to last a lifetime; the last thing Tess wanted to do was provide more fodder for her therapist.

"Sheriff Boyd and Ivy are just being dramatic," she called up. "No one is going to jail."

"Not yet, anyway," Ivy murmured. Tess glared so hard that Ivy had to cover whatever else she planned to say with a cough.

"Don't come down, Gertie. I'm heading up." Tess reached for the cellar ladder and was surprised to find Sheriff Boyd waiting to help her. He held the wooden frame with one hand, his other extended to give her a boost.

"Get her out of here, if you can," he said, his voice low. "Even with bones this old, we'll have to call the coroner in."

Tess felt her chest grow tight. No one knew better than Sheriff Boyd how a discovery like this could impact an impressionable teenager. There was a good chance Gertrude would treat it with the cavalier disdain she showed for pretty much anything that revolved around adults, but there was also a chance she'd take it deeply to heart.

"I'll do my best," Tess promised. When the sheriff didn't

let go of her hand right away, she hesitated. In the eight months she'd lived in the small, remote town of Winthrop—population of 466—she'd only touched this man a handful of times. They'd solved a murder together and faced immediate peril in each other's arms, but Sheriff Victor Boyd was a man who did things by the book.

In this case, the book said that a recently divorced thriller writer with a penchant for getting herself in trouble was not to be touched—or trusted—lightly.

"What is it?" she asked. "What's wrong?"

His glance fixed on the raw patch of skin around her wrists. "The next time you want to research kidnapping escape methods, I'd appreciate it if you didn't do it underneath a construction site."

Her heart gave a small stutter. "Why, Victor. Are you worried about me?"

He released her hand as quickly as he'd taken it. "Don't be ridiculous. I just don't want to have to deal with the media outcry. The last time you were involved in attempted murder, it took me six weeks to get rid of the reporters."

About the Author

Tamara Berry is the author of the Eleanor Wilde cozy mystery series and, under the pen name Lucy Gilmore, the Forever Home contemporary romance series. Also a freelance writer and editor, she has a bachelor's degree in English literature and a serious penchant for Nancy Drew novels. She lives in Bigfoot country (a.k.a. Eastern Washington) with her family and their menagerie of pets.

Find her online at tamaraberry.com.
facebook.com/TamaraBerryAuthor
Twitter: @Tamara_Morgan
Instagram: @tamaratamaralucy